Tears of a Hustler

A
Novel
By

$ilk White

GOOD2GOPUBLISHING

This novel is a work of fiction. All of the characters, organizations, establishments and events portrayed in this novel are either products of the author's imagination or are used fictitiously.

Published by:
GOOD2GOPUBLISHING
7311 W. GLASS LANE
LAVEEN, AZ 85339
www.good2gopublishing.com
QUESTIONS
G2G@GOOD2GOPUBLISHING.COM

THIRDLANE MARKETING: BRIAN JAMES
BRIAN@GOOD2GOPUBLISHING

AUTHOR: SILK WHITE
SILKWHITE@GOOD2GOPUBLISHING.COM
FACEBOOK.COM/SILKWHITE212
MYSPACE.COM/SILKWHITE
TWITTER@GOOD2GOBOOKS

Cover designer: Davida Baldwin
Edited by A. V. Finigan-Hutchines

ISBN: 978-1-453-62304-6

Thank you

First, I would really like to thank God for blessing me with this gift. Secondly, I would like to thank my queen for being by my side every step of the way. Thanks...you're the best (wink).

Next I would like to thank every single Silk White fan out there. I truly appreciate your loyalty and patience. Oh yeah, and shout out to Natasha; good looking on all the info you've given me, I appreciate it. Shout out to my man Ray and B.J. too. Oh, and my man Nelson, the Bronx bookman.

Last, but not least, big shout out to all my brothers and sisters locked up behind the wall...keep ya head up and ya eyes open...it gets greater later, you dig!!

Introduction

"Welcome to McDonalds. May I take your order," Nancy asked the overweight man that stood across the counter from her. "Yeah, let me get a number one with extra pickles." "And your drink?" "Let me get a coke with no ice," the greedy man said with authority. "Coming right up sir," Nancy said politely as she went to get the big man's fries ready.

Nancy couldn't stop looking at the clock because she only had thirty minutes left until she got off. Being five months pregnant didn't help, since her back was aching. Needless to say she couldn't wait to get off her feet.

"Thirty minutes and I'm gone," she kept telling herself. "Thank you. Come again," Nancy said nicely as she handed the big man his food. Once the big man disappeared through the front door, Nancy noticed a familiar face walk into the restaurant. It was her baby daddy, Dave. From the look on his face, Nancy could tell that he was in his usual foul mood.

"Hi. Welcome to McDonalds. May I take your order," she asked playfully. "Bitch stop playing with me and get my food," Dave snarled smelling like strong Vodka. "Nine piece nuggets with fries again," Nancy asked rolling her eyes. "Isn't that what I ask for every night," he replied coldly. "Well I'm sorry Dave, but it won't hurt you to tell me what you want again" "I don't like to repeat myself. Now go get my fucking food," he said with ice in his voice. "I'm sorry, but you're going to have to pay for your food tonight because my manager is still here. You came too early," Nancy said in a light whisper. "Bitch you must be crazy. I ain't paying for shit," he yelled way louder than he had to. "But Dave my manager is still here," she pleaded. "Fuck him. I'm your manager. Now go get my food or else," he warned.

"I can't stand this motherfucker," Nancy mumbled under her breath as she went to go get his food. "I don't know why you put up with that shit," Nancy's manager whispered as he walked pass. "I don't know why either," Nancy said to herself as she filled an empty cup to the top with sprite.

"Damn, hurry the fuck up. Does it look like I got all day?" "Dave I'm five months pregnant and I only got two feet, not to mention that I'm the only one in this relationship with a fucking job," she shot back. "Bitch, how dare you talk to me like that? I should smack the shit out of you. You know ain't nobody trying to hire a convicted felon. What, you want me to go back to the streets and risk my freedom? You want me standing on the corner at all times of the night? Huh? If I get locked up again I'm going upstate. The eight months I spent on Riker's Island was bad enough. You want me to get back into that lifestyle," Dave asked hoping she didn't call his bluff. “Baby you know I don’t want you back out there in those streets,” Nancy said feeling sorry for the worthless man standing in front of her. “I just need a little help,” she said handing Dave his food. “You know I love you baby. I’m outta here. Call me when you get home,” Dave said as he made his way towards the exit.

“I don’t know how you put up with an asshole like that all day,” the manager, Mr. Wiggins, said wiping down the counter. “I love him, but I hate him at the same time. Plus he told me that if I ever left him, he was going to kill me and I believe him,” Nancy said looking a little shook. “Kill you,” Mr. Wiggings asked in disbelief. “Child please, all that punk needs is a nice ass wiping. Just call the cops and put his punk ass in jail if he put his hands on you. “I thought about calling the cops, but that would be like sending another black man back to slavery, cause prison ain’t shit but modern day slavery. I would never send one of my people back to slavery no matter what he or she has done.” “Yeah that’s true, but you can’t just sit there and let him do whatever he wants to you just cause you don’t want to put him in jail,” Mr. Wiggings stated plainly. “Yeah, you’re right, but sometimes I just don’t know what to do.” “Don’t even worry about it sweetheart, you’ll figure it out. Why don’t you go home a little early and get some rest.” “Thank you, Mr. Wiggings. I could definitely use it,” Nancy said as she grabbed her things and quickly made her exit.

Nancy sat on the train, while thinking and feeling depressed. She was five months pregnant, and didn’t even have a bib for her baby yet. A million questions ran through her mind as she sat on the train.

Nancy wanted Dave to change his ways and start to help out a little more, but deep down inside she knew he wasn't shit and would never change. When Nancy stepped into the nasty apartment she lived in, she noticed her mother and her mother's boyfriend sitting on the raggedy couch watching T.V.

"Hey what's up ya'll?" No answer. Instead of arguing Nancy went straight to her room and closed the door. She hated living with her mother, Jasmin, and she really hated being in the house when her mother's boyfriend, Rick, was there. Ever since her mother started messing with Rick, Rick had been slowly but shortly turning Jasmin against her daughter. It was as if he wanted her all for himself.

As Nancy got her underclothes ready for when she got out of the shower, she heard a sharp knock on the door. Before she could ask who it was, the figure had already entered her room. Nancy was getting ready to bark on somebody for just busting in her room, until she realized that it was her best friend, Coco. Now Coco was what you called a project Barbie, and most of all she was a gold digger. She ran away from home at sixteen and had been taking care of herself ever since.

"Damn girl you still working at McDonalds," Coco asked already knowing the answer. "Yeah, unless you got a better way for me to make some money," Nancy countered. "Now that you mention it, I do got a new money scheme." "No, I'm not going out with no drug dealer and using him for his money, if that's what you were thinking," Nancy told her. "Girl that's a side hustle, and I'm talking about a permanent hustle," Coco confirmed. "So what do I have to do? Because I know ain't nobody just going to give us no money," Nancy joked. "Well I was chilling at club Spirit the other night when some guy named G-money came up in the club throwing money around like it was nothing."

"I already told you I ain't messing around with no drug dealer," Nancy cut in. "Wait let me finish," Coco said rudely as she continued. "So I'm in the club minding my business, when out of nowhere one of the men from G-money's entourage tapped me on the shoulder, and started to tell me how beautiful I was. I was thinking in my mind, "Yeah whatever." He then handed me a card with a number on it, and then he whispered in my ear, "If you need a job, call this number within forty-eight hours. In forty-eight hours this number will no longer be in service." Then before he left, he whispered in my ear again but this time he said, "You got some nice titties." Then he walked off."

"Oh my God, you're a prostitute now," Nancy joked playfully. "Fuck you bitch," Coco countered as she playfully pushed her friend. "So what happened," Nancy asked wanting to hear the rest of the story.

"Aight, so the next day I called the guy just to see what kind of job he was talking about. So he told me to meet him at this chicken spot in Harlem. So as I'm waiting at the chicken spot an all black Range Rover pulled up, and beeped the horn. As I approached the vehicle, the back window rolled down and inside of the backseat sat G-money. So I got in the backseat and we talked for about thirty minutes." "So get to the point," Nancy cut in once again. "Basically he told me that he needed a few chicks to bag up some coke for him and his partner Ali. I was like cool no problem, so that's what I've been doing. I can plug you in if you want?" "Are you crazy? I can't be around a whole pile of coke like that. Those fumes would kill me and the baby," Nancy stated plainly. "They give you a mask to cover your mouth and nose." "Thanks, but no thanks. I'll just stay at Mickey D's," Nancy said thinking slow money is better than no money.

"Girl you're going to be flipping burgers for the rest of your life. G-money is paying $100 dollars a night, so you do the math. No job you get is going to pay you a hundred dollars a day. Shit you can do both, work at McDonalds and get ya' side hustle on." "Nah, it sounds too risky. The cops can raid that place at anytime. I can't afford to take a chance like that."

"With both of us doing that, we can afford to get us an apartment, and then you can finally leave that loser, Dave. That nigga ain't gonna never be shit but a bum ass nigga and you know it." "You know Dave ain't letting me go nowhere," Nancy said letting out a light chuckle. "That mutha fucka ain't gonna do shit, but bring you down. The crazy part is that you know this," Coco said not understanding her best friend. "It's not that simple. If I told him that I didn't want to be with him no more, he would kick my ass and you know that," Nancy stated plainly. "That's why you have to get up and bounce. Don't tell that nigga shit. We would just get our apartment and be out," Coco said desperately trying to get her best friend to at least think about leaving her mother's apartment, and most importantly leave that bum, Dave.

"Okay Coco I'll think about it, but I ain't making no promises." "I knew you would come to your senses," Coco said playfully as she gave her best friend a big hug. "Easy bitch I said I'll think about it, now get up outta here so I can hop in the shower and get some rest. You know that I have to be to work early tomorrow," Nancy said escorting her friend to the door, so that she could get some sleep.

Chapter 1
G-MONEY

"What's good my nigga. We gonna do this or what," Skip asked getting frustrated. "Yeah, let me light this spliff up real quick," G-money answered lighting up the finger thick blunt. "Now I'm ready," he said letting out a light cough as he and his five man entourage hopped out of the Yukon, heading across the street to the bodega on the corner.

When G-money entered the bodega, he noticed that the small store was packed with customers. Immediately he went straight to the counter, skipping the long line. "What's up Oscar? You don't look too happy to see me," G-money said blowing smoke in the Spanish man's face. "G-money what's good? I was just about to call you," Oscar lied from behind the counter. "So what happen? Ya phone got cut off? You don't got no minutes? What?"

Before Oscar could reply a construction worker standing at the end of the line decided he should voice his opinion. "Hey mutha fucka I know you see this long line back here," he yelled out. G-money looked the construction worker up and down, and then turned to Skip and gave him the go ahead nod. Before the construction worker knew it, Skip pulled out his .45 and broke his nose, sending the big man crashing to the ground.

"Yo, everybody take whatever ya'll want and get up out of here," G-money ordered. Once the last customer exited the bodega, Skip closed and locked the front door.

"Every month it's the same thing, and you know Ali wants to get paid on the first of every month," G-money said putting his blunt out on Oscar's shirt. "Come on baby, you know I wouldn't fuck with you or Ali's money," Oscar said attempting to sound firm.

In one quick motion G-money slapped Oscar twice, and then snatched him over the counter. "Yo, open up the freezer in the back," he ordered as he watched his goons do as they were told. "Listen to me carefully Oscar," G-money said kneeling down so that he could have Oscar's full attention. "If I take you to that freezer you ain't coming back," he warned.

"Come on. All that isn't called for because I got the money behind the counter," Oscar announced through a pair of bloody lips. "So give me the fucking money so I can go already."

Oscar quickly scrambled to his feet to go fetch G-money his money. "Here you go. Sorry about that," Oscar said speaking with his head down. "All the coke you sell out of this bodega and you still playing games like a fucking kid? If Ali didn't like you so much I would've been smoked ya' stupid ass," G-money snarled looking Oscar up and down. "I'm sorry G-money. I promise that something like this will never happen again." "It better not! Have that protection money same time every month," G-money said as he and his crew exited Oscar's bodega.

Chapter 2
DETECTIVE NELSON

"Freeze! Put your hands where I can see them," Detective Nelson yelled as he aimed his .44 magnum at Ali and the Jewish man sitting next to him. "Don't even think about it," Big Mel yelled aiming his twin .45's at the Detective. "Damn you scared the shit outta me," Ali said as he gave the Detective a pound. "Big Mel its cool, Detective Nelson was just joking," Ali said to his twenty-four hour bodyguard.

Ali paid Detective Nelson $20,000 every month to keep the FEDS off of his ass and to keep his crew from behind bars. Detective Nelson also took care of all of Ali's competition. Detective Nelson would immediately shut down any crew that was making money, and then let Ali put some workers in that same spot. Ali had the master plan, and whoever didn't like it just stayed broke and hated from the sideline. He was the boss and G-money was the under boss.

"I'm glad you came over here cause, I need to holla at you," Ali said handing Detective Nelson a brown paper bag full of cash. "What's on your mind?" "I got a little problem. There's these cats out in Brooklyn that call themselves opening up shop. G-money's been begging me to let him go handle that, but I put him on hold because I don't want to draw up too much attention. You dig?" "Don't worry. I'll take care of it first thing tomorrow morning," Detective Nelson said as he stood up to leave. "Aight, let me know when you take care of that, so that I can send a few workers up there with some packs." "No problem," Detective Nelson responded. "Yo, Big Mel show Detective Nelson to the door," Ali ordered as he went and continued his conversation with his Jewish lawyer.

When Big Mel returned, Ali noticed that he had a sour look on his face. "What's wrong," Ali asked. "I don't trust that fucking cop. There's something fishy about that mother fucker." "I don't trust him either, but we gotta do what we gotta do, you dig? Everything with that white boy is strictly business; can't have friends like him because people like him will turn on you in a New York minute," Ali stated plainly. "Just be careful boss man, cause I don't like that fool," Big Mel replied.

Big Mel's job was to protect Ali from anything or anybody looking to hurt him. Big Mel was an ex-high school line backer. The only problem was that he wasn't too smart, so people in school called him dumb. But on the streets he was as smart as they came, and sharper than a thumb tack. Big Mel didn't talk much, instead he let his actions do all the talking for him.

"Yo Mel get G-money on the phone and tell him to make sure he has somebody pick up that protection money from all of our spots before the week is out," Ali ordered.

Chapter 3
I DON'T THINK THIS IS GOING TO WORK

"Only two hours left," Nancy said to herself as she glanced at the clock, then at the long line of customers standing in front of her cash register. Nancy served two of her customers when she noticed Dave enter the restaurant. From the look on his face she could tell that he was drunk.

"Hey baby what's up," Dave shouted loudly as he skipped the long line of customers making his way to the front of the cash register. "Look at you, looking all good and shit," he said as he leaned over the counter trying to give his girl a kiss. "Baby you can't do this while I'm at work," Nancy said leaning back refusing to give Dave a kiss.

"What," Dave growled looking Nancy up and down. "Bitch I'm your man. I'll kiss you wherever the fuck I feel like it," he snarled as he roughly kissed Nancy on the lips. "Now let me get a double cheeseburger, some fries, and a sprite." "Okay baby I got you, but I'm gonna need you to step to the side so I can take care of these customers first." "Fuck these customers. You serve your man first. You must've lost your fucking mind," Dave said loudly causing a scene.

Mr. Wiggins sat in his office in the back talking to his girlfriend on the phone, when he heard a loud commotion coming from the front. "What the fuck is going on," Mr. Wiggins said to himself as he took a look at the surveillance camera where he saw Dave acting a fool. "This mutha fucka must've lost his mind," Mr. Wiggins said to himself as he headed to the front of the store to see what all the commotion was about.

"Excuse me brother, is there a problem out here," Mr. Wiggins asked nicely. "Old man this ain't got nothing to do with you, so mind your business before you get knocked the fuck out," Dave said with ice in his voice.

Mr. Wiggins let out a light chuckle before he spoke calmly. "Nancy your fired. Get the fuck out of here and take your broke ass man with you." "Mr. Wiggins how can you do this to me?" "I didn't, you did it to yourself," Mr. Wiggins countered smoothly. "All this drama ain't good for business." "What am I supposed to do now," Nancy asked innocently. "Ask your big mouth boyfriend," Mr. Wiggins replied feeling sorry for his best worker.

"You ain't right; I bust my ass everyday in this mother fucker for you. Now you're just gonna fire me like I'm a piece of crap," Nancy said as tears ran freely down her face. "You know what? I'm better than this, so fuck you and Ronald McDonald. Both of ya'll can kiss my ass," Nancy snarled as she whirled on her heels, and stormed out of the restaurant. When she made it to the train station, she saw Dave standing there waiting for her.

"Davc don't even say shit to me right now," Nancy growled as she brushed past Dave heading downstairs to the subway platform. "Bitch who the fuck you talking to like that? I did you a mother fucking favor. I know you ain't want to work there for the rest of your miserable life, now did you?" "Dave a job is a job. I don't care where I'm working, as long as I'm getting paid. But some people wouldn't know shit about that now would they," Nancy countered looking Dave up and down, before she turned to get on the train.

"Well since money means so much to you, then I'm gonna get back on my grind out here in the streets, and risk my life and my freedom again," Dave said trying to make Nancy feel sorry for him like he always did.

"Dave honestly I don't care what you do anymore," Nancy said taking a deep breath. "You only care about yourself, what the fuck we gonna do now? I don't know if you forgot, but I'm pregnant" "Bitch I know. You better watch your mouth," Dave warned ready to put on a show for the rest of the passengers on the train.

Instead of arguing, Nancy just stayed quiet until it was time for her to get off of the train. She knew that arguing with Dave was a no win situation, so all she wanted to do was go home and take a hot shower.

"Why aren't you talking to me," Dave asked as he forcefully grabbed Nancy's wrist. "Because I don't feel like arguing with you tonight, that's why." "Oh what you mad because I embarrassed you in front of your old ass boyfriend, Mr. Wiggins?" Dave laughed as he staggered a little from all the alcohol he consumed earlier that day.

"Sometimes you can be a real asshole. You know that," Nancy said as she noticed Coco standing in front of the building waiting for her. "Bitch what I told you about your mouth," Dave snarled through clenched teeth. "Same thing I told you about your temper," Nancy shot back waving Dave off.

Before Nancy could take another step, she felt pain combined with a powerful force connect with the back of her head. It took everything she had inside of her to stay on her feet. Once Nancy regained her balance, she saw Dave charging towards her.

"Bitch you ain't going to be shit, just like your mother," Dave said as he stepped back, and hogged spit in his baby mother's face. Tears ran freely down Nancy's cheeks as she wiped the nasty spit mixed with phlegm from her face.

"You know what your problem is? You don't have no respect for nobody but yourself, but I'm about to teach you what happens when you disrespect somebody," Dave growled as he took his belt off, letting the buckle swing freely.

Before Dave got a chance to hit Nancy with the belt, Coco came to her rescue. "If you touch her with that belt your ass is going to jail tonight mutha fucka," Coco said in an icy tone. "Bitch you need to mind your business before you're next," Dave warned with fire dancing in his eyes. "Nigga please… I wish you would touch me, my brother would be up here so fast you wouldn't know what to do," Coco huffed shaking her neck. "Fuck your brother. I'll do him like I just did this bitch."

"My brother just came home from doing five years behind the wall. Please don't make me have to call him because it won't be a pretty site…trust me," Coco threatened. "Fuck you and your brother. I ain't hard to find," Dave slurred as he staggered across the street, in the opposite direction.

* * * *

"You okay," Coco asked as she helped her best friend back to her feet. "Yeah I'm fine," Nancy replied feeling shit on the inside. "I don't know why you don't leave that fool alone, all he's gonna do is keep treating you like a punching bag." "Yeah, but he won't let me leave," Nancy responded as the two hopped on the elevator of her building.

"What you mean he won't let you leave? Bitch you better stop playing and get lost on that clown. He don't do shit but whip ya ass, take your money, and blame you for all of his mistakes," Coco said hating the way Dave treated her best friend, especially while she was pregnant.

The two hopped off the elevator, and headed straight to the staircase. After everything that had just went on the last place Nancy wanted to be was home, so instead her and Coco sat on the steps in the staircase and continued their conversation.

Chapter 4
THE HOOD

"Yo, slow this mutha fucka down. Don't you see the cops right there," G-money barked angrily. "Man fuck the police," Skip shot back stopping at the red light. "I'll slap the shit out of one of those crackers if they try to arrest me." "I don't care about all that, just slow this mutha fucka down when you see the fuzz you dig?" "I thought if anything ever went down we could call that faggot, Detective Nelson, to get us out," Skip asked. "Fuck Detective Nelson. I don't trust nobody that got blue eyes, you smell where I'm coming from," G-money asked taking a long swig from his bottle of Henny that sat on his lap. "I can dig it, but if you're so worried about us getting pulled over, then why you got a big ass bottle of Henny sitting on your lap?" "Listen B, I'm a tell you like this." G-money hogged spit out the window before he continued, "I do this for all my niggas that's locked up, you dig? You know how many mutha fuckas in jail would love to be getting drunk right now? How many of them would love to be getting high right now, getting money, and fucking bad bitches every night? So that's why I do, what I do. It's a fucking war going on out here; us against the mother fucking police and right now we're losing. So I do this for all my niggas that's in jail who went out for theirs. This street shit is my life. All I know is money, drugs, cars, hoes, jail, and fiends…smell me? Its all a game and if I go to jail I lose, understand? And I ain't having that." "Yeah I can dig it," Skip replied as he double parked in front of Sumner projects. "I hope this mutha fucka don't take all day."

For some reason Brooklyn made Skip very uncomfortable. "There's that clown. Go right there. Pop the trunk so I can hit this fool off," G-money said as he slid out the passenger seat, and grabbed the duffle bag from the trunk. "Tray what's goodie," G-money asked giving the stocky man a pound. "You know, regular shit," Tray answered as he lead G-money into the building. "Yo, keep up the good work. Ali said every month your numbers been increasing. Keep that up and you might get a promotion…smell me," G-money said handing Tray the duffle bag.

"Come on, you know I gotta get this money by any means necessary," Tray capped as he handed G-money three large stacks of money. "Aight, I'm a swing back around here in two weeks to pick up that gwop. Everything's already packed up for you, so all you gotta do is hand out those packs, and make sure the count don't come up short, aight?" "You ain't gotta tell me twice," Tray said as he gave G-money a pound, then headed up the stairs.

As G-money made his way back to the car, he was cut off by some hood rat he piped a few weeks ago. "What's up G-money? I thought you was going to call me," the hood rat huffed standing pigeon toe. "Yeah I was, but I got caught up with some other shit ma. You know how that go," G-money said coldly as he brushed past the young lady. "Bitch ass nigga," she mumbled once G-money was out of ear shot.

G-money was very popular when it came to the women. Most girls said he reminded them of the rapper, Jim Jones, because of the way he wore his hair braided and kept his face unshaven. "Who was that bitch," Skip asked pulling out into traffic. "I don't even remember her name", G-money said before laughing hysterically. "Another one bites the dust, huh?" "You know I don't play no games," G-money boasted as he flipped open his ringing cell phone.

"What's up Coco," he answered. "Hey G-money, what's poppin," Coco asked in her sexiest voice. "Making my rounds for the day. Why, what's up? You wanna get up with me later," G-money asked looking at his watch. "Yeah that would be nice, but I was really calling because I need a favor." "A big favor or a little favor," G-money huffed. "Ummmm…..medium," she giggled. "Aight, what is it?" "Well its like this, I got this friend of mine who's having money problems, so I was wondering if you could maybe let her work with me and the other girls bagging up?" "I got you, babes, just bring her with you on Friday aight?" "Wait its one more thing….she's pregnant." "I don't give a fuck. It ain't my baby," G-money said coldly before he continued. "If she want to take that risk its on her, you dig? I'm just here trying to provide jobs for those who need employment because you know the man still isn't giving us no opportunities or jobs, especially all the people with felonies." "You right about that shit,"

Coco agreed. “But don’t worry about that because my girl is a soldier, and neither one of us is trying to work for the white man.” “You know I can dig it; but yo, I’m a little busy right now. Be ready at ten cause I’m a come through and scoop you up.” “Don’t worry daddy you know I’m gonna be ready. See you at ten.” “Aight one.”

* * * *

“Aight girl I got you in there, so now all you gotta do is get this money,” Coco said giving Nancy a high five. “Thanks girl, but you know I’m only doing this until I save up enough money so that I’m comfortable. Once I’m comfortable I’m gonna go find me another job.”

“Fuck getting a job,” Coco said aggressively. “Why get a job working for the white man when instead you can work for your own people?” “Because working with my people will fuck around and have me behind bars with the rest of my people,” Nancy said sarcastically. “Nancy you just a scaredy cat,” Coco joked turning on the stereo. “Thanks again for letting me stay here until I get my shit together. You’re a life savor,” Nancy said as Fantasia hummed through the speakers. “Girl don’t mention it, but you know that fool, Dave, is going to go crazy when he can’t find you.” “The only thing Dave can do for me is kiss my ass,” Nancy said glad to finally be free. “He can kiss my ass too while he’s at it,” Coco added as the two friends laughed.

“Girl let me go get my ass in this shower, so I can be ready by the time this fool gets here.” “Who’s that," Nancy asked nosily. "G-money with his fine ass; I hope he ain't looking too sexy tonight because I might have to go old school on him," Coco said seductively licking her lips. "Yuck! You're so nasty." "Oh yeah I forgot that you're a Christian. That's why you're pregnant now," Coco said jokingly as she headed towards the bathroom. Nancy didn't respond, instead she just laughed it off and stuck up her middle finger.

* * * *

"Yo who the fuck is Coco," Skip asked slowing down for the yellow light. "One of my P.Y.T's," G-money said lighting up another blunt. "Do she got a friend," Skip asked wanting a piece of the action. "I don't know, but I'll find out for you tonight. Oh shit, pull over real quick," G-money said as he took off his shades making sure his eyes weren't playing tricks on him. Immediately Skip pulled over across the street from the dice game.

"Yo, tell me that's not Calvin right there." "Yeah that's that bitch ass nigga right there," Skip confirmed. "What that clown owe you some money or something? "Yeah he fucked up some money back in the day, but Ali told me to give him a pass. He just told Calvin never to come back on the block. Now this nigga must think something is sweet," G-money said as he slid out the passenger seat.

As soon as Calvin saw G-money and Skip coming across the street, he already knew what time it was. "Look G-money its not what you think," Calvin said copping a plea. "I was just leaving." "So you mean to tell me you wasn't over here rolling dice," G-money asked getting all up in Calvin's face. "Nah I was just passing through," Calvin lied afraid to make eye contact with the killer standing in front of him. "How much money you got on you?" "Not much why?" "Listen I ask the questions around here chump," G-money said poking Calvin in his head with his index finger. "I got about five hundred on me" "Let me see that real quick," G-money said nonchalantly. "What…my money," Calvin asked somewhat confused. "You must think it's a game," G-money growled searching through the man's pockets vigorously, until he found what he was looking for. "Damn that's fucked up G-money," Calvin said in a light mumble. "What," G-money barked loudly causing Calvin to flinch. "You're lucky I caught you instead of Ali," G-money said as he chuckled lightly. "Enjoy the rest of your day brother," G-money yelled over his shoulder as he walked off. "I almost forgot to give this mutha fucka a warning," G-money said as he clutched his .45 and made a U turn.

Before he got a chance to even do anything, Skip had already sent a hot slug into Calvin's hip bone. G-money watched Calvin lay on the ground holding his hip. "Stay the fuck off the block next time," he chuckled as he and Skip hopped back in the ride and peeled off.

* * * *

"How do I look," Coco asked stepping out of the backroom. "Like a whore as usual," Nancy replied half-jokingly. Coco stepped out of the backroom wearing some black spandex fitting jeans, a black wife beater, along with some red four inch heel pumps to match her red headband that added more features to her pretty face. Coco favored Mariah Carey except her skin was a few shades darker.

"Yeah it's on tonight," Coco said excitedly as she poured herself a drink. "I don't know why you love going out with drug dealers and criminals all the time," Nancy said playfully. "Well at least they don't beat my ass," Coco yelled over her shoulder as she headed out the door.

Nancy sucked her teeth. "Fuck you. Ain't no man going to put their hands on me again." "I know because your girl is gonna always have your back, and hold you down," Coco said planting a kiss on her best friend's forehead. Coco's ringing cell phone interrupted the best friend bond.

"Hello," she answered. "Yo, I'm downstairs ma. Don't have me waiting all day," the voice on the other end said. "Okay I'm coming down right now," Coco said closing her cell phone. "Okay girl I'm out. Don't wait up for me." Coco grinned as she stepped out the front door.

As soon as Coco stepped out of the building she spotted G-money's black Range Rover. G-money hopped out of the Range sporting a snug fitting thermal shirt, with his jeans slightly hanging off his butt, along with a fresh pair of black Nike boots. The only jewelry that he wore was a nice watch, a chunky bracelet, and two diamond studded ear rings. "Hey babes what's up," Coco said as she gave G-money a hug followed by a kiss on the cheek. "Waiting to get up with ya sexy ass," G-money said cupping both of her ass cheeks in the middle of the street so everyone could see. "You got your license on you?" "Of course

I do. Why ,what's up," Coco asked curiously. "Because you're driving that's why," G-money said tossing her the car keys.

When Coco spotted the half empty bottle of Hennessy laying on the passenger's seat, she already knew what time it was. "So where we headed," Coco asked pulling out into traffic. "It's this nice Spanish restaurant called El Conde. I think its on 176th St and Broadway in the Bronx.

G-money turned up the volume on the new Lil' Wayne mixtape, pushed his seat back, and just stared out the window, watching the blur of faces pass by block after block. Before stepping out the vehicle G-money made sure he grabbed his .45 from under the seat and placed it in the side of his waistband. His pants hung so low that everyone in eye sight could see the firearm.

"Come on B. I'm hungrier than a mutha fucker," G-money huffed as the two entered the restaurant. "You don't think they might call the cops if they see that gun," Coco asked suspiciously. "Nah," G-money chuckled. "As much as I spend in this mutha fucka they would be crazy to do some shit like that."

The couple took a seat directly in front of the window. G-money always liked the window tables so that he could see everything. Immediately the waitress brought him and his lady two apple Martini's. "Yo let me get steak with rice and beans." "I'll have the same," Coco added as she handed the waitress back the menu. "You going to love the steak," G-money stated taking a sip from his drink. "G-money, can I ask you a question?" "Yeah, what's up?" "Why do you act so thuggish all the time?" "Act thuggish," he echoed loudly. "Listen sweetheart ain't shit about me an act, you understand? I been doing this since niggas was rocking high top fades and playing hop scotch you dig?" "I didn't mean it like…" "You better do your history, before you open your mouth. I'm banned from almost every club in New York. My name rings bells in every jail. I'm known by the whole NYPD, so believe me sweetheart what I do is no act" "Come here baby you need a hug," Coco said playfully as she got up and gave G-money a hug and a kiss. "Don't get it twisted like I'm bragging because that ain't shit to brag about. It's just how I was raised," G-money stated honestly. For the rest of the night the two talked, laughed, and enjoyed the rest of the night.

Chapter 5
THIS CAN'T BE LIFE

"God damn," Nancy said smugly on her hands and knees because with her face halfway in the toilet bowl. All day long Nancy had been feeling like shit. She woke up feeling like she had been partying all night long. "Damn this pregnant sickness shit is whack," she said to herself as she heard somebody entering the apartment.

Nancy stuck her head out the bathroom, and saw Coco heading towards the kitchen. "Damn bitch you just now getting back in from last night?" "Yup," Coco answered proudly. "And I thought I told you to be ready by eight o'clock?" "Sorry girl, but my stomach has been acting up all day," Nancy replied rubbing her five month pregnant belly. "Well hurry up and get dress because tonight is your first night at work and I already told G-money we were coming." "I don't know about this," Nancy said wanting to back out of the ugly situation that stood ahead of her. "It's too late for all that cause I already told them we were coming. Now go get dress," Coco said stuffing her mouth full of Ranch chips.

Nancy took a quick shower, and threw on some jeans and a tee shirt. "Come on, we gotta take a cab," Coco stated plainly when the two finally made it outside. Coco told the cab driver to let them out two blocks away from the spot, so they wouldn't draw any attention to themselves. Nancy took one look at the dirty looking building and wanted to do a 180. After walking up four flights of stairs, Coco did a special knock on the door that they were looking for.

"What's the mother fucking password," a deep voice boomed from the other side of the door. "Money over bitches," Coco answered quickly. Seconds later Nancy heard a series of locks being unlocked. When the door swung open, a big man wearing a wife beater and a pair of sunglasses greeted the two women with his shotgun resting comfortably on his huge shoulder.

"What's up Coco. Who's the new girl," the big man asked blocking the entrance. "What's up Big Bruce. This my home girl, Nancy. Tonight's her first night," Coco said flirtatiously. "Hold up, let me double check this real quick," Big Bruce said as he pulled out his cell phone and started dialing numbers. After a brief conversation, Big Bruce turned to Coco and said, "Sorry about that. I just had to check with G-money first to make sure every thing was every thing." The big man then stepped aside so that the ladies could enter.

When Nancy entered the work area, she saw a room full of topless women bagging up the poison, while wearing latex gloves, and a mask to cover their nose and mouth.

"I don't have to take my shirt off right," Nancy asked innocently. Big Bruce's roar of laughter was her answer. "I'm sorry sweetheart, but Ali's orders are that workers be topless, and that includes you," Big Bruce said wanting to see the pregnant goodies.

"Girl this is too much. I don't know if I can do this," Nancy whispered. "Damn," Coco huffed, followed by a suck of her teeth. "Yo, are you trying to get paid or what?" "Yeah...whatever," Nancy responded pouting like a baby. "Girl this shit is a piece of cake," Coco said as she removed her shirt, followed by her bra revealing her perky breasts that stood at attention.

Nancy wanted to say, "Fuck this shit," and go home, but she knew her baby would be the only one suffering. That's the only thing that made her stay. "Okay, get it together girl," she told herself as she slowly removed her shirt followed by her bra. Due to the fact that she was pregnant, her breasts were much larger than usual. Nancy put on the all white latex glove, and then followed Coco and got straight to work.

"How the fuck could a person smoke this or put this shit in their nose," Nancy wondered as she placed a small portion of the white powder in a small bag.

* * * *

"Yo you almost ready," Ali asked as he put on his double shoulder holster. "Yeah, where are we headed" Big Mel asked cracking his knuckles. "We gotta go pick up Little Spanky from the boxing gym. We going out to celebrate since he won his last fight," Ali answered sliding his twin 9mm's under his armpit and into the holster. "Yeah he did knock that punk ass white boy the fuck out," Big Mel added as he checked the baby Uzi he had holstered on his hip. "Yeah I taught that little muthafucka everything he know," Ali bragged as he and Big Mel stepped outside. "I don't know, little brother might be able to give the older brother a run for his money now," Big Mel said playfully as he hopped in the driver seat of the Denali with limo tinted windows. "Get the fuck outta here. I'll still whip his ass with my eyes closed," Ali snickered as he slid in the backseat. "Yo get G-money on the phone," he ordered as he checked his messages on his I-phone.

"Here boss man it's ringing," Mel said passing Ali the bum out phone as he stopped at the red light. "Hello?" "What's the deal my nigga," G-money's voiced boom through the phone. "You know the same shit different hour. But what's been going on with you?" "Making sure mutha fuckas got the count straight and all that. You know I'm all about getting this money. Ain't no paper out there that I'm scared of," G-money replied. "That's what I like to hear. But this faggot, Detective Nelson, is on my fucking back. He's talking about you bringing in too much heat and fucking up the deal we had." "Fuck that pale face coward. That clown talking like he's doing us a favor. He better shut the fuck up. I don't hear him complaining when he taking our money every month you dig," G-money huffed before he continued. "Plus I don't trust that mother fucker, you know how them crackers can get when they get mad? Detectives are worse than a fucking rattle snake, you understand? You my partner, so I'm trusting you know what you're doing, but I still don't trust that cock sucker." "Listen G-money this not a trust issue. What me and Detective Nelson got going on is just Business. We're going to use this crooked cop until we cant use him no more. I don't like him either, but our money count has increased forty percent ever since we started dealing with that clown. All I'm saying is just slow down a little and any problems Detective Nelson will handle it. All we gotta do is sit back and get paid." "I be trying to slow it down, but these clowns be forcing my hand out here. Oh shit guess who I ran into the other day?" "Who," Ali asked excitedly. "That bitch ass nigga Calvin." "Say word?" "Yeah I caught that fool slipping. I had to make him bite the bullet, you dig?" "Yeah, yeah I hear you, but you know we don't talk on the phone like that," Ali reminded him. "Yeah, you're right…my fault," G-money apologized. "But yo, we going to Eugene's tonight to celebrate. You rolling," Ali asked. "Oh yeah because Spanky knocked that white boy out, right? Aight, bet I'll meet ya'll muthafuckas down there." "Aight my nigga. See you at the club. One," Ali said as he flipped the phone close.

For the last eight years Ali and G-money controlled what went on in the streets. But they had been friends for over sixteen years, even though the two were like day and night. Ali was the smoother one and the streets loved him, but on the other hand the streets feared G-money. He was young, loud, wild, and just didn't give a fuck. He did what he wanted, when he wanted, and most off all G-money hated the police and showed them how much every chance he got.

"Yo, pull over right there," Ali instructed from the backseat. Big Mel did as he was told and parked directly in front of the boxing gym. When the two stepped foot in the boxing gym Ali, and Big Mel saw Spanky going hard with the speed bag.

"What's up champ," Ali shouted over the music that blasted throughout the gym and the constant bobbing of the speed bag. "I ain't the champ yet," Spanky replied with a smile. "When you gonna get your shot at the title," Big Mel asked jumping into the conversation. "When I beat these next four chumps they put me up against," Spanky answered looking at Big Mel never missing a beat on the speed bag. "Don't you mean if you beat your next four opponents," Ali corrected his younger brother. "No, when I beat all of them," Spanky capped back. "Nobody can beat me. I'm the best," he boasted laughing loudly. "It's always one person that has your number," Ali warned. "There's nobody out there that can fuck with me," Spanky bragged still working the speed bag. "Whoever can beat me I'll give them a hundred thousand dollars," he said nonchalantly as he began doing his sit ups. "Well you know your family will always be in your corner," Ali stated plainly. "Come on baby, you know I'm a team player when it comes to family," Spanky said reflecting on when he first started boxing. After Spanky's fourth professional fight, he gave Ali and G-money twenty four thousand dollars so they could buy a brick (kilo). Once Ali flipped that he made sure he paid his little brother back. Ever since the two were kids they always looked out for one another no matter what it was. The two were inseparable and took a vow that no one or nothing would ever come between them – Ever.

"But yo, Spank, the real reason I came here was because I wanted to talk about you and G-money," Ali said taking a seat next to his brother. "What about G-money," Spanky asked puzzled still doing his sit ups. "I noticed you and G-money been hanging out a lot lately." "Yeah and," Spanky answered breathing heavily. "Listen G-money is like my brother and all that, but you need to stay focused on boxing." "But you be with G-money all day," Spanky protested wiping the sweat from his face with a towel. "I'm a drug dealer and your not! You be with G-money and some shit pop off you're gonna be right in the middle of that shit. All this hard work will be all for nothing, you dig?" "Yeah I understand," Spanky huffed. "You right I should watch who I surround myself with." "That's all I'm saying, now go shower up so we can be out," Ali said as he ruffled Spanky's hair. The last thing Ali wanted was to see his little brother do something stupid and fuck up his whole career. Ali promised himself that no matter what he would keep his little brother on a straight path.

*   *   *   *

"Come on girl, lets get up out of here," Coco said as she put back on her bra. Nancy couldn't wait to leave the work place. "I hope the cops don't run up in here," kept running through her mind. "Damn this job ain't too bad," Nancy said to herself as Big Bruce placed cold cash in the middle of her palm for her day's work.

Coco noticed the look on her best friend's face as the paper made contact with her hand. "Yeah, don't front girl is this job the bomb or what?" "Yeah I can't even front," Nancy agreed with a huge grin on her face. "You know your girl ain't gonna put you on to no bullshit," Coco said in a matter of fact tone as the two made their exit. "We're going baby shopping first thing in the morning," Nancy said as her and her best friend stood on the platform waiting for the A train.

* * * *

"Yeah that's what the fuck I'm talking about," G-money said admiring all the beautiful women standing on line outside of the club. Every time G-money went to an event, he made sure he always rolled with at least ten thugged out goons, who he paid to take orders. Nine times out of ten, whenever G-money and his entourage stepped in a night spot something was more than likely to jump off.. G-money and his entourage skipped the long line, heading straight for the front entrance.

"Hey guys the line is back here," a guy wearing a buttoned up shirt with shades yelled from the velvet rope. "Nigga the line is wherever the fuck we say it's at, mutha fucka," Butch a former stick up kid and strong arm robber spat as he approached the man standing behind the velvet rope. "Yo chill, leave that clown alone," Skip chuckled as he threw his arm around G-money's newest soldier. "Yo Butch chill the fuck out," G-money yelled over his shoulder. "Damn let us get in the club first before you start acting up," he said letting out a light huff. "Yo Bobby what's good? It's me and ten of my niggas with me,"

G-money said giving the bouncer a pound. "Sorry G-money I can't even let you or your peoples get up in here tonight," Bobby said folding his arms. "What you mean we can't get in here," G-money asked. "Last time I let you and your peoples in here ya'll tore the fucking place up." "Dem Queens niggas was up in there fronting. That wasn't our fault," G-money protested. "Listen I've been given an order not to let you or your people up in here ever again," Bobby said increasing his tone a little. "Yo Bobby I'm a tell you like this, if me and my people don't get in this mutha fucka tonight we going to terrorize everybody out here on this line. Now try me if you think I'm playing," G-money said staring the bouncer down hoping he made a move.

"Hey is there a problem over here," a uniformed cop asked as he walked up on the scene, noticing a commotion. "Nah these gentlemen were just leaving," Bobby said as he turned and grinned at G-money. "We ain't going nowhere," G-money said as he hogged spit inches away from Bobby's shoes. "You heard what the man said," the uniformed cop barked placing his hand on his .357.

Before things got a chance to escalate Ali, Big Mel, and Spanky showed up right on time. "Is there a problem over here," Ali asked calmly. "The man here asked your friends to leave," the uniformed cop butted in, still with his hand on his .357. Big Mel stood looking at the uniformed cop, while his hand remained inside his jacket pocket where he had his .380 trained on the cop the whole time. "Yo Bobby you got my word G-money and the boys will be on their best behavior. Give 'em a pass this time," Ali said as he shot Bobby a private stare. "Okay, but if ya'll get into some shit this time it's a wrap for ya'll," Bobby said as he unclamped the barrier.

Once inside Ali and G-money were treated like celebrities. Ali didn't really care too much for the attention, but G-money, on the other hand, loved being in the spotlight. He lived for the attention. The entourage quickly made their way to the V.I.P section, where they ordered more bottles of Grey Goose then they needed. "Congratulations mutha fucka. All this is for you," G-money said throwing his arm around Spanky. "All that hard work is finally paying off," Spanky countered as he watched a pack of beautiful women "Pop lock and drop it." "You see this, the bullshit I be talking about," G-money said hotly. "Why the fuck is this big ugly mother fucker staring at me?"

Bobby stood a couple of feet away from G-money and his crew watching their every move. "Damn this nigga on our back, like a cheap suite," Skip added looking the bouncer up and down. "Listen, we're not here for him, we came here to celebrate," Ali reminded everyone. "Let that clown watch us ball out." "I don't know about ya'll, but I'm about to hit this dance floor because it's some bitches in here tonight," Spanky said as he popped open a bottle of champagne and headed to the dance floor along with G-money, and Skip. The club was jammed packed and jumping as usual. Spanky bumped and brushed pass what felt like a thousand people, before he and the crew finally made it to the dance floor.

Immediately G-money spotted a dark skinned chick with a short hair cut and a pretty face, but what really caught his attention was the young lady's ass. Her ass was so big that it looked like she had two asses in one. G-money quickly grabbed the dark skinned girl's wrist and pulled her towards him. The dark skinned girl took one look at G-money and came willingly. She aggressively threw her donkey ass on G-money's dick and started grinding to the beat. G-money rubbed all over the fat ass that stood in front of him as he got his swerve on.

Once Spanky saw G-money set it off, he immediately grabbed the dark skinned girl's friend and pulled her towards him. Ali sat in the V.I.P section with Big Mel watching his little brother have a good time, when he noticed a familiar face stroll into the club. "I know that's not who I think it is," Ali said to himself as he strained his eyes to get a better look.

Rell stepped into the club looking like new money, with his five man entourage behind him. Ten years ago Rell and his crew had the drug game on lock. A few people even called him the Michael Jordan of crack. His only problem was his temper. Rell was known for getting money and having a quick trigger finger. Rell wasn't the most attractive brother in the world, but somehow he always kept a bad bitch on his side. Rell made his way straight towards the V.I.P section where Ali and his crew were stationed.

"WOOOOO......," Big Mel said placing his big paw on Rell's chest. "Where the fuck you think you going?" "What?!" Rell countered slapping the big man's hand down. "Chill Mel, he's cool let him through," Ali yelled before Big Mel got ignorant. "Ali what's popping my nigga," Rell asked as he gave Ali a pound followed by a hug. "Ain't shit. When you get out," Ali asked downing the remainder of his Grey Goose in one gulp. "Them fucking pigs finally let me out yesterday," Rell answered helping himself to a drink. "You know can't no jail hold a nigga like me, but fuck all that I hear you the man out here on these streets now, and that punk Gerald oh excuse me I mean G-money. "Yeah me and G-money running the whole show now," Ali said emptily. "That's why I came here to talk to you," Rell said moving his chair closer. "I need to get this money out here. I know I've been gone for a while, and I don't want to cut nobody's throat. That's why I'm coming to you first." "So what did you have in mind," Ali asked uninterested. "Well it's too hot for me to be on a block or corner, so I was thinking maybe you could break me off a few housing projects – you know the concrete jungle." "The concrete jungle, huh," Ali echoed. "Listen check this out, the best I can do is give you one housing project to run, but the split is gonna have to be fifty, fifty. Now I usually don't do shit like this, but since you're an O.G. and you just came home I'm going to look out for you aight. I'm going to have my workers run the shit, so you don't have to get your hands dirty you dig?" "Thanks, but no thanks. I got my own workers," Rell said flatly helping himself to another drink. "Well I'm gonna have to have a few of my workers in there to make sure ain't no funny business going on," Ali stated plainly. "What you don't trust the God," Rell asked defensively. "Fuck trust, this is business. You know how the game goes, Rell, you're an O.G," Ali said downing his drink only to fill his glass right back to the top. "Yeah, I forgot you learned from the best," Rell chuckled as he noticed G-money step into the V.I.P section followed by his goons.

"Who the fuck is this clown," G-money asked not caring about the man's feelings that stood in front of him. "Come on, you don't remember me, Gerald," Rell said with a smirk on his face. The five men who came with Rell laughed loudly only making things worse. "It's me Rell," he said extending his hand. G-money shook it bloodlessly. "Yo, I remember when I used to make you fight when you used to be scared," Rell said looking G-money up and down like he was still a child. "Looks like that tough love did you some good." "Yes it did," G-money countered as he removed a big wad of cash from his pocket.

Rell thought G-money was going to hand him the money as a welcome home gift, but instead G-money turned towards the crowd and made it rain hundred dollar bills. "Yo Rell we getting money over here, why don't you go snatch a pocketbook or something," G-money said before he broke out into a laughing fit. "You little punk mutha fucka," Rell growled as he jumped up and charged G-money. Before he could reach G-money Spanky caught him with a lightning fast right hook, lifting Rell off of his feet, knocking him out cold.

As soon as Rell's body hit the floor Skip, Butch, and the rest of the goons were on him; stomping him like vultures who smelled fresh blood. Big Mel's baby Uzi kept Rell's goons under control.

When Bobby saw the fight breakout, he quickly ran over there knocking down fifty to sixty people in the process. "I told this mutha fucka I wasn't playing with his ass," Bobby said to himself as he finally made it to the fight. He quickly pushed as many people off of Rell as he could.

When G-money saw Bobby enter the V.I.P section, his face immediately wrinkled as if he smelled some shit. G-money snatched the Grey Goose bottle from off of the table and swung it with bad intentions until it reached it's destination. The bottle shattered violently over the bouncer's head, instantly knocking him out cold. "Fuck face faggot," G-money chuckled as he stepped over the big man's body heading towards the exit.

Once everybody was outside, Ali made sure he pulled G-money to the side. "What the fuck is your problem," Ali growled. "You need to start thinking before you react." "Fuck that. That clown was trying to play me," G-money responded placing a blunt in his mouth. "Listen, we need order around here. If niggas see you wilding all day, then they gonna think they can do the same thing." "They're soldiers, what you expect them to do," G-money asked bluntly. "Do you know what you just did," Ali asked. "Yup," G-money answered as he broke into a coughing fit from the haze in his lungs. "Fuck Rell, he can't see us anyway…fucking old timer."

Ali couldn't do anything but chuckle, his partner's head was hard as a rock and backing down was not in his vocabulary. "Yo, I'm out. Holla at me tomorrow," Ali said as he noticed several cop cars pull up to the scene. Big Mel watched the cop cars disappear through the rearview mirror, as he fled the scene.

Chapter 6
WHEN IT HURT SO BAD

"I'm going to hurt this bitch when I catch her," Dave said to himself as he entered Nancy's mother's building. "KNOCK, KNOCK, KNOCK." "Who the fuck is it," a male's voice boomed from behind the door. "It's Dave. Is Nancy home," he asked patiently waiting for an answer. Seconds later Rick swung open the door. "Man, that bitch ain't here," he said emotionlessly. "Ya'll don't know where she's at," Dave asked stepping into the apartment. "Nope, but wherever she is, she need to keep her freeloading ass over there," Jasmin cut in. "Okay if ya'll see or hear from her be sure to let me know," Dave said as he made his exit. Not being able to locate Nancy only made Dave's anger grow twice as much. He was broke and in a great need of some pussy. Dave checked all the spots that Nancy could be, with no luck. The longer it took for Dave to find her, the more pain he planned on dishing out.

Chapter 7
FINAL WARNING

"I don't know why you thought you could trust a bunch of niggers," Detective Bradley said sipping his morning coffee. "All them mother fuckers are the same; they will lie without even thinking twice," the white detective said openly. "Not all of them," Detective Nelson corrected his partner. "Ali is cool it's that fucking G-money that's giving us problems." "I say we bust that mother fucker's head, and then maybe he'll get the message," Detective Bradley said not hiding the fact that he didn't like black people. "Yeah we do that and then we fuck up our money. I don't know about you, but I like taking money from them every month," Detective Nelson said placing a Winston between his lips. "Me too, but with all those shootings, and people getting sent to the emergency room sooner or later somebody's going to have to take the fall for that, cause it makes us look like we're not doing our job." "Yeah you're right about that. I think I'm going to have a little chat with our friend Ali," Detective Nelson said as he picked up the phone in his office, and began dialing the number.

* * * *

"Is this count straight," Ali asked taking the small duffle bag from Butch. "Yeah it's all there," Butch answered assuredly. "Yo Mel, put this paper through the money machine and make sure it's twenty," Ali said tossing Big Mel the duffle bag. "If you keep running those projects how you're doing, you're going to be up for a promotion soon, you understand," Ali asked trying to feel the young man out. "That's what I'm talking about, moving up the ladder. Maybe you can put me with Skip and the rest of the soldiers, so I can start putting in some work," Butch said making a gun with his fingers. "Easy young hopper, we take things one step at a time around here. Just be patient and you'll get your turn," Ali assured the young man. "So you've been following all the rules, right?" "Yeah," Butch answered quickly. "Nobody gets high or drunk while they on the clock. And nobody is to be strapped while they're on the grind, just in case the boys roll up," Butch said repeating the rules. "And what's the main rule?" Butch raised his hand and said, "Chief, the crew is to be clean at all times while on the clock." "Remember those rules and you'll last long in this business," Ali said proudly. "Yeah it's all there boss man," Big Mel cut in tossing the duffle bag back to Ali.

"Aight, get up outta here. G-money will swing through later with the re-up." "What time," Butch asked foolishly. "Whenever the fuck he get there," Ali barked dismissing the young street thug. "We gotta start tightening up around here," Ali said looking at Big Mel. "I'm checking up on all our spots tonight myself to make sure mutha fuckas ain't taking no short cuts or getting lazy, smell me?" "Yeah I can dig it," Big Mel said as he felt his cell phone vibrating. "Yo it's that punk ass Detective," he said tossing Ali the phone. "What the fuck this mutha fucka want," Ali said out loud as he flipped open the cell phone. "How can I help you," Ali answered. "I'm going to skip through all the bullshit. Your boy, G-money, is out of control," Detective Nelson said getting straight to the point. "If you don't control your partner, then there's little I can do for you. I'm trying to help you, seriously I am Ali, but you're going to have to control that mother fucker or I'm going to have to come down on you and your team. And if I come, you know I'm coming hard! So please let's avoid all of this, and continue to do good business together." "Listen, I understand what you're saying, but you're not the one out in them streets all day. That shit you're talking about is easier said than done. I'm going to talk to G-money one more time, but you're gotta keep in mind that in this business you can't just talk everything out, you dig?" "I hear what you're saying, now hear what I'm saying, when people get shot and we don't have a shooter my boss puts the pressure on me. And when he puts the pressure on me, I'm going to put the pressure on you and that's just how it works," Detective Nelson said flatly. "Like I said, I will have a word with him

Detective, you have a nice day," Ali said ending the conversation.

Chapter 8
A FRESH START

"KNOCK, KNOCK, KNOCK." "Who the fuck is it," Big Bruce yelled from behind the door clutching his twelve gauge shot gun. "Open this mother fucking door."

Immediately Big Bruce recognized the voice and opened the door. "Boss man how's it going," he asked stepping to the side so that Ali and Big Mel could enter. "You tell me," Ali countered giving the big man a pound. "You know I got shit under control down here, boss man," Big Bruce said in a matter of fact tone. "That's what I like to hear," Ali said as he looked around making sure that everything was in order. He quickly stuck his head in the room full of topless women. He didn't say a word, he just nodded in agreement. "Keep up the good work brother," Ali said giving Big Bruce a pound. "You leaving already, boss man?" "Yeah, you know I'm not staying a minute longer than I have to," Ali said as he and Big Mel made their exit.

* * * *

"Okay Big Bruce you have a good night." "You too Nancy," Big Bruce said looking at the pregnant woman's ass jiggle in her snug fitting stretch pants. "Make sure you go home and feed that baby," he joked. "Fuck," Nancy said out loud. It was pouring down raining and she didn't have an umbrella, newspaper or anything. "Fuck this shit, I'm taking a cab home tonight," she said to herself as she swiftly walked to the corner to catch a cab. Nancy stood on the corner flagging down cab, after cab just to have cars fly by like she was invisible.

As Nancy stood on the corner soaking wet, a all black Denali came to a stop directly in front of her. Seconds later the back window came rolling down. "What's good sweetheart. You look like you can use a ride," Ali said smoothly from the backseat. "No I'm alright," Nancy replied looking down the street to see if she saw any more cabs coming in her direction. "Come on ma, let me get you out this rain." "Thanks, but no thanks," Nancy responded again as she began to stroll towards another corner. As Nancy walked down the wet sidewalk she noticed the Denali slowly cruising behind her. "Why are you making things so difficult," Ali asked as he slid out of the backseat of the Denali. "You shouldn't be out here in this kind of weather," he said noticing her stomach poking out.

Ali quickly removed his jacket and placed it over the young lady's shoulders. "All I want to do is give you a ride home." Nancy took one last glance down the street to make sure she didn't see any cabs coming before she made her final decision. "A ride home, and that's it," she asked as she slid in the back of the truck with the stranger.

"So would you like a drink," Ali asked pouring himself a shot of Hennessy. Nancy looked down at her stomach, then back at the handsome young man. "My fault, I'm bugging," Ali said apologizing. "So what's your name?" "Nancy," she answered. "So Nancy, what are you doing in this kind of neighborhood at these hours, especially while you're carrying," Ali asked throwing the shot back. "Minding my business," Nancy capped. Ali just sat back admiring the young woman's beauty. Nancy looked like Lil Kim before all the plastic surgery. Her wet hair only made her face look even more exotic. "Why are you so cold inside," Ali asked pouring himself another shot. "I'm not being cold, I'm just being real with myself," Nancy said staring emptily out of the window. "All men are full of shit. What's with the thousand questions?" "Just trying to get to know you," Ali replied with a smile. "Get to know me? I don't talk to strangers, I don't even know your name." "My name is Ali," he answered proudly. Oh, so you're the infamous Ali, huh," Nancy chuckled. "What's so funny," Ali asked curiously. "Because you asked me what I was doing out here at this time of night, remember?" "Yeah I remember." "Well I was working for you," Nancy stated plainly. "Get the fuck out of here," Ali said in disbelief. "You don't believe me," Nancy asked laughing. "Why don't you just ask Big Bruce if I'm lying?"

Big Mel glanced at Ali through the rearview mirror, and then back to the road. "I'm sorry Nancy, but I'm not going to allow you to work there any more." Ali looked at Nancy for a comment. "What you mean I can't work there any more," Nancy asked angrily. "How you just going to stop my money flow like that?" "Because I'm the boss," Ali answered flatly. "Fucking greedy motherfucker," Nancy said under her breath as a tear escaped her eye.

It seemed like every time things started to go good, something or someone always went wrong. "Ali please I need money for my baby," Nancy begged. "Where's your baby daddy?" "I left him because he has a hand problem," she pouted like a child. "I'm sorry, but if I could help you I would," Ali said as the Denali came to a stop. "Yeah whatever," Nancy said as she hopped out of the truck. Then she handed Ali back his jacket and said, "Here's your jacket."

Ali just sat in the backseat staring at the pregnant girl until she disappeared inside the building. "I want G-money in my office first thing in the morning," Ali said with a sharp edge in his voice. "Can you fucking believe this shit? A fucking pregnant girl working in the shop." "Yeah G-money's bugging out with that one," Big Mel stated plainly, his eyes never leaving the road. "Shit is getting too mother fucking sloppy around here," Ali said throwing back another shot.

Chapter 9
GETTING BACK TO OLD TIMES

"Click Clack, yo I say we go twist them niggas caps the fuck back right now," Debo said loading his dessert eagle. "Be patient. G-money and the rest of those clowns are going to get what's coming to them," Rell said pacing back and forth in his small one bedroom apartment's living room. "First thing we gotta get our money right. Can't go to war unless your paper is up feel me?" "I feel you. So we just let G-money and those chumps get a pass," Debo asked somewhat confused. "Negative; at the end of the month we make our move on those chumps." "But why so long," Debo asked ready for some action. "Listen Debo, you're going to have to trust me. I've been doing this for too long not to know what I'm doing, feel me? Niggas don't call me MJ for nothing. The one thing I've learned from sitting in a cage for all those years is that you must have patience. Now we already took over four corners. By the end of the week we should have eight corners," Rell said looking at his right hand man. "You can't do shit without money." "Yeah, you're right about that shit," Debo responded cracking his knuckles.

Debo was what you called a beast. He stood at 6"4 and weighed 250 pounds solid. Rell met Debo in prison and kind of put the big man under his wing. He made him read plenty of books, and also schooled him on the game, not the drug game but the game of life. Rell promised Debo that if he stuck with him, and remained loyal, that he would make him a rich man. And everybody who knows Rell, know that when he makes a promise he keeps it.

"Damn I feel sorry for Gerald. The crazy part is I used to like the boy," Rell said letting out a light chuckle. "Come on lets go pick up this money." "Lets do it," Debo replied as the two exited the small apartment.

Chapter 10
CLEAN UP TIME

"What's good, you wanted to see me," G-money said entering Ali's office. "Yeah, close the door and have a seat," Ali said leaning back in his chair. "Who let that pregnant girl work in the shop," Ali asked getting straight to the point. "This shorty that works in the shop asked me if I could put her pregnant girl friend on the clock, so I was like fuck it why not." G-money shrugged nonchalantly. "That chick could've brought us all down if something would've happened to that baby in her stomach," Ali lightly scolded. "Yeah, but I felt sorry for the bitch. Her friend was telling me how she ain't have no money or shit for the baby, and how her baby daddy be whipping her ass for no reason. So I thought I would give the bitch a break, smell me," G-money said helping himself to a drink. "Yeah I feel you, but we gotta protect ourselves at all times," Ali said leaning forward. "It's time for us to start cleaning shit up. That fucking cock sucker, Detective Nelson, said one more incident from anyone on our team, and our deal goes out the window. So basically I'm about to tighten up the whole operation because we can't afford no mistakes or nobody getting locked up." "Yeah I can dig it. I never liked Detective Nelson anyway," G-money stated plainly.

"But anyway, you ain't hear nothing on that old school nigga, Rell?" "That clown don't want no trouble with us. All I did was bring him back to reality because that fool was talking like he was still in the eighties," G-money said as the two busted out laughing. "Don't sleep on that fool though, because you never know," Ali warned. "Come on, the way we chumped that fool, he gon' have to come back, without a doubt. And when he do, I'm going to end his career point blank," G-money said giving Ali a pound. "Oh yeah, ya man, Butch, been holding down the projects by himself and he been doing a good ass job too." "Yeah I saw that fool when I went to go drop off the re-up. Nigga think he big time now", G-money joked as he stood up to leave. "Let me get up out of here and check up on this bitch; she been texting me all day," he said looking at his cell phone.

"Hold up, before you go let me get that girl's address who put you on to the pregnant girl." "Why what's up," G-money asked suspiciously. "I'm going to drop her a couple hundred, just to make sure she keeps her mouth shut, you dig? We don't need no bullshit going on right about now," Ali said strongly. "Yeah you right about that," G-money agreed as he scribbled the address down on a piece of paper, then made his exit. "That's a crazy motherfucker," Ali chuckled as he stared blankly at the address on the paper.

Chapter 11
ANOTHER DAY ANOTHER DOLLAR

"You ain't never seen them pies? I'm talking so much white it'll hurt ya eyes," Butch hummed Young Jeezy's words as he sat on the bench listening to one of his runner's radio. Butch sat on top of the bench scanning the whole hood, when he saw a light scuffle break out. "What the fuck is going on now," He asked himself, as he got up to investigate the situation. "Yo, what the fuck is going on over here," Butch yelled out causing his workers to stop beating up on a crack head. "What's the problem," he asked. "Yo dis dirty muthafucka owe me fifteen dollars," the young runner said angrily. "Fifteen dollars," Butch asked in disbelief. "So you gonna kill the man over fifteen dollars?" "I ain't gonna kill him, I'm just gonna whip his ass," the young runner said without a care in the world. "Yo money get up out of here," Butch said helping the fiend to his feet. "The object of the game is to make money, not chase money away." "But the mother fuc…" "What's your name lil' nigga," Butch asked cutting the young kid off. "Andre," the young man answered. "Okay Andre listen, if you choose to let the fiend build up a credit for fifteen dollars then that's on you. If the muthafucka don't pay you back he's only hurting himself because now when he's a little short motherfucker gotta pay the full price. Within a week I bet that fool pays you what he owes you," Butch said kicking some knowledge to the youngster. "That corner boy bullshit is dead from now on, we going to look at this game like business men," Butch said repeating something Ali told him not too long ago. "You about your business right?" "All day," Andre replied placing a Newport between his lips. "Aight, then get back to work and lets get this money," Butch said smoothly as he headed back over to the bench where he came from.

Butch's job was to keep the traffic in the projects, as well as the money coming in at a fast pace. Butch spent one year as a look out, and two more years as a worker to finally become a crew chief. It wasn't that he was a good worker, but Ali wanted to test his loyalty as well as his hunger. Now three years later Butch was in charge of the whole operation, and still moving up on the ladder. Butch watched the fiends come and go, realizing that he would probably be bone dry in two hours if that. He quickly reached for his blackberry. Ali had supplied everybody on the team with a blackberry, but the phone was not to make calls, it was supposed to be used to get in contact with him or G-money by email only in case of an emergency. Anybody caught using their blackberry for any other reason would have a hell of a price to pay. Everything was about discipline.

Butch smoothly slid his blackberry out of it's case as he typed G-money a message. "Yo I'm thirsty, bring me something to drink." He then placed his blackberry back in it's case, and waited patiently for his re-up to arrive.

Chapter 12
SOME TIMES PAIN TURNS INTO PLEASURE

"What you mean he said you can't work there no more," Coco asked with a nasty attitude. "Yeah that's what Ali said," Nancy said heatedly. "Mutha fucka just mad cause I was getting mines." "I'm going to holla at G-money, next time I see him because this is some bullshit," Coco said angrily like she was the one who couldn't work there any more. "Girl I'll be back in a few hours. I gotta go take care of something real quick," Coco said as she grabbed her purse, and headed out the door.

Nancy just sat on the couch searching through the classified ads in the newspaper, hoping to obtain employment as soon as possible. But she knew it wouldn't be easy with her condition. "Who am I kidding? Nobody is going to hire a bitch who's six months pregnant," Nancy said tossing the newspaper across the floor. She couldn't think of one person who would hire her. On top of that, she wanted to at least have five hundred dollars saved up for the baby. Nancy wanted to kill Dave since it was his fault why she got fired from McDonalds in the first place. Nancy's cruel thoughts came to an end when she heard somebody banging on her door like the police.

"Who is it," she yelled out walking to the door. No answer came back. "I said who is it," she said as she reached the peephole. Nancy huffed loudly when she noticed who it was. "What do you want," she asked in a nasty tone. "I just want to talk to you," Ali yelled from the other side of the door. "We don't have a mother fucking thing to talk about," Nancy said snaking her neck as if Ali could see her through the door. "Come, this won't take long, plus I'm not leaving until you talk to me," he threatened.

Ten seconds later Ali heard a series of locks being unlocked. "You got two minutes, so make it quick," Nancy said peeking her head from behind the door. "May I come in," Ali asked taking a step further. "Nah you good," Nancy said stopping Ali in mid-step. "Damn sweetheart I was just coming to bring you a gift for the baby," Ali said handing the beautiful woman who stood in front of him a thick envelope. "Nah I'm good, I don't want no hand outs. This ain't no charity case," Nancy said as she refused to take the envelope. "This ain't no hand out sweetheart, this is a gift from my heart," he said extending his arm once again. "Thank you very much. Is there anything else I can do for you," she asked her tone dropping a notch. "No sweetheart that will be all," Ali said politely as he and Mel headed back down the hallway heading towards the elevator.

Nancy quickly shut the door, and proceeded to open up the envelope. Beasting to see what was inside, she ripped the envelope in four different places. Once she finally got it opened, she found that inside the envelope was a nice size stack of money along with a letter. "I don't believe it," Nancy said out loud as she began to count the money. Her final count was three thousand dollars. "Damn that was very nice of him," Nancy said to herself as she sat down, and read the letter.

Dear Nancy,

If you are reading this, that means you have accepted my little gift. First of all let me start off by saying the money is not to try to buy you or your friendship that money is for that little one in your stomach. Me being a black leader and all feel it's only right to look out for my people because if I don't who will? But moving along I was wondering if maybe one day we might can go out and grab us something to eat if that's okay with you. If so give me a call at (917) 555-0000. If you are not interested still give me a call. I've only spent twenty minutes with you and from that short time I could tell that you a sweet and special girl. Not to mention it's plain to see you have a good heart. Well I don't want to bore you, so I'm going to end this letter.

P.S. I hope to hear from you soon!!

When Nancy finished reading the letter, she thought that she was going to melt on the couch. Nobody had ever talked to or spoken about her like that in her entire life. For once in her life she felt special and good inside. "Nah he gotta be running game on me because he's a drug dealer and I know it's plenty of women who are with him or dying to be with him," Nancy said to herself, trying to talk herself out of liking Ali and falling for his game. Nancy didn't know what kind Ali was playing, but she definitely wasn't interested. Besides, what would a handsome young man with money want with someone six months pregnant? Her thoughts were quickly interrupted, when she heard her microwave beeping. She rushed over to the microwave, and fetched out her butter popcorn, that she had been craving all day. As Nancy sat on the couch, eating her popcorn, she re-open Ali's letter and read it over again.

Chapter 13
BROTHERS FROM ANOTHER MOTHER

"Five hundred I make this shot," G-money challenged dribbling the basketball between his legs, in street clothes. "That's a bet, and you've been drinking today," Skip said snatching a big wad of cash from his pocket. "Nigga must think he Tom Sheppard." "Aight, let me get a warm up shot first," G-money said still dribbling the ball. "Nah fuck that warm up shit, just shoot," Skip said getting all up in G-money's ear. "Yeah make the shot when the pressure is on nigga, you balling right? Five hundred ain't shit to you, right?" He taunted as G-money got ready to shoot.

As G-money was about to take the shot, he noticed a crowd form. Seeing other gamblers make side bets only got G-money even more hyped. "Let's go three, two, one," G-money said as he shot the jumper a few feet behind the three point line. The whole crowd erupted in a loud, "OOOOH," when the shot bounced off the rim. "Nigga must think he Jordan," Skip said as he broke down into a laughing fit. "Yo son gimme my money." G-money quickly peeled five hundred dollars off his stack of money and handed it to Skip. "Small thing to a giant. There's plenty more where that came from."

"Come on we like family, I don't like taking your money like this; its too easy," Skip boasted as he threw his arm around G-money's shoulder. "Nigga you only took five hundred from me, you talking like you a million or something," G-money replied still a little salty that he had missed that shot. "You talking like you wanna run it back," Skip challenged counting G-money's five hundred dollars in his face, just to rub it in. "Nah maybe later, we gotta go take care of something real quick," G-money replied as he deactivated the alarm, and started up the engine to his Benz just by a press of a button on his key chain.

"When are you going to get you one of these joints," G-money asked pulling out into traffic. "Not my style B." Skip said placing a blunt between his lips. "You know I save all my money, you never know what might happen." "Yeah you know in this business you might get ya head blown off tomorrow", G-money said half jokingly. "Then all that money is going to go to waste." "God forbid if I get killed tomorrow, I know my son and his mother will be straight," Skip said letting out a light cough. "Plus that's what its all about anyway my little man. I work for him, so when he gets older he ain't gonna have to work for the white man or no bullshit like that. Why you think white folks are so far ahead of us? Because white people are born with an option, either they can work if they want, or they can not work if they don't want. You know why? Because their parents done already put in the work so their kids won't have to, you dig?" "Yeah I can dig it," G-money said taking in the knowledge his friend was throwing at him. "Yeah well that's what I do with my money," Skip said passing the blunt to G-money.

"Damn nigga why you always wet the shit all up," G-money complained as he pulled up right in front of the boxing gym. "Why you stop here," Skip asked curiously. "I gotta go holla at Spanky real quick," G-money answered quickly as he slid out the driver's seat and disappeared inside the gym.

* * * *

Spanky stood in the middle of the ring in the gym going hard with a sparing partner. For Spanky it was like fighting a girl the way he landed any punch he wanted to his sparring partner's exposed face and head gear effortlessly. "Okay that's enough," Old school Freddie said tired of watching Spanky beat up on the other fighter. Old school Freddie was a boxing expert, and one hell of a trainer. He had been training Spanky since the first day he stepped foot in the gym. Freddie saw fire, and hunger in the young man's eyes since day one, not to mention Spanky loved to hurt people. When he first started boxing, he never went for the knock out. Instead he would talk shit to his opponent while landing vicious blows. His plan was to try to in flick as much pain as possible. That was until Freddie told him to stop playing around in the ring and go for the kill. He would always tell Spanky, "A ring is no place to play, even if you know you can beat your opponent because one punch can change a fight."

"Yo Freddie get ya old ass out the ring before I come in there and knock you the fuck out," G-money yelled staring down the old man. "You young punk mother fuckers swear ya'll so tough. Anybody can shoot somebody, but can you fight? Come in this ring and I'll show you what real tough guys do," Freddie said opening up the ropes inviting G-money into the ring. "Old man I wouldn't even brake a sweat," G-money countered as he gave Spanky a pound.

"You better stop fucking with Freddie, his hands are still kind of nice," Spanky said in a matter of fact tone. "I'll wash that nigga up stupid quick," G-money said waiving off the old man. "But anyway what's good? You ready to make this move?" "Yeah, come with me to the locker room real quick," Spanky said leading G-money towards the back. "I don't be wanting people all up in my business," Spanky said once he and G-money were alone in the locker room.

Spanky quickly unlocked his combination lock and grabbed a book bag from his locker. "Clock work," he said handing G-money the book bag. "That's what I'm talking about," G-money said looking at the neatly stacked money in the book bag. He quickly thumbed through the bills just to make sure everything was straight. "You been doing a good job," G-money said reaching down in his draws removing a healthy Ziploc bag full of Ecstasy pills.

"Yo this a double; you think you can handle this," he asked handing Spanky the Ziploc back.

"Yeah Christie should be able to handle this," Spanky replied as he quickly stuffed the Ziploc bag in the small pocket of his duffle bag. "Ali doesn't know anything about this right," G-money asked curiously. "You crazy! It look like I'm trying to get killed," Spanky said seriously. "Ali don't want me involved in no kind of street activities." "Because you got a career and a future; me and Ali ain't never going to be shit but criminals you understand? I don't even know why you fucking with these pills for anyway," G-money told him. "I understand what ya'll saying, but if Christie got the clientele then I'm going to supply her," Spanky looked at G-money for a comment. "Supply and demand, Ali taught me that, plus more money is always better. You can never have enough money." "You right about that," G-money agreed.

"So what's good? You still rolling to the strip club with me tonight," Spanky asked. "No doubt we in there," G-money replied rubbing his hands together. "Aight, so I'm about to go shower up, and I guess I'll meet you there."

"Aight bet. I'm a call you when I'm on my way," G-money said as he gave Spanky a pound, then headed towards the exit. When G-money made it back to the gym area he saw Old school Freddie doing some push ups. "You need to be working out your jaw instead of your arms" G-money said breaking down into a laughing fit. "My jaw is far from glass, young brother," Freddie challenged. "One of these days I'm a whip your old ass up and down this gym," G-money said as he made his exit.

Chapter 14
IT'S STRENGTH IN NUMBERS

"Yo that nigga, Michael Vick, is about to go to jail son," Dave said standing on the corner drinking a forty, talking to his friend Maurice. "You crazy. Vick got too much money to go to jail; niggas with money don't never do no jail time," Maurice told his friend. "Damn B, I might have to catch a jux (commit a robbery) tonight," Dave said looking at Maurice. "Why, what's up?" "Nigga I'm broke," Dave said patting his pockets. "What happened to that shorty you had? I thought she was holding you down," Maurice asked looking at his friend for an answer. "Man fuck that bitch. She ain't shit but a gold digger," Dave said turning up his forty ounce. "I tell you this though, when I find her I'm a put my foot in her ass." "Why don't you just let that girl be?" "What the fuck you mean," Dave barked. "Bitch keeping me away from my seed, I don't play that shit." "Damn, I didn't know all that was going on, but if I see her I'm a definitely let you know," Maurice assured his friend.

Before Dave could say another word, he noticed an all black S.U.V. pull up to the curb. The smoked black tinted window made it impossible to see inside. Immediately Rell hopped out of the S.U.V. and made his way towards the corner with Debo right on his heels. "Yo Dave what's good my nigga," Rell asked giving Dave a pound skipping right past Maurice. "Oh shit Rell, what's poppin? When you get out," Dave asked smiling from ear to ear. "I been home for a couple of days now, but fuck all that I came to see if you still about your money," Rell said looking Dave up and down. "You know I'm about my paper. I just don't got nothing popping right now," he said throwing back his forty. "So you telling me you and ya man standing on this corner right now just for fun," Rell asked sourly. "Basically," Dave answered shame fully. "My money is kinda funny right now, but you know I'm a bounce back like I always do."

"Aight this is the deal, this corner right here," Rell said pointing to the ground, "this my corner now! But I want you to run it for me. I'm going to get you a hammer, workers, and all that; all you have to do is sit back and make this money." "Aight bet. That's what I'm talking about," Dave said giving Rell a pound followed by a hug. "That's why I respect you so much, you always looking out for ya boy." "If I don't then who will?" "I'm a put this block on the map. You don't have to worry about shit, just hit me with that product and it's on," Dave said convincingly. "Aight, but I'm a tell you from the jump that we can't afford no fuck ups, you dig," Rell said as he, Dave, and Debo stepped inside the bodega. "Come on B, fuck ups ain't even in my vocabulary," Dave said grabbing another forty from the freezer. "Aight, I'm just letting you know cause if you have any fuck ups you gonna have to report to the big man," Rell said pointing at Debo. "Nah baby I got this, all I ask is that you let me put my man, Maurice, on so he can hold me down," Dave asked twisting open the cap on his forty. That's your call, but we about to do it real big out here, so I hope you ready like you say you are," Rell told him. "Rell you know I'm always ready to get this money. You know how I get down." "You might even have to bust that ratchet," Rell reminded him. "You know my gun game is still serious," Dave boasted. "Time will tell. I'm a send somebody around here to hit you off tomorrow," Rell said as he gave Dave a pound, and broke out.

"That bitch ass nigga talks too fucking much. I hope his bite is louder than his bark," Debo said once he and Rell were back in the whip. "He was stunting back there but, what fool can't watch over the block," Rell said splitting open a Dutch. "But he should be able to handle that block, if not we'll just replace him," Rell said shrugging his shoulders.

"Aight cool, but what's up with that bitch ass nigga, G-money," Debo asked with ice in his tone. "I'm ready to get at that fool." "Who Gerald," Rell chuckled. "We ain't gonna kill him just yet ,that's soon though. First we going to hit that clown where it hurts the most." "And where's that," Debo asked confused. "We gonna hit his pockets first," Rell said as he sprinkled the crunked up spliff in the Dutch. "Getting into a man's pockets is worse than shooting him. Plus once you in his pockets, his mind is next, then once we in his mind he's a dead man walking. Trust mc, I got this whole shit already planned out," Rell said giving his partner a wink.

For the past five years Rell sat in his cell coming up with the master plan, and now was the perfect time to execute his plan.

Chapter 15
THE NIGHT LIFE

"Ahwww shit," Eric mumbled under his breath, as he noticed G-money followed by at least fifteen thugs behind him. "What's going brother, how you feeling," Spanky asked giving the strip club's bouncer a pound followed by a hug. "I'm cool," Eric replied emotionlessly. "We not gonna have no problems in here tonight are we," the big bouncer asked focusing all his attention on G-money and his entourage. "Nah baby, we chilling tonight," G-money assured the big man as he slipped a hundred dollar bill in his hand.

"Okay gentlemen, ya'll enjoy yourselves tonight," the bouncer said letting the group pass through the velvet rope, and enter the club. Once inside the strip club, G-money and his entourage took a seat and enjoyed the show one of the strippers on the stage was putting on. "Damn that bitch's ass is stupid fat," Skip said out loud as he watched the stripper do a hand stand, and pop her pussy at the same time. "That's what I'm talking about, baby you earning this money," G-money yelled as he tossed a hand full of one's at the sexy dancer. "You see shorty right there is about her paper," he boasted to the rest of his crew.

Meanwhile Spanky just sat quietly on the sideline until he saw the person he was looking for. Christie came from the dressing room wearing nothing but a sky blue thong, and a pair of sky blue stiletto's to match. Her meaty thighs along with her fat ass caused every man in the spot to redirect their attention to her goodies. Christie wasn't skinny, but she wasn't fat either, she had a pretty face and a hustler's tongue.

"What's good with this lap dance," G-money asked flashing a hand full of singles. "Boy move out of my way," Christie said as she playfully pushed G-money to the side. "Heeeey baby," she said poking out her full lips that were covered in strawberry lip gloss as she bent down and kissed Spanky on his lips. "Hey baby, how you feeling," he asked. "I'm feeling much better now that you're here," she replied as she took a seat next to Spanky and held his hand.

"Yo what time you get off," Spanky said jerking his hand loose to look at his watch. "You see that's the shit I be talking about," Christie huffed then sucked her teeth. "Every time you come in here you act like you're embarrassed to be seen with me." "I am embarrassed! You know I don't want you shaking your ass in front of all of these perverts. I make enough money so you don't have to do this," Spanky countered. "You hear what you just said? You make enough money; that's your money. You make your money how you do, and I make mines how I do, you feel me?" "No." "Baby your missing the whole point. If you were to leave me today I would be good. You know why? Because I make my own money, and I like having my own, plus I don't like what you do for a living and I don't see you quitting your job," she said sarcastically.

"Listen, I didn't come here to argue with you," Spanky said pulling Christie closer to him. "You know I love you right," he asked in a hushed tone. "Of course I do. Baby I promise I won't be working at this job much longer." "Thank you Jesus," Spanky said playfully.

Spanky and Christie had been together for four years. Spanky hated the fact that his girl friend was a stripper, but what could he say, she was a stripper when he first met her. Christie wanted to stop stripping a long time ago, but just wanted to save up enough money just in case anything ever went wrong. Depending on a man was one thing Christie vowed she would never do, especially after growing up watching her mother have to do some wild things because she didn't have her own. Christie promised herself she would never be like her mother.

"Aight baby let me go make this money," Christie said as she kissed Spanky on the cheek. "Hold up baby I got something for you," Spanky said discretely handing Christie a brown paper bag. "This feels a little different," she said noticing the package felt a little heavier than usual. "Yeah that's double right there," Spanky said looking both shoulders suspiciously. "Can you handle that?" "I can handle anything you throw at me and I do mean anything," Christie replied raising an eyebrow. "I'm a see you later on tonight big daddy," she said as she disappeared to the other side of the club.

G- money sat sipping on his cup of Hennessey as he watched his crew make it rain on the strippers. His soldiers worked hard, so he enjoyed watching them have a good time. G-money's thoughts were interrupted when a stripper approached him from behind.

"You look like you could use some company," the stripper whispered seductively licking her lips. "Now that you mentioned it, I could use some company," G-money flirted after taking one look at how big the stripper's ass was. Without hesitation the stripper bent over and started shaking her ass in G-money's face. The stripper's ass cheeks were so fat that each time she shook her ass it made a loud clapping sound. "That's what I'm talking about," G-money said with a thirsty look in his eyes as he stuffed single after single in the young woman's thong.

After chilling in the strip club for about forty minutes Spanky had seen enough. "Yo I'm about to breeze. I'm a holla at you tomorrow," he said as he gave G-money a pound, then made his exit. "Aight bet, scream at me tomorrow," G-money said redirecting his attention to the fat ass in front of him.

* * * *

When Spanky finally made it home, he quickly took off all of his clothes and hopped into the shower. Twenty minutes later, Spanky hopped out of the shower and was quickly caught off guard as he heard Ne-yo humming through his living room speakers. Instantly Spanky reached under his bathroom sink, and pulled out the .380 he had stashed there. He slowly stepped out of the bathroom, making sure he tiptoed not to make any loud noises. When Spanky reached his bedroom, he opened the door cautiously only to find Christie spread out across his bed butt naked.

"What the fuck you doing here," Spanky asked lowering his gun. "What does it look like," she replied seductively spreading her pussy lips apart with her two fingers.

Spanky quickly sat his gun down on the dresser as he made his way over towards the bed. "I been thinking about my dick all day," Christie whispered as she continued to play with her pussy in front of her man. She could see the hungry look in his eyes. Spanky quickly got on the bed and started kissing on Christie's thighs. It wasn't long before he made his way up to her sweet spot. Christie let out a loud moan when she felt Spanky's tongue hit her clit. Every time she tried to pull away, Spanky would pull her back down with his tongue moving a thousand miles per second. Christie wasn't allowed to leave, until she came five times. Her pussy was so wet that she could feel her upper thighs feeling wet and sticky. She slowly removed Spanky's towel, and was happy to see that his dick was already hard. She quickly pushed him on his back and climbed up on top of him. Christie's pussy was so wet that Spanky's dick just slid right in with no problem. She then planted her feet on the bed and rode Spanky's dick like it was a new motorcycle for the rest of the night.

Chapter 16
YOU CAN'T LOSE IF YOU DON'T PLAY

Nancy sat in the house bored as hell. She had been watching Lifetime movies all day, and was sick of watching T.V. She was also still mad about not having a job, but the three thousand dollars Ali had given her came in handy. She made sure she spent the money wisely. Ever since Nancy read that letter, she couldn't keep her mind off of Ali. He was so sweet, but at the same time Nancy knew he had to have a mean side to him because of the type of business he was into. But that still didn't stop Nancy from wanting to get to know him better.

"Should I call him or not," Nancy asked herself looking down at her stomach. "Fuck it dinner can't hurt," she said as she picked up the phone and began dialing the number he left in the letter.

*   *   *   *

Ali sat in his office along with Big Mel watching a video of Spanky's next opponent. "You see them Spanish mother fuckers don't be caring if they get hit, as long as they get in one good hit," Ali said studying the Spanish man on the tape. "This Spanish guy is tough," Big Mel added rubbing his chin. "As long as Spanky trains how he's suppose to, he'll destroyed this clown," Ali said nonchalantly knowing his little brother's skills were way better than the Spanish man's. "Yeah, but this Spanish mutha fucka got a lot of heart and a good chin," Big Mel said as he reached for the ringing cell phone on the table.

"Who dis," he barked into the receiver not recognizing the number. "Hello, may I speak to Ali please," a soft voice asked on the other end. "Who's calling please," Big Mel asked lowering his voice a notch. "Could you tell him it's Nancy please?"

"Hey boss man it's some chick calling for you named Nancy," Big Mel said with his hand covering the receiver. "Yeah let me get that," Ali said reaching for the phone. "Hello," he spoke smoothly. "Hey what's up?" "You tell me beautiful. I've been waiting for you to call," Ali said in his best mac daddy voice. "Ummm…I was calling about that offer you made me in your letter." "And what offer is that? I make a lot of offers," he told her. "The dinner offer you made me," she reminded him. "I made you a dinner offer,"

Ali asked dumbfounded. "Never mind, maybe I got the wrong number." "Okay, okay I was just fucking with you," he said before she hung up. "You pick whichever restaurant you want and that's where we're going." "Well I don't really go out too much, so I wouldn't know a good restaurant if it slapped me in the face." "I know the perfect spot, start getting dressed and I'll be over there to pick you up at nine o'clock. Is that okay," he asked. "Sure, that will be perfect," Nancy answered looking at her watch that read eight twenty. "Okay I'll see you then," Ali said ending the conversation.

Nancy hung up the phone with a huge smile on her face. Fucking with a loser like Dave for so long, Nancy almost forgot what it felt to be treated like a real woman. It didn't matter anyway because Dave was old news and Ali was looking like a prince in shining armor coming to rescue her.

Nancy stood in front of her mirror, applying her make up when she heard a light knock at the door. She quickly glanced at the clock on the wall that read ten after nine. She put one more coat of lip gloss on before she headed to the door. "I thought you got lost for a second," Nancy said stepping out into the hall way. "Nah, sorry I'm a little late but I had to take care of something before I came over here," Ali said pulling a dozen roses from behind his back. "These are for you." "Ahww thank you," Nancy said blushing. This was the first time any man had ever brought her flowers. "They're beautiful." "Beautiful flowers, for a beautiful woman," Ali countered.

"Give me one second, let me go put these in some water," she said stepping back inside the apartment. Seconds later she returned, still blushing like a little school girl. When the two stepped out of the building, there was a light breeze flowing as they made their way to the curb where the Range Rover awaited them. Once the couple was in the back seat, Big Mel put the pedal to the metal.

"So where are we going," Nancy asked not able to hide the excitement on her face. "It's a surprise," Ali answered popping open a bottle of champagne. "That's cool, I love surprises." "I'm pretty sure you're going to love this one as well," Ali said filling his glass up to the rim.

As Ali poured the champagne into his glass, Nancy noticed the gun sitting in Ali's shoulder holster. At first she wasn't going to say anything, but she knew if she didn't ask the question would haunt her all night long. "So what's the gun for," she asked suspiciously. "What you mean," Ali asked not understanding the question. "I mean we only going on a date, is the gun really necessary?" "Very necessary," he answered downing his drink in one gulp. "Why does me having a gun bother you," he asked. "No it doesn't bother me, I just don't see the point." "Listen sweetheart, since I was young I've always been told it's better to have a gun and not need it then to need a gun and not have one," Ali stated plainly. "So do you take a gun everywhere you go?" "No sweetheart, I take two guns with me where ever I go," he answered honestly. "Okay, to each its own I guess," Nancy said dropping the subject. "Shit, if I sod drugs all day to a bunch of thugs I guess I would carry a gun everyday too," Nancy said to herself as the Range Rover came to a stop.

Ali made sure he helped Nancy out of the truck as they made their way into the restaurant. Once inside the restaurant the host greeted Ali with a handshake. "Right this way," he said in a weird accent as he lead the couple to a table all the way in the back. Nancy was shocked when the host lead them to a table with two lit candles on top.

"Is everything okay," Ali asked noticing the strange look on Nancy's face. "I'm cool, I just never had a candle lit dinner before," she said honestly. "Well there's a first time for everything," Ali whispered softly as he pulled out Nancy's chair her.

As the couple sat down looking over the menu, Big Mel sat close by keeping an eye out for anybody or anything that looked suspicious. "So I take it you don't get out much," Ali asked looking over the menu. "Not really," Nancy answered quickly as the waiter approached the table. "Are ya'll ready to order," he asked. "Yeah, I'll have the lobster dinner," Nancy answered. Handing the waiter back the menu, then winked at Ali. "I'll have the same thing," Ali added handing the waiter back the menu. "Oh and can you bring me a bottle of champagne, and some water for the lady." "Coming right up," the waiter said politely as he headed back around the corner.

Once the waiter was out of ear shot Ali continued with his conversation. "So why is it that a pretty lady like yourself don't go out much?" "Well I'm going to be honest with you, my last boy friend was very abusive." "I'm sorry." "What are sorry for? Its not your fault that he's an ass hole." "I meant to say I feel sorry for him. If I ever catch that faggot," Ali said with a chill in his voice.

Nancy was happy when she saw the waiter approaching the table. She hated talking about her past, every time she did, all of the hurtful things Dave did to her came back to haunt her. "Before we eat, I would like to make a toast," Ali said filling his glass with champagne. "To us and our future, the past is the past," he said raising his glass. "I will definitely drink to that," Nancy said as she grabbed her glass of water and held it up in the air. "To us and our future," she said as the two glasses clinked. Once dinner was over, Ali pulled out Nancy's chair like the perfect gentleman, and escorted her back to the vehicle. For the entire ride home the couple didn't say a single word to each other, instead Nancy curled up in Ali's arms as the two listened to Alicia Keys humming softly through the speakers.

"Ya'll lovebirds wake the fuck up. We got some company," Big Mel yelled over his shoulder as he noticed the cop car lights flashing in the rearview mirror. "Damn these mutha fuckas ain't got nothing better to do," Ali huffed sitting his glass of champagne down. "Yo pull this mutha fucka over." Seconds later two red neck officers came strolling to the vehicle shining their flashlights inside the vehicle.

"What seems to be the problem officer," Big Mel asked uninterested. "License and registrations shit head," the officer barked shining the bright light in the big man's eyes. Big Mel slowly reached for his wallet, and removed his license and the card Detective Nelson gave him in case him or Ali ever got pulled over or arrested. "Here you go officer," Big Mel said placing the card on top of his license.

The officer studied the card for about thirty seconds before he spoke. "Where did you get this card from?" "Detective Nelson," Big Mel answered quickly.

Three minutes later the officer returned to the driver side window, and handed Big Mel back his license, and the card. "Sorry for wasting your time. You enjoy the rest of your night," the officer said tipping his hat. "No problem officer," Big Mel replied as he pulled back out into traffic.

"I can't stand those racist muthafuckas," Ali huffed in a tone of disgust as Big Mel pulled up in front of Nancy's building. As Ali walked Nancy to her building, all of the local thugs and drug dealers who stood in front greeted Ali with a head nod. "You know those guys?" "No, but I'm sure they know me," Ali replied as the two stepped on the elevator.

"I really had a nice time tonight," Nancy said as she and Ali walked down the narrow hallway heading towards her apartment. "Well I hope this won't be the last time we get to be with each other," Ali hinted.

"Can I ask you a question," Nancy said fishing in her purse for her keys. "I'm pretty sure you get your fare share of pussy, and I'm also sure that women throw themselves at you everyday, so I asked myself why would you want to be with somebody like me?" "What do you mean somebody like you?" Nancy didn't answer, instead she just looked down at her six month pregnant belly. "Oh that," Ali said letting out a light chuckle. "Listen sweetheart, I don't care that you're pregnant, and I don't care about what people have to say about me either. But I'll tell you one thing I know; I know what I like and what I want, and I like and want you," he said pointing at her. "But why me," she asked. "Because you're beautiful and I'm not just talking about your looks I'm talking about your inner beauty. Its hard to find a person that's beautiful on the inside and outside, and that baby in ya stomach is a blessing, and I would be honored to help you raise that baby in your stomach."

Those last words caught Nancy off guard. "You're sure that you really want to be with me exclusively," Nancy asked looking into Ali's eyes for an answer. The look Ali gave her said all she needed to know. "Listen Ali, I'm going to need to think about this for a day or two because I just got out of a horrible relationship and…" "That's all you have to say, I already know how it is coming out of an abusive relationship," Ali said cutting her off. "Thanks for understanding," Nancy said as she kissed Ali on the cheek. "You got my number, so don't be a stranger." "I won't sweetheart. You have a good night," Ali said as he watched Nancy enter her apartment. He didn't leave until he was sure she was inside safely.

Once inside of the apartment, Nancy felt like jumping up and down, but she decided against the idea because Coco was in the living room. "Hey girl, where you coming from," Coco asked noisily. "I had a date," Nancy answered nonchalantly. "Bitch stop lying. Who you went out on a date with being six and a half months pregnant." Coco laughed loudly slapping her thigh for extra emphasis. "For your information, I went out with Ali," Nancy said placing her hand on her hip. "You are such a liar," Coco said not believing her best friend. "Okay don't believe me then," Nancy said shrugging her shoulders as she headed for the bathroom. "Girl stop playing around…are you serious," Coco asked again in disbelief. "Yeah girl, why would I lie?" "Okay get over here and tell me all about it," Coco said thirsty for the gossip. "Well we just went out to eat at a nice restaurant, and just talked for the whole night trying to get to know each other better," Nancy said making a long story short. "Damn, I thought you had something juicy to tell me," Coco said disappointed it wasn't the gossip she was looking for. "No bitch, I'm not a whore like you," Nancy yelled over her shoulder as she disappeared inside of the bathroom.

Once inside of the bathroom Nancy quickly removed her clothes and stepped inside of the shower. She still had a big smile on her face. She couldn't remember the last time she had such a good time. As Nancy stood in the shower replaying the whole night over again in her mind, she couldn't help but notice that her pussy was soaking wet. Immediately Nancy spread open her pussy lips with her two fingers and began playing with herself, until she came twice. Once out of the shower, Nancy slid in the bed and stared up at the ceiling until she felt her eyes getting heavy and drifted off to sleep.

Chapter 17
LIFE IS SHORT

"Come on, I don't got all day how many you need," Andre snarled, looking over both shoulders. "Hold on, gimme a chance to count my money," the fiend shot back trying to iron out his crumbled up bills. "You should've been had ya money ready before you came over here," Andre said as he snatched the fiend's money. "You probably can't even count," he said quickly adding up the money in his head. "Here," Andre said in a nasty tone as he handed the fiend two small bags of crack. "Come on, I don't want this flakey bullshit. Let me get two of those pregnant rocks," the fiend complained making a scene. "Get up outta here B. You making it hot," Andre said excusing himself leaving the fiend standing there. "Bitch ass nigga," the fiend spat once Andre was out of ear shot. "Nobody don't tell me what to do," he slurred as he pulled his stem and sprinkled the product inside of it and proceeded to light it up.

Butch sat at the flagpole talking to one of his shorties when he thought he was seeing things. "I know this mutha fucka is not out here getting high in broad day light," he said to himself as he stood up. "Yo ma I'll be right back. Let me go take care of something real quick," Butch said as he headed in the crack head's direction. "Yo what the fuck is wrong with you," Butch barked as he slapped the fiend's stem out of his hands. "Come on man, I ain't doing nothing wrong," the fiend slurred with a pile of white slime caked up on both corners of his mouth. "Listen, when you get ya fix next time you go smoke that shit across the street, inside the building. I don't give a fuck, just don't smoke it outside aight?" "Man you trippin," the fiend slurred obviously too high to know who he was talking to. Seconds later the fiend felt the concrete slap him in the face. Butch had dropped the fiend with one punch to the back of the head. After Butch knocked the crack head out, he walked inside of the building like nothing had ever happened. Once inside of the building, Butch hopped on the crowded elevator, and pressed his floor. When the elevator finally reached his floor, Butch quickly made his exit and headed towards the door he was looking for. Once in front of the door, Butch did a special knock. Seconds later, he heard some feet shuffling from behind the door. "Its about time you got here," Stacey said looking Butch up and down. Stacey was a two hundred and fifty pound chick who was on G-money's pay roll. Her apartment was used as a stash crib. Stacey was also known for throwing wild house parties. "Don't be rushing me, I get here when I get here," Butch said playfully as he brushed past Stacey. Butch wasn't surprised to see that the house was packed with neighbors, and friends from the hood. "Damn you stay with a packed house." "You know I throw card games every weekend," Stacey said in a matter of fact tone. "Yo, just take ya big ass in the kitchen and fix me something to eat," Butch said as he headed down the hallway to the backroom. He quickly pulled out a set of keys, and unlocked the room door. Inside of the room was money, guns, and plenty of product. Butch quickly made his way towards the dresser, and proceeded to fill a zip lock bag up with crack.

* * * *

"Yo pull over right here," Rell ordered from the backseat. "There go one of them niggas right there," Debo said pointing at the young kid selling drugs in the open. "You want me to take care of that clown," Debo asked sternly. "Nah, I got this one." Rell said as he threw on his hoody, and slid out of the vehicle. When Andre saw the hooded man coming in his direction, he immediately assumed he was a fiend. "What's up, you need something," he asked looking over both shoulders. "Yeah, let me get five of them thangs," Rell said digging in the small of his back. In a blink of an eye Andre found himself staring down the barrel of a snub nosed .38. Immediately his urine broke, spilling out of him effortlessly. "Tell that faggot Gerald he's next," Rell smirked as he pulled the trigger. His smirk quickly turned into a grin when he saw Andre's brains pop out of the back of his skull. Before Rell left, he made sure he pumped the five remaining bullets into the young kid's lifeless body. Andre's body jumped from the weight of the shots as Rell quickly fled to the get away car.

*　　*　　*　　*

Butch found himself caught up in a shit talking contest with one of Stacey's guest when he heard a loud series of gunshots. He quickly dashed back into the bedroom, grabbed a .380, stuck it in his back pocket, and then headed out of the door. "Yo keep this door locked and don't open it for nobody until you hear from me," he yelled over his shoulder as he disappeared in the B staircase. When Butch finally made it outside, he saw that a big crowd formed at the spot he last saw Andre standing. "Oh hell naw," Butch said out loud when he saw Andre sprawled out on the concrete. "Fuck," he cursed loudly as he quickly pulled out his cell phone and quickly emailed G-money.

Twenty minutes later the cops finally arrived on the scene. "Yo what happened," G-money asked calmly with about fifteen to twenty goons behind him. "I don't know. I was in the stash crib grabbing some more jacks when I heard like six shots go off." "So did he get robbed," Skip asked jumping in on the conversation. "Nah, he ain't have nothing heavy on him because I was bringing him a new pack," Butch stated plainly. "So mother fuckers just killed him for no reason," G-money asked. "I guess so because he ain't have shit for them to take," Butch answered shrugging his shoulders. "Aight, you keep running this mother fucker how you been doing; just keep your ears open," G-money said as he and his entourage made their exit. As G-money and his crew made their way back to their vehicles, they never noticed Detective Nelson watching their every move.

Chapter 18
WHAT A DIFFERENCE A DAY MAKES

"A yo, go get me a pack of Newports," Dave ordered as he handed the young lookout a twenty dollar bill. Dave was really feeling himself now that he was making money. He went out and bought all new clothes, and a used 2001 Yukon. The way Dave lived in the past was nothing but a memory. According to Dave, he was the man; he had power and was loving every minute of it. All he did was collect the money, count it, and report back to Rell. His main man, Maurice, was the one doing most of the work, watching workers, paying the lookouts, and bagging up while he took all the credit.

"Hey daddy, you still out here working," Rita asked in a nagging tone. Rita was Dave's new girl friend. The two met each other at a night club. When Dave saw the pretty chocolate skinned woman dancing by herself he knew right then, and there he had to have her. "Yeah, you know I gotta make this money," Dave replied as he hungrily undressed Rita with his eyes. "What time you gon' be finished daddy? I wanted to go see that new Denzel Washington movie," she whined, pinning her neatly twisted dreadlocks up in a bun. "Damn I forgot that shit came out today," Dave said as his lookout came back with his cigarettes. "Good looking lil' homie, keep the change," he said putting on a show because his girl was present. "Aight baby, go get in the truck, we're going to the movies. Let me just go holla at Maurice real quick," he told her. "Yo hold the block down, I'm going out with my shorty," Dave said proudly. "Damn nigga again? This the forth time this week ya'll going out." "What, you my parole officer or something," Dave shot back looking at his friend. "I'm just saying we both suppose to be holding down the block," Maurice said as he gave Dave a pound.

Chapter 19
CHANGING THE GAME

"So in two weeks it's the big day, huh," Ali asked sipping on a glass of Grey Goose. "In two weeks I'm going to knock this Spanish mutha fucka out," Spanky boasted as everybody bursted out laughing. "I'm putting a hundred thousand dollars on this fight, you better not let me down kid," Mr. Goldberg added as he sipped from his champagne glass.

Mr. Goldberg was a Jewish lawyer that Ali hired to pick up any case he or anybody on his team caught. No matter how small or big the case was, if you was down with Ali then Mr. Goldberg was going to be your lawyer no questions asked. "If you were smart, you would bet two hundred thousand," Spanky told him.

The foursome's conversation was rudely interrupted when they heard a loud knock at the door. "Click, Clack...Big Mel go check that out," Ali ordered as he cocked back one of his 9mm's. "Who the fuck is it," Big Mel yelled as he slid a shotgun from under the couch. When Big Mel looked through the peephole he was shocked to see Detective Nelson standing on the other side of the door. "It's this faggot ass detective," Big Mel said looking at Ali for approval to let the detective in. "Let him in," Ali ordered as he slid his 9mm back into it's holster. "Out of my way big man," Detective Nelson barked as he brushed past Big Mel. From the redness in his face you could tell that the white detective was smoking mad. "Hey, I thought we had a deal mother fucker," Detective Nelson growled pointing his finger in Ali's face. Out of reflex Ali slapped the detective's hand down. "Yo chill the fuck out," he warned. "Chill the fuck out," Detective Nelson echoed with a devious grin on his face. In one quick motion Detective Nelson flipped the table that the four men sat at upside down spilling champagne and liquor everywhere. "Is you crazy," Big Mel yelled as he grabbed Detective Nelson and rushed him, pinning his back to the wall making sure he placed his forearm under the detective's throat. "Take your filthy paws off me or else," Detective Nelson whispered as he struggled to break the big man's hold. "Listen detective, you're in my mutha fucking spot. Respect it or you'll get treated accordingly," Ali warned. "Let him go Mel." "Fuck you Al. We had a deal and you broke it," Detective Nelson snapped. "What the fuck are you talking about? My people have been cool," Ali said pouring himself another cup of Grey Goose. "Bullshit, G-money and his crew just murdered a young kid in the projects yesterday," Detective Nelson grumbled.

Another knock on the door startled the five men in the office. "Go check that out," Ali ordered. "Oh it's G-money," Big Mel said as he unlocked and opened the door so that G-money, and the four soldiers he had with him, could enter. "What's poppin," G-money asked giving Big Mel a pound. "Uninvited guest," Big Mel replied in a hushed voice. "What's good, ya'll having a meeting up in here without me," G-money asked as he gave Ali a pound followed by a hug. "Nah ,Detective Nelson just dropped by talking about you and your peoples murdered some kid yesterday," Ali said taking another sip from his glass. "Get the fuck outta here," G-money said waving the detective off. "Does Deandre Johnson ring a bell," Detective Nelson asked with a chill in his voice. "Fuck is you talking about," G-money sighed. "Lil Andre was one of my workers. Somebody came through and smoked him yesterday. Why the fuck would I smoke one of my own people?" "Either way it goes the kid got murdered because of you whether you admit it or not; probably one of your million enemies," Detective Nelson said in a icy tone. "Fuck you and the whole NYPD. The whole force can kiss my ass. My lil' homie got smoked last night and instead of looking for his killer, you're over here harassing us. Get the fuck outta here with bullshit," G-money spat helping himself to a glass of Grey Goose. "People like you kill me," Detective Nelson chuckled as he moved in closer towards G-money. "You think you're so fucking tough." "I talk tough because I do tough things," G-money shot back. "Let me ask you a question tough guy," Detective Nelson said now face to face with G-money. "You think you're untouchable?" The murderous look G-money gave him answered his question in more ways than one. "I bet you can get touched," Detective Nelson threatened. "Listen, anybody touch a cornrow on my head and they gonna be getting fed through a fucking tube, smell me? And that goes for anybody, including you detective," G-money said in a challenging tone.

"Ali I'm going to give you another chance to do business with me because you're a cool guy, but only under one circumstance…you must drop this cock sucker from your team," Detective Nelson said pointing at G-money. The whole room erupted with laughter after that last comment. "Sorry detective, but G-money is family and we take care of our own around here," Ali said strongly. "Big mistake, I thought you were suppose to be the smart one, but instead you're just as dumb as this Nigger." "Yo, who you talking to like that," G-money swelled up but was held back by Big Mel. By this time Detective Nelson's face was as red as an apple. "I guarantee all of you motherfuckers will regret this. Ya'll must not know who ya'll fucking with, but around here I'm Mr. Untouchable," Detective Nelson growled as he stormed out of the office heated.

"Aight everybody listen up," Ali said grabbing everyone's attention. "We're gonna keep running things how we've been doing. Just spread the word that we might be under a microscope, so I want everybody to cover their asses. We can't afford no fuck ups. G-money, I want you to be extra careful because we know for a fact that Detective Nelson got something up his sleeve for you, so stay on point. For right now, we're just gonna play it by ear and see what happens."

Chapter 20
RACIST PROFILE

Nancy sat in the tub soaking and relaxing as "Donny Hathaway" Flowed through her bathroom radio speakers. She had to have some relaxing music playing every time she took a bath. For the past two weeks Nancy had been in the best of moods, especially since her and Ali had been spending almost everyday with each other. Once she got out of the tub, she quickly lotioned up her body and got dress. Nancy had a lot of shit to do today; first she had to pick out a cake for her baby shower, not to mention she had to do a little shopping for her and the baby. Nancy threw on some comfortable stretch pants, some flat sandals, put her hair in a pony tail, threw on her Chanel shades and was out of the door. Her first stop was to 116th Street and St. Nicholas to a store called "Make My Cake." She heard that they made the best cakes for special occasions, so she figured why not show them some love.

As soon as she stepped into the store, she was amazed at the kind of cakes that they had on display. “Wow this is nice,” she said to herself as she saw a cake with the cover of the F.E.D.S. magazine on it. “Yeah I’m getting something just like this,” she said admiring the F.E.D.S. magazine cake. “Hey, can I help you,” a short brother asked politely from behind the counter. “Yeah, I was wondering can ya’ll put any picture on a cake?” “Yes if it’s a clear picture,” the short brother answered quickly. “Okay then I’m going to have to come back when I know what I want. I just wanted to see some of your work, and I must say I’m very impressed. Do ya’ll have a card,” Nancy asked. “Sure, here you go,” the brother said politely handing the pregnant woman the card. “Thank you. I hope I see you soon.” “Don’t worry you will,” Nancy yelled over her shoulder as she exited the store.

Once out of the store, Nancy quickly flagged down a cab and headed to her next destination. After five hours of shopping, she figured that she should start heading home. Nancy laughed to herself as she flagged down another cab because she had spent five hours shopping and still didn’t get everything that she wanted. As Nancy stood on the corner waiting to flag down a cab, she heard a group of footsteps coming from behind her. Nancy quickly spun around with a fright.

“Excuse me is your name Nancy,” Rita asked sucking her teeth with two of her home girls behind her. “Yeah I’m Nancy, do I know you?” “Listen bitch I’m going to tell you this one time, and one time only, stay the fuck away from my man.” “Who is your man,” Nancy asked curiously. “Now she wanna play stupid," one of Rita's home girls jumped in the conversation. "Dave is my man bitch and I don't want you blowing up his cell phone at all times of the night no more," Rita said popping her lips and rolling her eyes. "Dave," Nancy echoed as her face wrinkled up. "Please, I have a real man now, a real man, and I'm the one who broke up with Dave in the first place," Nancy informed her. "Listen bitch I'm tired of listening to all these lies. If you wasn't pregnant I would tear ya ass up," Rita growled swelling up in the middle of the street. "Well bitch I won't be pregnant forever, all I got is a month and a half left. I'll be more then happy to whip ya ass," Nancy told Rita as a cab pulled up right in front of her.

"You see a bitch, you slap a bitch," Rita grumbled moving in a little closer. "Listen, I got better things to do than argue in the streets with a bunch of hood rats. Excuse my back," Nancy said smoothly as she slid into the backseat of the cab. "Yeah you better run bitch," Rita spat loudly as she kicked the back door of the cab. Before the cab pulled off, Nancy mouthed the words, "Fuck you bitch," as the cab driver bent the corner.

"I'm gonna bust her ass next time I see her," Rita promised as she and her crew went on about their business.

When Nancy finally made it home, she immediately plopped down on the couch from her long adventure. "Can you believe the nerve of this bitch," Nancy said out loud to herself as she picked up her cordless phone and dialed Coco's cell phone number.

*   *   *   *

Coco sat at a fancy restaurant on a double date with G-money, Skip and his wife, April. They all sat enjoying a good meal and good conversation when Coco heard her phone ringing in her bag. Instantly she recognized the number and answered. "Hey girl what's up?"

"You ain't gonna believe what happened to me while I was out shopping," Nancy said cradling the phone between her ear and shoulder as she got up to go find herself something to eat. "I'm on the corner trying to catch a cab, when out of nowhere Dave's new girl friend runs up on me talking about I better stay away from Dave or else she going to bust my ass." "Girl tell me you're lying," Coco said in disbelief. "Nah, I'm dead ass. She ran up on me with two of her girl friends poppin shit like she's about that." So what did you say," Coco asked hungry for some gossip. "I told that dirty whore once I had this baby, I was going to kick her ass. You know I don't play that shit," Nancy said venomously. "That bitch better fall back before she get her ass stomped out," Coco spat not caring how loud she spoke. Where you at? I thought you would be home by now." "I'm on this double date right now with G-money and one of his home boys, and his girl." "Oh aight, why didn't you say so. I'll just holla at you when you get home." "Aight later," Coco said ending the conversation.

"Everything good," G-money asked overhearing a little bit of Coco's conversation. "Yeah everything's cool. My girl just got into a little confrontation with some bum ass bitch; nothing serious," Coco replied knifing off a small piece of steak, and shoving it into her mouth.

"So you really think that chump, Detective Nelson, gonna start harassing us," Skip asked pouring everybody at the table another glass of wine. "Fuck that white boy," G-money said waving Skip off. "Well I think we should come up with a plan, just in case this cracker try to teach us a lesson or prove how much power he has," Skip said seriously. "I already got a plan; if he start acting up, it's on simple as that," G-money slurred. "Come on G, use your head. You're trying to fight a battle you know we can't win," Skip stated plainly. "Skip, you already know how I get down, and you know I don't give a fuck about no cops. How I look letting a faggot ass cop herb me? It's not happening. Both of my uncles are in jail for killing a cop, I think that shit just runs in my family," G-money said nonchalantly.

"Sometimes talking to you is like talking to a fucking building," Skip said shaking his head. "Come on baby you ready to go," Skip asked looking at April. "We all came together, so we're going to leave together," G-money said flagging down the waiter for the check. "You mad at me baby, you need a hug," G-money asked playfully reaching for Skip's hand. "You think everything's a joke," Skip huffed as he placed a few twenty dollar bills on the table.

"Put that money back in ya pocket. Your money is no good when you're with me. Every time we go out, I pay," G-money said placing two hundred dollar bills on the table. Skip quickly snatched his money off the table, and stuffed the bills back into his pocket as the four of them made their exit. "Here baby, you drive," G-money said handing Coco the keys to the Range Rover. Coco quickly pulled out into traffic, and made a left turn, then stopped at a red light. "Yo the fucking cops are behind us," Coco announced nervously. "Are they signaling you to pull over," G-money asked curiously. "No, they're just riding behind us," Coco answered. "Yo Skip you strapped?" "Of course," Skip answered from the backseat. "Aight, gimme your hammer so I can put it on the glove compartment." "What," Skip blurted out. "You know the rules…never put you or Ali in jeopardy." "Fuck that, you got kids," G-money reminded his friend. "It's all in a day's work," Skip said extending his arm. G-money quickly removed his .45 and handed it to Skip. The Range Rover made it about six more blocks down the street when the cop car signaled for it to pull over.

"Aight everybody just be cool," G-money ordered as Coco pulled over on the side of the road. As soon as the officer approached the Range Rover, Coco could feel the bright light from the officer's flashlight abusing her eyes. "Driver keep your hands on the steering wheel," the officer barked as he clicked his walkie talkie and called for back up. "Nobody make any sudden moves and we won't have a problem."

Seconds later, an unmarked detective car pulled up on the scene. Skip immediately shook his head in disbelief when he saw Detective Nelson stepped out of the vehicle. By the look on Detective Nelson's face Skip knew it was about to be trouble. Detective Nelson quickly pulled out his .44 magnum when he reached the passenger window. "Well, well, well, look at what the cat drug in," Detective Nelson chuckled aiming his .44 magnum directly at G-money's head.

"What seems to be the problem Detective," G-money asked with ice in his tone. "You have the right to remain silent," Detective Nelson quickly shot back as he reached and opened the passenger door. “Keep your hands where I can see them, and step out of the vehicle slowly,” he instructed without taking his gun or focus off of G-money. “What’s the charge,” G-money asked. “Shut your fucking mouth boy,” Detective Nelson snarled as he violently shoved G-money against the hood of the Range Rover. The menacing look G-money gave the Detective screamed trouble. “This is what you wanted right tough guy,” Detective Nelson whispered in G-money’s ear as he roughly patted him down making sure he wasn’t strapped. G-money didn’t respond instead he just kept quiet as Detective Nelson handcuffed him, and roughly sat him down on the curb. “Put your hands on the hood boy,” the uniformed officer said harshly as he shoved Skip against the vehicle. “This is bullshit,” Skip capped back refusing to cooperate. Immediately the uniformed officer roughly tackled Skip, slamming him down on the concrete. Skip wasn’t going out without a fight; he continued to squirm, and resist to cooperate. April quickly slid out of the vehicle when she saw the officer struggling to apply the handcuffs on her man. “Hey what are you doing,” she yelled as she got ready to jump on the officer’s back. “Take another step bitch, and I’ll blow your fucking head off,” Detective Nelson yelled aiming his gun at April, freezing her in mid-stride. “Get over here bitch,” he growled grabbing a fistful of April’s hair. “Hey stop moving or I’ll blow this bitch’s brains all over the sidewalk.”

When Skip saw April defenselessly in Detective Nelson’s grasp he quickly surrendered, and let the officer handcuff him. The uniformed officer then quickly cuffed Skip, and sat him down on the curb next to G-money. “What were you going to do;

jump on my back," the uniformed officer asked placing a fake smile on his face as he walked over towards April. "No I wasn't, I was just…"

April lost her train of thought when she felt the officer slap the shit out of her. "You just what," he yelled forcefully grabbing April by her collar, pinning her back against the Range Rover. "I'm going to fucking kill you mutha fucka," Skip screamed out in rage as he tried his best to get back to his feet. Immediately Detective Nelson violently busted Skip on the top of his head with his .44 magnum. As Skip's body jerked from the impact of the blow, the .45 fell from his waistband. "What do we have here," Detective Nelson said with a big smile on his face, as he picked up the handgun. "You got a permit for this," he asked with a smirk on his face. "What else you got on you," he asked as he roughly searched Skip only to find another .45 in the small of his back. "Jackpot," Detective Nelson laughed loudly as he headed back over to his car.

"Do you have any drugs or weapons on you," the uniformed officer asked in a seductive tone. "No I don't have nothing on me," April answered quickly. "Well I'm just going to have to see about that." The officer chuckled as he roughly shoved April on the hood of the Range Rover, and began to frisk her. Immediately the officer started at April's ankles and worked his way up to her legs where he rubbed, and caressed her inner thighs the whole time never taking his eyes off of Skip. "Don't even worry about it, this mutha fucka is already dead he just don't know it yet," G-money whispered as he saw the defeated look on Skip's face.

Once the uniformed officer finished caressing April's legs, he quickly slid his hand up to her pussy.

Out of reflex April's body jerked when she felt the white man's hands in a place where they shouldn't have been. "Don't fight it baby, you know you like having a real man touch you the right way," the uniformed officer whispered in April's ear as his hands slid from her pussy up to her breast. "Don't you wish you had a real man in your life," he asked spinning April around so that they could be face to face. April didn't answer, she just looked at the officer in disgust as tears ran freely down her cheeks.

"Hey what the fuck are you doing over there? Cuff the bitch and let's go," Detective Nelson ordered as he violently snatched Coco out of the vehicle, and threw her against the hood. "Got any drugs or weapons on you," he asked as he began to frisk her. "You know I don't got shit on me, you're just fucking with us because we're black," Coco replied as she sucked her teeth, and rolled her eyes. Detective Nelson quickly handcuffed Coco and spun her around so that she could see his face. "You think I'm a racist," he asked her. "I don't think, I know you're a racist. You didn't even read us our rights," Coco replied smartly. "Okay you got the right to remain stupid," Detective Nelson said as he quickly punched Coco in the stomach causing her to drop to her knees. "Come on let's get these scum bags in the car," he ordered as he tossed Coco in the backseat of his unmarked vehicle. The uniformed officer grabbed G-money, and helped him up off the curb, forcefully shoving him towards the car. "I'll be seeing you real soon Officer Allen," G-money said as he glanced at the officer's name tag. "Was that a threat boy," Officer Allen asked as he pulled out his night stick, and jabbed G-money in the stomach. "Hold on," Detective Nelson yelled as he snatched the night stick from officer Allen's hands. "Let me get some of this," he said as he hit G-money several times with the night stick before he shoved him in the backseat. "Get a good look at my face faggot because I guarantee you'll be seeing a lot of it after tonight," G-money warned as Detective Nelson threw his unmarked car in drive, and headed to the station.

Chapter 21
SHIT HAPPENS

"Aight, so you got all the paperwork and everything for this new restaurant, right," Ali asked sipping on some yak. "Yeah, everything is all ready to go," Mr. Goldberg answered taking a double take at the paperwork that was in front of him. "Aight, so we already got some people working in the pool hall, and the small coffee shop downtown, right," Ali asked as he checked his emails on his I-Phone. "Yeah that's correct; we just moved the crew you had on 119th street off the corners and into the stores, just like you asked," Mr. Goldberg answered again. "Aight, so we're right on schedule then. After the restaurant opens, then we're going to move on to the cab service." "Hey boss man, what's up with all these businesses you're opening up," Big Mel asked curiously. "What? You forgot why we even started hustling?" "To make money, right," Big Mel asked dumb founded. "Not only to make money, but to create jobs, and opportunities for other black people," Ali said in mid-sip. "If we don't look out for us, who will?" "Is that a trick question," Big Mel said playfully. "This hustling shit is just a stepping stone to get our foot in the door. Plus we can't do this shit forever. These judges giving out life like its water, smell me? Mother fucker won't be throwing the book at me," Ali chuckled as he watched Big Mel reach for his cell phone.

Yeah, who dis," Big Mel answered the restricted call. "Yo, it's me G-money," he spoke excitedly. "Me, Skip, and our ladies got locked up this faggot mutha fucka, Detective Nelson, harassing us and shit. Tell the big man to send bail money, and Mr. Goldberg down here to get us out, you dig?" "Say no more, it's already done," Big Mel replied ending the conversation. "That was G-money, he said Detective Nelson locked him and Skip up while they were with their shorties." "You see that's what the fuck I'm talking about. Once all our businesses are up and running, I'm taking all the crews off the corner," Ali stated strongly. "Go grab some bail money out of the safe." Big Mel quickly grabbed twenty thousand out of the safe, and handed it to Mr. Goldberg. "If it's more than that just put up the money and I'll pay you back once you find out the total," Ali said reclining back in his seat.

* * * *

After spending fourteen hours in a small holding cell, G-money, Skip, Coco, and April were finally released. "Take a cab home ladies, me and

Skip gotta go handle something real quick," G-money said as he handed both ladies a hundred dollar bill. "Be careful…I love you baby," April whispered kissing Skip on the lips. Before Coco could even say a word, G-money and Skip were already headed down the street on foot. By the look on both of their faces Coco knew the two of them were on they way to do something stupid.

Chapter 22
IT'S NOT A GAME

"Why you always walking past me like you ain't feeling me," Butch asked in a smooth tone. "Butch, you know I don't deal with guys who live in the projects. Ya'll don't know how to keep ya'll mouths shut," the hood rat stated plainly as she started walking off. "Well fuck you then bitch," Butch yelled as he placed his 9mm in the garbage can just in case the cops ran up on him, he would be clean not to mention if Rell came through he wouldn't be naked. Butch sat on the bench watching two girls who had been arguing for the past twenty minutes.

"Why don't you just slap that bitch already," he said to himself hoping to see a good fight. Butch's mind frame quickly changed when he heard one of his look outs scream 5-0. When Butch looked to his right he saw Detective Nelson quickly approaching.

Immediately he hopped up off the bench, and started walking in the opposite direction.

"Get over here big time," Detective Nelson spat as he violently threw Butch up against the black gate that surrounded the projects. "Is there a problem detective," Butch asked smartly. "Yeah, I have a problem with seeing you sitting on this same bench every day, all day for no particular reason," Detective Nelson replied as he handcuffed Butch then proceeded to search him. "Okay where did you hide the drugs and guns," he asked upset that he didn't find anything on the suspect. "Come on detective you know I just say no to drugs," Butch chuckled noticing that he was getting under the detective's skin. "Come on, let's go," Detective Nelson growled as he pulled Butch off of the black gate, and lead him towards his vehicle. Where the fuck you taking me," Butch asked nervously. "I'm taking you downtown to see if you have any warrants," Detective Nelson stated. "Tell your buddy, Ali, from now on you and a few of your partners will be getting locked up everyday – is that understood? Every time I see you in that projects, I'm going to put cuffs on you," he added as he vigorously shoved Butch into the backseat of his car.

*   *   *   *

After Detective Nelson finished beating Butch down with a night stick for fifteen minutes, he needed a drink. "Hey Officer Allen, how about a few beers," Detective Nelson said as he noticed Officer Allen filling out some paperwork. "I wish, but I got a lot of papers to fill out; I arrested eight of Ali's men tonight," he boasted. "That calls for a few drinks, plus I'm buying," Detective Nelson huffed not taking no for an answer. "Okay," Officer Allen said throwing his hands up in surrender. "No way I can turn that down." As soon as the two stepped outside the police station, the cool night air slapped them in the face. "Damn it's kind of breezy out here tonight," Officer Allen said out loud as he looked up, and saw a brown station wagon coasting down the street with three shooters hanging out of the window wearing ski masks and clutching fully automatic weapons. "Holy shit," was the last word the officer spoke before the shooters opened fire.

The next ten seconds sounded like the fourth of July. The loud roar from the machine guns caused Detective Nelson to jump out of fear. Instantly he felt a bullet rip through his shoulder, causing blood to splatter all over his grey suit. Officer Allen didn't stand a stance, as the gunmen riddled his body with bullets. By the time Detective Nelson pulled his gun from his holster, the station wagon was already turning the corner. "Fuck," Detective Nelson growled with a sharp edge in his voice as he looked over and saw Officer Allen's dead body sprawled out on the ground with his eyes open, where he laid silent forever.

* * * *

"Yo make sure you dump this mutha fuckin station wagon," G-money ordered as he and Skip hopped out of the vehicle. "I got you. I'm a ride out to this chop shop that's right around the corner, and tell them to strip this mutha fucka clean," Diesil assured G-money. "Don't worry, we won't let you down," Benny said from the passenger seat. "Aight, give me your guns," G-money said as he took Benny's tech 9, and placed it in a duffle bag along with the other weapons. "Ya'll get rid of the car and I'm gonna get rid of these guns," G-money told them as he and Skip slid into the S.U.V. that awaited them.

"You seen the look on them fools faces when they seen us," Skip laughed loudly taking his eyes off the road to look at G-money. "Them mutha fuckas ain't know what to do," G-money boasted as he lit up a blunt. "Them fucking crackers crossed the line when they fucked with my wife," Skip said sourly as he slowed the car down when he reached the Brooklyn Bridge. Immediately G-money hung out the window, and tossed the duffle bag full of guns down into the Hudson River. "Aight, now we have to go change, then head to Madison Square Garden so that we can make it to Spanky's fight on time," G-money said fiddling with the radio. "Oh yeah, I forgot that shit was tonight," Skip said out loud as he put the pedal to the metal.

* * * *

"Tonight is just the beginning baby," Freddie said out loud as he massaged Spanky's shoulders as he got his hands wrapped inside the locker room. "I'm going to beat the shit out of this Spanish mutha fucka," Spanky said sternly as he cracked his neck. "You think I put in all those hours in the gym to lose tonight? Fuck outta here. If that Spanish cat wants to win, then he's going to have to kill me in that ring," Spanky continued his rant.

"Tonight is your night baby," Christie whispered as she planted a soft kiss on Spanky's lips. "I'm going to knock this clown the fuck out tonight just for you baby," he said giving Christie a wink. "I know you are boo," she replied as she noticed Ali enter the locker room with a pregnant woman on his heels. "Long time no see," Ali said as he kissed Christie on the cheek. "I been busy working, trying to blow up like you, big time," she said playfully.

"What's up champ," Ali barked playfully throwing a left hook to see if his little brother was on point. "You going to have to come better than that," Spanky said easily blocking his older brother's left hook. "That's what I like to hear," Ali said as he gave his brother a hug. "Good luck out there; me and my new girl friend, Nancy, are going to be in the front row cheering you on," Ali said introducing Nancy to everyone in the locker room. "I should fuck you up," Spanky said playfully before he continued. "Why you ain't tell me you was having a baby?" Ali let out a light chuckle before he spoke, "Nah it's not even like that. She was pregnant when I met her. Our connection was so tight that once I met her, I just couldn't let her go. You know what I'm saying?" "Yeah I feel you, whatever makes you happy," Spanky said uninterested as a weird silence fell upon the locker room. "Well I'm Christie and it was very nice meeting you," she said breaking the silence.

"Hey I'm going to need everybody to get the fuck out of here. We got a fight in twenty minutes and Spanky needs to stay focused," Freddie growled as he tied up Spanky's left glove. "Aight, good luck out there. We're all going to be in the front row to support you," Ali said as he and the girls headed for the door. Spanky nodded in agreement as Freddie tied up his right glove. "It's show time baby," Freddie spoke loudly to encourage and hype Spanky up. "It's either going to be him or it's going to be you," his voice boomed as he slid the punching mitts on his hands. "One, two, three, just like we do it in the gym," Freddie said placing the mitts eye level. With the quickness of lightning, Spanky threw a jab, followed by a right hook, ending it off with a vicious uppercut. "That's what I'm talking about," Freddie continued to speak loudly for extra emphasis.

* * * *

"You ladies need anything from the concession stand," Ali asked. "No thank you baby; I'm fine," Nancy answered. "How about you, Christie?" "I'm so nervous, I can't eat a thing," she replied as she sat cross legged. "I'm so scared Spanky might get hurt," she said as her eyes got watery just from the thought of her man getting hurt, let alone knocked out. "Spanky is a soldier. You know that better than anybody," Ali tried to cheer Christie up as he saw G-money, and Skip searching for their seats. "Yo, over here," Ali stood up waving his arms like he was signaling a plane.

"Ya'll just made it to the fight; it starts in about five minutes," Ali informed the two. "You know I wouldn't miss this for the world," G-money said as he kissed Christie on the cheek, he stopped short when he noticed Nancy sitting next to Christie. "What she doing here," G-money questioned. "Nancy is my new girl. Nancy this is G-money, G-money this is Nancy," Ali introduced the two. "I know who she is. She the girl who's man used to whip her ass," G-money spoke openly. "Don't be ignorant all your life," Ali said sharply as his brown eyes glittered dangerously. "It's not her fault that her last man was a coward that liked to abuse women. All that matters now is that she's with me and I would appreciate it if you wouldn't disrespect her." "You right, my bad. We gotta start taking better care of our sisters out here," G-money replied as he gave Nancy a hug. "Welcome to the family." "Thank you," Nancy shot back happy to be apart of Ali's family.

"Check this out, I gotta talk to you about some serious shit," G-money said as he and Ali stepped off to the side. "What's up," Ali asked sensing that it had to be something bad. "I know you heard the other night me, and Skip got locked up, right?" Ali answered with a head nod. "This mutha fucka, Detective Nelson, violated us and our shorties, so we went and wet up the whole precinct" G-money said nonchalantly. "You did what," Ali barked. "He left me no option; I had to do it," G-money said as he lowered his head shamefully. "Do you know what the fuck you just did?" "Yeah, I fucked up," G-money replied. "Now we going to have to shut everything down for a while and sell our packages wholesale until this heat dies down," Ali growled angrily. "Not to mention you going to have to lay low for a while now." "Nobody saw my face." "It doesn't matter. We going to take the heat for it anyway since we got the biggest crew out. What other crew got the balls to do some shit like that?" "Yeah, you right," G-money nodded his head in understanding. "You have to start using your head. We not in this shit for the reputation no more, we been past that bull shit. It's all about the money now B," Ali stated sternly. "We almost done with this drug shit anyway, remember this shit is nothing but a stepping stone. In about six to eight months all of our businesses will be up, and running. All we have to do is stay afloat and out of trouble until then, aight?" "Yeah, I know I shouldn't have did that shit, but I just had to. I can't stand that punk ass detective." "Well did you at least kill him," Ali asked. "I'm not sure. I know for a fact I hit that fool though," G-money boasted. "Who went on the hit with you?" "Me, Skip, Diesil, and Benny." "What," Ali asked not believing his ears. "You took big mouth Benny with you?" "Yeah, I needed another shooter," G-money replied emptily. "I want you, and Skip to leave town for a little while; just until things cool down. I'm a holla at Diesil myself." "What about Benny," G-money asked. "I'm going to handle that clown myself," Ali said as he noticed his brother's opponent making his way towards the ring. "We going to talk about this later," he said distractedly as the two headed back to their seats.

"This Spanish mutha fucka is kind of brolick," Skip said out loud looking at how cut up and ripped the Spanish man's body was. "None of that matters. It's all about your skills," Ali added as they all stood up and cheered when they saw Spanky and Freddie making their way to the ring.

As soon as Spanky stepped into the ring, the first thing he did was size up his opponent. "I got this," he told himself. Spanky noticed that the majority of fans in the crowd were Spanish or Mexican, so he knew he would have to perform well because the judges usually showed favor to the fan's favorite.

"Take it to him from the beginning of the round to the end," Freddie whispered in Spanky's ear removing Spanky's hooded robe as the two fighters made their way to the center of the ring so that the referee could run down the rules to them one last time. "Okay I want a nice clean fight. When I say break, I expect for ya'll to do so; okay fellas keep it clean, and good luck…touch gloves," his voice boomed through the microphone as the crowd cheered in anticipation of a good fight. "This chump is standing in your way, get him out of your way, and get your title shot," Freddie announced placing Spanky's mouth piece in his mouth.

Once the bell rung, it was on and poppin. The Spanish fighter quickly rushed Spanky back against the ropes, throwing wild vicious haymakers. The crowd quickly erupted when they saw the black fighter up against the ropes, trying to block each shot. One haymaker broke through Spanky's guard and connected with his jaw. Immediately Spanky clinched the Spanish fighter then whispered in his ear, "You hit like a bitch." As the referee untangled the two. The Spanish fighter tried to rush Spanky again, but to no avail. Spnaky quickly sidestepped the blow catching the Spanish fighter with a clean uppercut to the chin, followed by a left hook that made a loud clapping sound as it connected on the Spanish man's eye. Spanky quickly noticed blood trickling down the fighter's right eye; he also noticed the Spanish fighter held his hands up a little higher leaving his body wide open.

Spanky quickly attacked like a young lion going after a wounded animal. He threw a lightening quick jab at the Spanish fighter's face, followed by a hook to his body. "Puta," Spanky growled through clenched teeth as he noticed the Spanish fighter was doubled over in pain from the body shot, before he caught him with one last right cross before the bell rung. "You my bitch," Spanky said staring the Spanish man down as he made his way to his corner. Before he sat on his stool he looked over and winked at Christie who still looked a little nervous.

"That mutha fucka is already out of gas," Freddie spoke confidently noticing the Spanish guy looking winded and out of breath. "His body is his weak spot, make sure you work that jab then set him up for a good body shot," he instructed. Spanky didn't speak, he just nodded his head in agreement as he heard the bell ring, signaling for the beginning of round two. Again the Spanish man came charging like a wild bull, but Spanky's jab stopped him in his tracks. The Spanish man was no match for Spanky lightening jab. He landed his jab easily for the majority of the round that was until he saw an opening.

Spanky quickly faked a jab and instead came with an uppercut, breaking the Spanish man's nose. Once Spanky saw what he had dropped on the Spanish man, he quickly threw a series of combinations. The referee immediately stopped the fight when he saw the vicious blows connect with the Spanish man's unprotected face.

"That's what the fuck I'm talking about," Ali stood up to cheer his brother on. "You did it baby, you earned your title shot," Freddie said hugging Spanky in the middle of the ring. "Do me a favor and tell Spanky I said I'm proud of him, and congrats," G-money said as he stood up to leave. "Where you going," Ali asked. G-money leaned closer to Ali's ear. "I think I'm a go to Atlanta and take a little vacation just until things cool down." "Sounds like a good move," Ali agreed. "I'm going to keep in touch," he said giving G-money a pound followed by a hug. "Holla at ya boy," G-money said as he and Skip made their exit.

Chapter 23
VACATION TIME

Before G-money headed to the airport he made a quick stop. "Knock, Knock, Knock," G-money waited patiently for someone to come to the door. Seconds later Coco opened the door wearing nothing but some boy shorts, and a wife beater. "Hey, what you doing here," she asked stepping to the side so that he could enter. "I was about to head out of town for a little vacation," G-money said lighting up a blunt. "Where you going?" "Atlanta," he answered in between puffs. "And I was wondering if you would like to join me?" "Hell yeah, I wanna go," Coco said excitedly seductively biting her bottom lip. "Get over here and give me a hug with ya sexy ass," G-money said inhaling Coco's sweet scent. Before Coco knew what was going on, her boy shorts were around her ankles and G-money was fucking the shit out of her. Coco bent over the arm of the couch as G-money long dicked her. She screamed out in a mixture of pleasure and pain until her cum drenched her inner thighs.

Once G-money finished laying his pipe game down, Coco quickly took a quick shower, and packed a few of her belongings, and was ready to go.

* * * *

"Go pack you and lil' man's shit; we going on a little vacation," Skip announced as soon as he stepped foot inside his five bedroom house. "Where are we going," April asked curiously. "We going to Hawaii," Skip said noticing the smile on his wife's face. "Why you smiling for," he asked playfully. "Because my husband is taking me to Hawaii," April celebrated doing a dance she must've picked up from either BET or MTV. "Stop acting like I don't be taking you nowhere," Skip said checking his Rolex. "Aight hurry up; our plane leaves in about two hours," he notified her.

Chapter 24
THE TAKE OVER

"Oh shit that's the bitch ass nigga. That sucker punched me in the club that night," Rell said looking at Spanky on Sport Center. "Yeah that is that bitch ass nigga," Debo said squinting his eyes to get a better look. "I didn't know he was a boxer." "Me either," Rell added lighting up a Newport. "Too bad because when I catch him I'm going to break both of his arms." "I would kill him if I was you," Debo said adding his two cent. "Nah, you see with a nigga like that if you break his arms that's even better than killing him," Rell said as he noticed Beverly enter the living room. "Hey daddy can I get you anything," she asked politely. "Yeah fry me and my man some fish." "Okay daddy," Beverly said heading towards the kitchen to fix her man his food.

Beverly was a white girl with blue eyes, and blonde hair. She may have been white, but she knew how to take care of her man. The reason Rell made Beverly his wifey was because while he was behind the wall all the sistahs he had been dealing with all turned their backs on him do to the fact he had such a long bid. But not Beverly, she stuck behind Rell for his entire bid. Once he was released, he vowed that he would never date another sistah, and he planned on keeping his word.

"How that chump, Dave, been holding up," Rell asked. "He been doing aight; his count is always straight," Debo said quickly snatching his .45 from his waistband when he heard somebody banging on the door like the police. "Who the fuck is that banging like the fucking cops," Rell said out loud grabbing his P89 from off of the coffee table as he made his way to the door so that he could investigate. "It's the cops," Rell said signaling Debo to put away his gun.

"Greetings officer," Rell said addressing the detective. "Hi, how are you doing Rell, my name is Detective Nelson. I need some help taking a few guys down, and I was told you could help me," he said as the two exchanged glances. "I'm sorry Detective, but I'm afraid someone gave you some incorrect information," Rell said flatly as he went to slam the door but the detective's foot stopped him. "Listen, the word on the street is you want G-money dead," Detective Nelson said lighting up a Winston. "I can help you get rid of him." "Why the fuck would you want to help me," Rell questioned. "Let's just say I owe him one," Detective Nelson said averting his eyes towards his arm cradled in the sling.

With that being said, Rell stepped to the side so that the Detective could enter. "Okay, I'm going to get straight to the point. Me and Ail used to do businesses, but he bit the hand that fed him now he's finished. Meaning there's a position open for a new street legend. This game is all about longevity, and with me on your side there's no telling how for we can go together." "What's in it for you," Rell asked as he studied the detective. "Twenty thousand every month," he answered quickly. "That's not going to work; I'm barely pulling in twenty thousand a month now," Rell said not liking how that sounded. "You see you still thinking like a nickel and dime hustler," Detective Nelson said shaking his head. "Once you're connected you'll be making triple that amount in a week. This is how it works, any block you want to take over, you just let me know and I'll arrest the crew who's selling on that block. That's when you bring your people in and take over, but we must get rid of G-money because he's going to cause a problem." "What about Ali," Debo asked speaking for the first time. "Yes, Ali must go as well," Detective Nelson stated firmly. "You know that's going to get real ugly, right? Not to mention the lost I'm gonna be taking when my men start getting arrested," Rell said unsurely. "Anybody from your crew get locked up, I'll have them released within twenty four hours." "Let me talk it over with my man real quick," Rell said as he, and Debo stepped in the next room to weigh their options. Ten minutes later Rell and Debo reappeared from the backroom. "Looks like you got your self a deal," Rell said shaking the detective's hand. "I just want to let you know that now that I have the green light it's gonna be a lot of blood spilled." "I hope so. I'll contact you in thirty days for my money," Detective Nelson said greedily as he made his exit. "Put a tail on that mutha fucka," Rell said lighting up the clip of haze that sat in the ashtray. "What's up? You want him dead," Debo asked with a menacing look in his eyes. "Nah, I just need to know more about him; it's something fishy about that mutha fucka," Rell said with concern. "Say no more, I'll take care of that first thing in the morning," Debo said as the two men sat down, and enjoyed their fish.

Chapter 25
IGNORANCE

"Damn I see you getting all this money up in this mutha fucka," Benny said noticing all the drug traffic coming in and out of the projects. "Yeah, you already know how we do it," Butch replied munching on some barbeque chips. "So what brings you down to the projects?" "This where all the bitches at," Benny said as if he were at a whorehouse. "You see the same ole tired ass bitches every time you come up this mutha fucka." "Yup and every time feels like a new one," Benny chuckled as he saw three girls heading in their direction. "Hey Butch," the prettiest one out of the three spoke. "Who got smoke out here?" "My man in the lobby of that building right there can help you," he replied pointing to the building to his left. "Aight, good looking Butch," the girl said as the three headed towards the building before Benny stopped them. “Hold up for a second ma,” Benny said grabbing the prettiest one by the wrist. “I got what you need right here,” he said revealing a Ziploc bag full of purple haze from his pocket. “How about all four of us go back to my place, and get zooted.” The girls giggled before the pretty one spoke. “We good, maybe next time,” she replied. “Damn baby, why you playing hard to get with a nigga? You so fine I’ll do anything for you , even kill a mutha fucka,” Benny joked. “Yeah right, you probably never even shot a gun before,” the pretty one yelled over her shoulder as the three headed to get some weed. “Bitch, it’s obvious you don’t watch the news because if you did you would of heard about that precinct I shot up,” Benny yelled hoping the threesome heard him.

“Yo, are you stupid or dumb,” Butch asked not believing his ears. “What you talking about? I’m just having fun with the bitches,” Benny said nonchalantly. “Yo, you a dumb ass nigga,” Butch said hotly as he got up and left Benny sitting on the bench all by himself. “Lil’ weak ass nigga,” Benny said out loud once Butch was out of ear shot. Benny sat on the bench alone until it started to drizzle. “Damn what else could go wrong,” He said out loud as he jogged to the corner store so that he could get out of the rain.

Seconds later Diesil pulled up in his 2002 Escalade. “What’s good son,” Diesil yelled beeping the horn. Once Benny saw who the driver was, he quickly ran and slid into the passenger seat. “Yo, I gotta hurry up and get me a car, son,” Benny said not liking how everybody around him seemed to be doing better than he was. “Things come to those who wait,” Diesil said making a left turn down a naked alley. “Where the fuck we going,” Benny asked curiously.

"Some fucking idiot can't keep his mouth shut, so I have to shut it for him." In a quick motion he snatched Benny out of his seat by his collar. "What the fuck you doing man," Benny squealed. "Shutting up your big mouth," Diesil replied aiming his 9mm at his old friend's head, whose life was silenced by five messengers of death.

Chapter 26
A DAY OFF

"So what's so important that you interrupted my precious beauty sleep," Nancy asked playfully as she and Ali took their seats in the soul food restaurant. "I thought I told you I had something important to talk to you about," Ali smiled as he picked up his menu. "So spit it out," Nancy shot back waiting for Ali to spill the beans. "I want you to move in with me." "Are you serious," Nancy asked excitedly. "Yeah, I been thinking about this for the past month, and I think now is the perfect time," Ali announced. "I don't know about that, I don't want to be free loading; if I do move in with you I would have to contribute." "You see, you worrying about the wrong thing," Ali said sharply as the waiter approached their table. "Are ya'll ready to order," he asked politely. "Yeah, I'll have some fried chicken wings, barbeque chicken, macaroni and cheese, and some collard greens." "I'll have the same thing with a pink lemonade," Nancy said handing the waiter back the menu.

Once the waiter was out of ear shot, Ali continued where he had left off. "I already got everything worked out, after you have the baby I was going to open up a business for you." "What kind of business," Nancy asked. "I'll let you pick," Ali said winking at his woman. "That way you can make your own money, and spend it how you see fit." "Why are you doing this," Nancy asked not understanding. "Doing what," Ali asked curiously. "Being so good to me." "Because I love you and I see something inside of you, something I've never seen in a woman before," he told her as he sipped from his wine glass. "You are truly a blessing from God," Nancy slurred as a tear escaped her eye. "It's like God sent you down from heaven right on time, right when I thought my life was over. You don't know how many times I contemplated taking my life, but I just couldn't because of the unborn life in my stomach," she said rubbing her stomach. "Listen, that's weak talking you doing. You're much stronger than that and you know it," Ali stated firmly. "All that's over and done with; today is a new day now can you please answer my question." "Yes, I would love to move in with you," Nancy announced smiling like a kid in a candy store. "A yo, Big Mel, she said yes," Ali yelled over his shoulder. Big Mel didn't respond, he just threw two thumbs up. After dinner, Nancy and Ali slid into the backseat of his Range Rover, while Big Mel hopped in the driver's seat and headed to Ali's house. "So where do you live? I don't believe I've been with you all this time and I don't even know where you live."

"I live in Jersey," Ali answered quickly. "Why have I not been there yet," Nancy asked curiously. "No woman has ever been to my house before," Ali stated plainly. "And why's that?" "What you think, I just be bringing mad chicks in and out of my house? Nah, bitches will kill you faster than a man would."

Chapter 27
THAT'S HOW THE GAME GOES

"Listen, if you don't got no fucking money then you just assed out," Butch spat coldly showing the crack head no respect. "Come on I thought we was brothers," the crack head said hoping Butch would cut him a play. "Yo, listen to me carefully, I'm going to count to ten in my mind and at the count of ten if you're still in my eye sight I'm going to bust a cap in ya dirty ass," Butch growled sick and tired of playing crack head games with the fiend. "Yo Butch we almost on E one of the young workers whispered in his ear. "Aight shorty I got you," Butch replied hopping off of the bench as he headed to Stacey's crib.

Butch stepped off the elevator only to find himself looking down the barrel of Debo's shotgun. "Hey Butch we've been waiting for you," Debo said with a wicked smirk on his face. "What's this all about," Butch questioned throwing his hands up in surrender. "Shut the fuck up," Debo growled as one of his soldiers quickly patted Butch down. Once Debo was sure Butch was unarmed, he roughly grabbed him by the back of his neck, and directed him into the apartment. Immediately Butch felt his stomach start to do flips as he stepped over Stacey's dead body followed by the dead bodies of all the people who attended her party that night. "What the fuck is this all about," Butch asked again. "What ya'll want; money?" "Fuck ya money," Rell said entering the living room with the whole stash in three duffle bags. "I already got that and all the product you had in the backroom," Rell spoke calmly. "Then what is it you want," Butch asked looking at, at least six different guns pointed in his direction. "I want you to tell me where I can find Ali and G-money," Rell said as he grabbed the Grey Goose bottle from off the kitchen table and turned it up. "Fuck you," Butch growled waving Rell off. "This little nigga tougher than he looks," Rell chuckled as he violently bust the Grey Goose bottle over Butch's head. "Do what you gotta do," Butch spoke in a soft tone as blood trickled down his forehead. "Well actually, I need you to deliver a message for me." "Why don't you deliver it yourself," Butch snarled. "Because I rather it come from you," Rell said calmly as he slowly pulled out his P89. Butch swallowed hard before he spoke. "I ain't delivering shit."

Rell didn't speak instead he aimed the barrel at Butch's legs and sent three hot slugs in each leg.

Butch screamed out in pain as he just laid helplessly on the floor. "I'm sure G-money and Ali will get the message loud and clear," Rell chuckled as he and his crew made their exit, leaving Butch for dead.

Chapter 28
NEEDS

"Let me see what you working with," G-money requested as he laid on the king size bed at one of the fanciest hotels in Atlanta. "That's what you want," Coco asked in a seductive voice as she slowly slid out of her robe. "That's exactly what I want," G-money answered distractedly as he tried to unglue his eyes from Coco's sexy chocolate body. Coco quickly made her way towards the stereo system, and popped in a reggae C.D.

Coco slowly and sensually began to gyrate her hips to the music that flowed through the speakers. After about eight minutes of watching Coco mimic the moves of a stripper, G-money couldn't take it anymore. "Bring that ass over here," he demanded. Coco quickly complied as she crawled on the bed like a lion getting ready to attack. G-money intensely watched as Coco took his erect manhood in her warm mouth and didn't release the hold she had on it until his fluids filled her mouth. Coco greedily swallowed as much as she could, while the remainder of it dripped down her chin. After a performance like that, G-money couldn't help but notice Coco's pussy was soaking wet. "Come get this pussy," Coco said in a light whisper as she laid on the bed spread-eagle style waiting to get fucked. Without thinking twice G-money climbed on top of Coco and handled his business. The two went at it like wild animals in the jungle for at least four more rounds.

After G-money finished laying down his pipe game, he quickly grabbed his blunt off the dresser and fired it up. "Damn you smoke more than an Indian," Coco commented half-jokingly. "I'm about to get my drink on too," he said in between puffs, as he headed to the small mini bar and poured him and Coco a glass of Hennessey.

Before G-money could even sit down he heard his I-phone ringing. Instantly he knew it had to be important because only four people had that number, he mostly used that phone for it's access to the internet and it's built in I-pod. "I'm listening," he answered. "What's good, Mike can you talk?" Instantly G-money picked up the voice and knew it was Diesil. Everybody in the crew always asked to speak with Mike when they had something important to say, just in case their phones were tapped or bugged no one would get in trouble because Mike didn't exist. "Yeah I can talk what's up?" "Yeah we got a little problem up here. A boy that go by the name Rell came and smoked everybody in Bank of America (The code name for the stash house) and put six in the oldest boy's legs," Diesil coded his words the best he could. “Word,” G-money asked downing his shot of Henny in one gulp. “Yeah, word is that boy got snow white (Detective Nelson) backing him up.” “I already suspected that was coming,” G-money thought out loud. “Word is he’s looking for you and the big man.” “Well he won’t have to look too hard because I’m coming back tonight.” G-money’s voice boomed through the phone. “Aight that’s cool because the whole family is hungry, but we didn’t want to start dinner without you, smell me?” “I can dig it,” G-money said blowing out a puff of smoke. “It’s definitely going to be a big dinner (War).” “Yeah the big man ain’t happy about this either,” Diesil said in a light whisper. “I could imagine,” G-money said shaking his head. “So who’s running Bank of America now?” “Who else can handle that job better than me?” “Oh the big man gave you the position,” G-money questioned. “Yeah because he knew if I go out I’m going out on some terminator shit, you dig,” Diesil boasted. “You know I can dig it,” G-money replied. “But yo I’m going to holla at you when I touch down. I don’t want to talk too much on this phone, smell me?” “Say no more. Scream at me when you touch down one,” Diesil said ending the conversation.

“Is everything okay,” Coco asked sensing something was wrong. “We going to have to cut this little vacation short. Some shit came up and I have to get back to the city,” G-money said placing the roach in the ashtray. “That’s cool, I have to get back and throw this baby shower for my home girl any way,” Coco stated plainly as she finished up her glass of Henny. “Next time I’ll take you to an island or something, aight,” G-money said over his shoulder as he started packing up the little bit of shit he had. The only thing on his mind was getting back to New York.

* * * *

Ali woke up to the smell of some fresh bacon, eggs, and pancakes flowing through his nostrils. He immediately jumped out of his king sized heated water bed, and grabbed his twin 9mm's off the night stand, heading towards the kitchen where the smell was coming from.

Nancy dropped a glass plate when she saw the two pistols in her face. "Oh shit baby I'm sorry," Ali said lowering his 9mm's when he realized it was Nancy cooking. "Sorry baby, I'm not used to living with a woman. When I heard somebody fooling around in the kitchen I immediately thought the worse." "It's okay boo; I thought you might be hungry when you woke up," Nancy said as she watched Big Mel run up in the kitchen carrying some kind of machine gun. "It's just me Big Mel, I was just fixing us all some breakfast. Sorry if I startled ya'll," Nancy apologized. "You don't have to apologize for that cause you know a brother likes to eat," Big Mel said greedily rubbing his belly. "This nigga will eat anything literally," Ali joked sipping on some orange juice. "You know that's right," Big Mel capped as he picked up his ringing cell phone.

He spoke briefly before hanging up. "Yo let me holla at you for a second," Big Mel said as the two stepped into the living room so that they could talk in private. "That was Diesil on the phone. Looks like we got a problem." "What else is new," Ali said sarcastically. "What's the problem now?" "Diesil said that nigga, Rell, and his peoples just shot up Butch and everybody who was in the stash house." "Did we take a hit," Ali asked. "Yeah twenty thousand; ten in cash and ten in work. He also said that the word on the streets is Detective Nelson is now backing up Rell," Big Mel said shaking his head. Deep down inside he knew that them two together was definitely going to be a problem. "Did Diesil take care of loud mouth Benny like I asked him to?" "Yeah he took care of that the other day." "Aight tell Diesil it's his turn to step up to the plate. Tell him to pick up a small package from the other stash crib, round up a couple of workers, and look outs, and set up in the projects," Ali said pacing back and forth. "And tell him I'm going to get him some muscle to hold him down. We have to do whatever we have to, to keep those projects."

With that said Big Mel quickly got Diesil on the phone and gave him the run down. "Diesil said he's going to take care of that right now," Big Mel announced. "Aight get dressed we have to go see this connect, it's re-up time," Ali said as the two quickly got dressed and headed out the door.

*   *   *   *

"Damn it's dumb cold out here today," Dave grumbled blowing and rubbing his hands together. "You don't grind, you don't shine," Maurice reminded his partner. "Yup and you know I'm going to get my shine on tonight at Rell's party," Dave boasted. "Where's he throwing this party at?" "Downtown somewhere, it's suppose to be a lot of strippers there. I think one of his home boys just got out of jail," Dave said as he noticed Rita stepping out of a cab.

By the look on her face he could tell she was mad about something." "Hey baby what you doing here," he asked. "Don't give me that baby shit, I've been calling you all day, why you ain't been answering your phone," she snapped. "Don't come down here with that bullshit because I ain't even in the mood," Dave warned with a cold chill in his voice. The look Dave gave her made Rita stop dead in her tracks. Just the other day she got punched in her face for talking reckless, so she tried a different approach. "I'm sorry daddy, you know I hate when I can't get in touch with you," she said her voice changing to a whining, pleading note. "So what's so important that you had to come all the way down here?" "I was trying to call you and tell you I seen ya raggedy ass baby mother the other day," Rita said popping her gum like a true chicken head. "Word," Dave said lighting up a Newport. "Where you saw her at?" "I saw that bitch on 125th street. If she wasn't pregnant I would've bust her ass." "I'm going to kill that bitch if I catch her," Dave growled cracking his knuckles. "Don't even worry about that daddy, I'm going to handle that bitch for you, because you know I don't play when it comes to my man," Rita said snapping her fingers and making an "S" in the air. "Plus I heard her baby shower is next week." "Where did you get that info from?" "We both get our hair done at the same spot and I overheard the girls talking about it," Rita told him knowing what his reaction would be before she even spoke. "Do you know where and when the baby shower is being held," Dave questioned. "Of course I do," Rita announced proudly. "Well I guess I better go get her a gift," Dave chuckled as his mind began drawing up a plan.

*　　*　　*　　*

Big Mel pulled into the driveway of the mansion and as always the site of the huge house brought a smile to his face. "When it's all said and done I'm going to get me a crib just like this," he told himself. "Don't worry it won't be long, this nightmare will be all over soon," Ali said patting Big Mel on the back as the two hopped out of the vehicle. "Hey come on in guys," Frankie said welcoming his guests. Frankie was an arrogant fast talking Italian. Ali only dealt with him because of the quality of his product, if it wasn't for that the two wouldn't have shit to talk about.

"What's up Frankie," Ali said brushing past the Italian man with Big Mel on his heels. "Can I get ya'll something to drink," Frankie asked pouring himself a glass of Vodka. "Nah, let's just get down to business," Ali stated firmly. "I'm sorry Ali, but I'm not going to be able to continue to do business with you," Frankie said. "Here we go," Ali sighed. "Why can't you do business with me any more? What my money ain't good," Ali asked sarcastically. "It's not that, you know me and you never had any disagreements before," Frankie commented. "It's that fucking Detective Nelson; that prick strolled up in here the other day talking about if I sell you a gram of anything he's going to throw me under the jail." "It's all good Frankie, I understand," Ali said as he and Big Mel stood up and headed for the door. "I'm sorry about this, really I am. I hope it's no hard feelings," Frankie said walking his guests to the door. "It's all good," Ali said frustrated as he and Big Mel hopped back into their vehicle.

"What do we do now, boss man?" "First we have to find the rat in our crew," Ali replied blankly staring out of the window. "You think somebody in our crew is snitching," Big Mel asked curiously. "Of course, how the fuck Detective Nelson know where we cop from? How the fuck did Rell know which apartment was the stash crib? You think he got that information off the internet or something," Ali chuckled. "You right, I never looked at it like that," Big Mel said pulling into a Popeye's drive thru. "So how do you want to handle this?" "We going to smoke him out," Ali stated plainly. "If it's one thing I hate more than a faggot, is a fucking snitch."

"Damn this mutha fucka is good," Big Mel said out loud looking at his cell phone. "What happened," Ali asked. "Diesil just sent me an email. Five more of our soldiers just got locked up and two of them were killed by the police," Big Mel said shaking his head.

"Take me to Detective Nelson's office now," Ali ordered from the passenger seat. Detective Nelson had just crossed the line, and Ali had played the nice guy long enough, now it was time to get back on his bullshit.

Ali stormed into the precinct with Big Mel on his heels. "I need to speak to Detective Nelson now. Tell him it's urgent," Ali growled to the uniformed officer who sat behind the desk. "Detective Nelson is busy right now, would you like to leave him a message or something," the officer asked rudely never taking his eyes off of the paperwork in front of him.

"Listen officer, time is money and I don't waste either one. Now I would appreciate it if you would go back there and tell Detective Nelson somebody out here would like to speak to him," Ali said with a sharp edge in his voice. "Listen buddy I just told you…"

In one quick motion Ali slapped the papers off of the officer's desk. "Have you lost your damn mind," the officer barked as he shot to his feet snatching his night stick from off of his hip as he came from behind his desk ready to get his Rodney King on. The officer quickly thought twice when he saw thirty rough looking black thugs storm into the precinct all dressed in black standing behind Ali.

"Now I'm only going to ask you one more time, go tell Detective Nelson that someone out here wants to see him," Ali took a step closer tensing his muscles, ready for action. Thirty seconds later all of the officers in the precinct came rushing to see what was going on. "Is everything okay out here," an older officer asked with his hand on his pistol. "There's no problem officer. We would just like to have a word with Detective Nelson," Ali spoke calmly.

"Somebody go get Detective Nelson," the older officer commanded. Everyone could feel the tension as the two sides had a stare down until Detective Nelson came strolling nonchalantly from the back.

"Somebody looking for me," Detective Nelson asked sarcastically making his way to the front line with his .357 magnum in his hand. "Yeah, I need to have a word with you alone," Ali stated looking around at all the officers for extra emphasis. "First get your posse out of here," Detective Nelson said staring at the sea of black faces.

With a snap of his finger, Big Mel quickly escorted all of the soldiers outside. "That's more like it," Detective Nelson chuckled placing his .357 back in it's holster. "Right this way," he said leading Ali to his office. "Okay, now how can I help you," Detective Nelson asked with a wicked grin on his face. "Is this how you want to play it," Ali asked firmly. "What are you talking about," Detective Nelson asked faking ignorance. "You know exactly what I'm talking about. We can definitely go body for body if that's what you want," Ali threatened. "You don't have the man power for that and you know it. You made your choice and this is what happens when you bite the hand that feeds you." "I don't have the man power," Ali echoed. "You must not know how we get down in the concrete jungle. Trust me Detective you might want to quit while you're ahead." "Listen boy." He made sure he dragged out the word. "Me and you don't have shit else to talk about, you hear? You made your bed now sleep, don't make me out to be the bad guy." "Yeah you right, we don't have shit else to talk about," Ali said calmly as he stood up to leave. "Ali," Detective Nelson called out. "No hard feelings right?" Ali didn't answer he just looked Detective Nelson up and down then made his exit. Once Ali was gone Detective Nelson quickly pulled out his cell phone and dialed Rell's number.

"Yo what's good," Rell answered. "I just had a confrontation with Ali. I thought you were going to take care of him and that fool G-money?" "Yeah I am, but it's not that simple. We going to have to keep chipping away, you keep locking up members from his crew and my crew will keep taking out as many of his soldiers until there's nobody left to protect them." "Yeah well we're going to have to speed up this process a little because they have to go," Detective Nelson said with fire in his voice. "You need to calm down and let your hair down in about three months. Ali and G-money will be done, they don't even have a spot to get no good work from," Rell laughed loudly. "Why don't you come to my party tonight and enjoy yourself." "I might just do that," Detective Nelson said ending the conversation.

* * * *

"I just got an email from G-money; he and Skip are back in town," Big Mel told Ali. "Good, tell him it's time to strap up; we going to show this faggot mutha fucka, Detective Nelson, who runs the streets," Ali stated helping himself to a glass of Gin and juice. "Mr. Goldberg left me a message last night talking about the new restaurant is ready for business." "Oh word," Big Mel asked pulling out into traffic. "Yeah, we need to swing by the projects real quick so I can find a few female waitresses and put them on the payroll."

"Thanksgiving is next week, what you got planned?" "Mel you know we do the same shit every year. The day before we going to give out turkey's to the whole community then on Thanksgiving day the whole crew is going to have Thanksgiving dinner together." "We going to have to rent out a different spot because this year we got double the soldiers we had lost year," Big Mel said keeping his eyes on the road. "That's what it's all about; multiplying. There's strength in numbers, beside we all family and family should spend Thanksgiving together, you dig? We almost got enough businesses up and running to leave this drug shit alone," Ali said helping himself to another glass of Gin and juice. "Leave it alone and never look back." "But why leave? The game has been good to us," Big Mel questioned. "You're smarter than that Mel. You know this game is set up for us to lose, especially now that Detective Nelson has it out for us," Ali chuckled. "So you really just going to leave the game just like that?" "Just like that," Ali said snapping his finger for extra emphasis. You one crazy mutha fucka, Ali." "No, I'm a smart mutha fucka." Ali corrected him. Big Mel laughed loudly. "What's so funny," Ali asked. "That shit you talking is easier said than done. You know how many brothers said the same shit you just said?" "Those other fools were just talking; I'm going to let my actions do the talking for me like always," Ali said felling the affect of the Gin and juice.

"Well let me just thank you now for everything you did for me and my family," Big Mel said as he doubled parked in front of the projects. As soon as Ali stepped foot in the projects all the local thugs, and people who resided there greeted the man who gave so much back to the community.

"What's good, how's it looking in here," Ali asked giving Diesil a pound. "Shit been looking regular ever since we took that hit," Diesil replied scanning the hood. "Aight, you been switching the stash crib every other day like I told you to?" "Yeah, but the workers been complaining about that." "Listen, tell those mutha fuckas to keep their mouths shut and do what they get paid to do," Ali stated plainly. "Mutha fuckas complain about anything."

"Yo, did my man, Wise, ever come through to see you," Big Mel asked. "Nah who the fuck is

Wise," Diesil asked dumbfounded. "That's my man who just came home, he's a real wild DMX type of nigga," Big Mel said pulling out his cell phone. He spoke briefly before hanging up. "Yeah he said he's right around the corner; he'll be here in five minutes." "Aight so this guy Wise is suppose to do what exactly," Diesil asked. "He's just extra muscle," Big Mel hissed. Ali quickly pulled Diesil to the side where they spoke in hushed voices. "Yo, I think we gotta snitch in our crew. Have you been noticing anything or anybody doing anything unusual?" "Nah not that I know of, but I will definitely keep an eye open and let you know if I see or hear anything," Diesil responded. "Aight you do that and stay on point out here," Ali yelled over his shoulder as him and Big Mel made their exit.

* * * *

Diesil sat on the bench just chilling, when he noticed some dark skinned guy with a bald head walking in his direction. "Yo who's name is Diesil out here," the bald head man asked looking Diesil up and down. "That's me, you must be Wise," Diesil said extending his hand. "My man, Big Mel, told me you could use a little back up out in these projects," Wise said shaking Diesil's hand. "Yeah, we had a little situation up in here last week so now the big man is being extra cautious." "Who's the big man," Wise asked curiously. Diesil chuckled. "You mean to tell me Big Mel didn't tell you who the big man is," Diesil asked suspiciously. "Nah it must've slipped his mind," Wise said giving Diesil a look that said are you're going to tell me. "Don't feel bad, I don't know who the big man is either," Diesil said lying with a straight face. "Let me give you a tour around this mutha fucka," Diesil said changing the subject as he showed Wise the in's and out's of the projects.

*   *   *   *

"Hold up something ain't right," Ali said snatching his twin 9mm from it's holster. The apartment that he used as an office, front door was wide open. "Cover me," Big Mel said holding his Uzi with two hands as he slowly crept towards the door with caution. "Okay it's clear."

As soon as Ali stepped foot inside of his office, he couldn't believe his eyes. Someone had broke in and trashed the place. His sixty inch T.V. was smashed up, file cabinets were in the middle of the floor along with scattered papers all over the place. "It's on now," Ali said to himself as he just stood there looking at his office in disgust. He quickly picked up his throw away phone and made a quick phone call.

Chapter 29
LET'S GET THIS PARTY STARTED

Rell's party had brought out all the hustlers in the city ,not to mention all the hoes. The place was packed with wall to wall dealers, strippers, pimps, prostitutes, gold diggers, models, hoes, and most of all the toughest thugs in New York city. "All this is for you," Rell yelled over the blaring music pointing at the crowd.

"Thanks, I really appreciate this," Mad Dog said giving Rell a hug. "Well show me how much you appreciate it by keeping ya ass out of jail," Rell capped handing Mad Dog a bottle of Belve. "Definitely, my main focus is getting this money this time around. I ain't got time for no bullshit. Oh, but don't get it twisted, I'll still bust a nigga's head in a minute," Mad Dog chuckled meaning every word he spoke.

Meanwhile in the parking lot G-money pulled into the club's parking lot six cars deep. "I heard mutha fuckas was out here looking for the kid," G-money slurred reeking of alcohol. Before G-money exited his vehicle he made sure he grabbed his bottle of Grey Goose from off the floor as he and his entourage headed towards the entrance.

"How much is it going to cost for me and my crew to get up here without waiting on this long ass line?" G-money asked the big seven foot tall bouncer. "I'm sorry brother, but this is a private party, besides you and your crew don't meet the dress code requirements, so there's nothing I can do for you, sorry," his voice boomed. "Listen, I don't think you understand," G-money said taking a step closer. "I need to get in there and speak to the man who's throwing the party." "No, I don't think you understand," the bouncer growled talking way louder than he had to. "This is a private fucking party."

Before G-money could respond, police cars came from every direction trying to box off G-money and his entourage. Out of reflex G-money and his crew scrambled trying to escape. Each man in his entourage was carrying a fire arm and more than likely had a warrant out for their arrest or were on parole.

After a short pursuit, a uniformed officer had tackled G-money in the process of trying to put the cuffs on G-money. G-money found a way to grab his .45 from his waistband. Immediately he pumped four bullets into the cop, causing blood to splatter across his face. Once G-money's entourage heard the shots go off they immediately opened fire not caring who they shot.

* * * *

"Yo, it's a shoot out going on outside right now," Debo told Rell and the rest of the crew. "Let's go check it out," Rell said snatching his P89 Ruger from his waist leading his crew towards the entrance.

* * * *

Once G-money rolled the cops dead body off of him, he quickly shot the next cop closest to him. Seconds later G-money noticed at least five more cop cars pulling up to the scene. "Fuck," G-money growled as he tossed his .45 and laid spread out on the ground with his hands behind his head so he wouldn't get shot.

Meanwhile the rest of G-money's entourage continued to bang out with the police, everyone except for Skip he smoothly ran around the corner tossing his dessert eagle under a parked car as he walked regular trying to blend in with the regular club goers.

Once the rest of G-money's entourage saw that they didn't have a chance to win the gun fight they quickly surrendered. When it was all said and done five police officers were killed to go along with the seven dead members of G-money's entourage.

* * * *

By the time Rell and his crew made it outside the police had full control of the situation. “This stupid mutha fucka fell right into the trap,” Rell said out loud shaking his head.

By this time Detective Nelson had already made his way to the crime scene. “You just can’t do right can you,” Detective Nelson knelt down to speak to G-money who was laying face down on the concrete handcuffed. “You set me up you fucking cock sucker,” G-money barked. “No, I just out smarted you,” Detective Nelson corrected him. “And it was way easier than I thought it would be,” he laughed loudly. “We’ll see who gets the last laugh,” G-money snarled already planning on getting revenge on the detective.

* * * *

Skip stood across the street with the rest of the bystanders watching the show, when he noticed Wise jogging down the street looking back over his shoulder. “Damn he must’ve of gotten away like I did,” Skip said to himself as he pulled out his cell phone and dialed Big Mel’s number.

“Yo, what’s up? Can I speak to Mike,” Skip said speaking in codes. “Tell the big man everything is fucked up, over seven people from our crew got locked up, and tell him Grandma (G-money) too.

"Aight get low," Big Mel said quickly as he ended the conversation. "Yo that was Skip on the phone, he said G-money and about seven soldiers just got locked up."

"Fuck," Ali cursed angrily. "Get Goldberg on the phone and get him down there ASAP," Ali stated as he turned on the T.V. and saw the whole shit already on the news. The reporter spoke with fire in his voice as he announced that there were twelve dead bodies on the scene and five of them were cops.

"Damn," Ali whispered as he picked up his throw away phone and dialed a number. Diesil answered on the fifth ring. "Yo what's good?" "You tell me," Ali responded. "I'm pulling up right now," Diesil replied. "Okay come see me when you're done," Ali said clicking the phone dead.

* * * *

Diesil pulled in front of the precinct on his motorcycle. He quickly scanned the front before he made his move. He quickly hopped off the bike leaving the engine running as he leaned it on the kick stand.

Once inside the precinct, Diesil made sure he drew the string tight on his hooded sweatshirt as he made his way to the front desk. "How you doing officer? I have a note I need you to give to Detective Nelson for me if it's not too much trouble," Diesil said politely as he handed the officer the note.

"What the fuck is this," the officer growled looking down at the note. Before the officer could lift his head back up Diesil aimed the nozzle of the silencer on his .380 at the officer's head and squeezed the trigger five times before he quickly made his exit. Once outside, Diesil hopped back on his motorcycle, revved the engine, and left the smell of burnt rubber in the air.

Chapter 30
SCOPE THE COMPETITION

"You see this mother fucker is slick," Freddie commented as he and Spanky watched tapes of his next opponent. "His foot work is outstanding." "It's aight," Spanky hated. "You're really going to have to bring you're A-game if you expect to leave that fight with that man's belt," Freddie added. "I came too far not to take that title from that clown. This is what I been training for all my life," Spanky said seriously. "We going to really have to study these tapes because it's hard to fight mutha fuckas who fight in that awkward Roy Jones style." "Honestly Freddie, do you think I can take this chump," Spanky asked seriously. "Yeah I know you can take him; it's just going to take hard work and discipline," Freddie replied unsurely. "You know you the underdog right?" "Word? Damn that's fucked up, a lot of people going to lose their hard earned money because I'm not playing with this clown. I'm a go in that ring and try to kill that fool;

people must've of forgot I'm still undefeated." "So is he," Freddie reminded him. "Fuck you Freddie. I can see it in your eyes, you think I can't beat this mutha fucka," Spanky shot to his feet and threw on his hoody. "I didn't say that Spanky," Freddie pleaded. "You didn't have to, it's written all over your face," Spanky stated as he headed towards the door.

"Where you going Spank," Freddie yelled out. "I'm going to put these miles in," he said placing his I-pod ear phones in his ear, then made his exit.

Spanky decided to jog all the way home, something he had never done before. The whole time he jogged down the street he visualized his opponent standing in front of him as he threw the one, two. Two hours later Spanky had finally reached his house. When he stepped foot in the house he was shocked when he saw Christie sitting in the living room watching the same video of his opponent.

"Hey baby I didn't even hear you come in," she said turning off the T.V. "What you watching," Spanky asked turning off his I-pod. "Oh," she began quietly. "Uhm, I saw the tape of your next opponent sitting on the table so I thought I would just check it out." "So what do you think," he asked. "He's real good," Christie said turning to face her man. "He's going to be the toughest person you ever fought or maybe ever fight."

"You think I can win," he asked. "Of course I think you going to win. You ain't never lost a fight just like him, what makes him better than you?" "Thanks boo, I needed to hear that," Spanky said giving his wife a big hug. "Did you sign the contract yet," she asked. "I signed it earlier today," Spanky chuckled. "What's so funny?" "It's funny because whether I win or lose, we still going to be rich."

"Baby we already rich." "Well excuse me, I meant to say we'll be richer." The two laughed.

"So when is the fight?" "Nine month from now," Spanky whispered as the two headed to the bedroom to get their freak on for the last time until the fight was over.

Chapter 31
WHEN IT RAINS IT POURS

"Come on girl you gonna fuck around and be late to your own baby shower," Coco said playfully. "Sorry but I can't move like I used to," Nancy replied as the two headed out the door.

Big Mel held the back door open so the two beautiful queens could enter the vehicle. "Thanks Mel," the two said in unison. Once everyone was in the vehicle safely, Big Mel headed towards the baby shower. By just looking at Nancy's face you could tell that she was nervous and happy at the same time. "You beautiful girl, don't even worry about it," Coco said joyfully. "Thanks girl," Nancy replied as the two sat listening to their favorite songs for the rest of the ride.

* * * *

When Dave and Maurice stepped inside of the warehouse they were shocked to see twenty soldiers all dressed in black wearing black gloves holding assault riffles. "I'm glad ya'll could make it on such short notice," Rell said handing the two men a pair of black jeans, a sweater, and gloves.

"What's this all about," Dave asked curiously. "I just got the word last minute that Ali and his crew is going to be attending a baby shower out in Brooklyn," Rell said nonchalantly. "So what's the plan," Dave asked. "We going to kill everybody up in that bitch," Debo answered for Rell. "Hold on, I think we got a problem," Dave said nervously. "What's the problem Dave," Rell asked stepping in Dave's face. "You scared," he asked challenging Dave's manhood. "Nah, I ain't scared it's just that, that's my baby mother's baby shower," he told him. "Get the fuck outta here, you bullshitting," Rell laughed out loud. "So Ali out there piping ya BM (baby mother) and you don't wanna do shit about it?" "I'm going to smoke that faggot," Rell said trying to sound extra tough. "Just let me go in there for five minutes and let me try to persuade her to leave with me if that doesn't work, then we can shoot up the whole place. All I need is five minutes," Dave said damn near begging.

* * * *

Nancy sat greeting and mingling with all of her guest as they continued to file in, while the other guests just sat stuffing their faces. "Damn, I didn't know you knew this many people," Coco commented. "Me either," Nancy replied as the two woman broke out laughing. "Hey girl, you look bigger than a house," Christie said making her entrance as she hugged Nancy and handed her a gift. "Thanks girl, you better go get you some food because these people up in here acting like they never ate before." "You don't have to tell me twice," Christie replied as she headed over to the food section.

Nancy was really having a good time. She had never thought in a million years that she would be having such a big baby shower like this. In the middle of her thoughts she saw her knight in shining armor coming her way. "Hey baby everything alright," Ali asked kissing Nancy on the lips. "Yeah, life couldn't be better thanks to you," she said giggling like a little school girl. "Likewise baby, today is your day so enjoy it. I'm going to be over there with the guys. If you need me just holla." "Okay baby," Nancy replied as she watched her man walk over to where all the guys were standing in a huddle.

"As soon as I walked in the house, she was already naked," Diesil said standing in the middle of the huddle. "I pulled out my dick and she was on it like it was the last dick she would ever see again in her life." "Nigga stop lying," Wise cut in. "Chill, don't interrupted my story; this is a true story," Diesil continued. "Aight so check it, I'm blowing shorty back out, right…then out the blue something told me to look up. I look up and what do I see? Her twin sister standing in the door way butt naked watching my performance." "Yo this nigga is lying son," a soldier commented from the side line. “You buggin, you know how much pussy I get,” Diesil asked.

Suddenly the whole room got quiet when Butch rolled up in the place in his wheel chair. “Oh shit look at this mutha fucka,” Diesil yelled out as everyone went to greet the fallen soldier.

Meanwhile Nancy sat down with Coco and Christie enjoying some fried chicken, yellow rice, and some macaroni and cheese. “Damn this shit is delicious. Who cooked this shit,” Coco asked. “Ali hired a chef to cook all this food,” Nancy answered stuffing her face. “I think this is the best food I ever tasted,” Coco stated as she helped herself to another plate. “Girl how’s everything going with G-money,” Christie asked sipping on a glass of homemade lemonade. “Not good. His first court date is tomorrow, so I’ll know a little more when I speak to his lawyer tomorrow,” Coco said hoping everything would be okay. “You know I’m going to be praying for you,” Nancy said trying to comfort her best friend.

“Oh shit, is that Dave right there,” Coco asked looking towards the entrance. “You better stop playing like that,” Nancy chuckled thinking her best friend was just joking around. “Nah, I’m serious…look,” Coco said pointing towards the entrance. By the time Nancy looked up, it was too late because Dave was already heading in their direction.

“What, you thought you could hide forever,” Dave asked helping himself to a seat. “Dave why don’t you do us all a favor and leave,” Coco snarled rolling her eyes. “Bitch mind ya mutha fucking business,” he warned. “I’m here to get my family back.” “Family,” Nancy echoed. “Nigga, you must’ve lost your rabbit ass mind.” “Listen, watch your mouth before you have blood in it,” Dave threatened. “Now listen, shit is going to be different this time around," he said pulling out a huge wad of cash. "Together we can do big things." "Like what, rob a liquor store," Coco said sarcastically. "I ain't going to tell you again, mind ya business." The look in his eyes screamed trouble. "I'm sorry Dave, but you're a little too late. I have a new man now." "A real man," Coco cut in again. "We can do this the easy way or the hard way, but either way you're coming with me," Dave said getting loud, revealing his ignorance. "I'm not going anywhere with you," Nancy said in a matter of fact tone. "Bitch who you talking to like that?" Dave shot to his feet and viciously grabbed Nancy's arm. "Take your hands off of me," Nancy demanded as she tried to pull away. "Get off of her Dave," Coco screamed as she jumped on Dave's back, and started choking him so that he would let Nancy go. "Get the fuck off me bitch," Dave barked as he viciously flung Coco over his shoulder, and slammed her to the floor causing her body to make a loud slapping sound against the floor.

Dave quickly turned and tried to grab Nancy again, but Ali's right haymaker hit him dead in his face, causing Dave to stumble backwards. Dave quickly regrouped and threw his hands up, but it was no use. Fists came flying from every direction until Dave laid in the middle of the floor knocked out cold.

"You alright baby," Ali asked Nancy as he helped Coco back to her feet. "Yeah, I'm fine; that was just my old boyfriend," Nancy said feeling embarrassed. "Oh that's him right there," Ali growled. All he could think about was the stories he heard about with Dave beating and torturing Nancy, along with a whole bunch of other bad things that he had done to her. With that last thought Ali snapped, even though there were at least twenty goons still stomping, and kicking Dave's unconscious body.

Ali quickly shoved everybody out of the way as he snatched one of his Berettas from his holster and knelt down. "You fucking scum bag," he growled as he proceeded to rearrange Dave's face with the handgun. Ali pounded Dave's face in with his gun until he was sure every bone in his face was broken, to go along with the teeth he had knocked out.

When Ali slid his Beretta back into it's holster, everyone was so quiet you could hear a pin drop. "Get this piece of shit out of my presence," he ordered as he went and helped himself to a drink. Five minute later the music was playing again, and everyone carried on like nothing ever happened.

Big Mel and a few goons carried Dave's lifeless body outside where they tossed it into the trunk of one of the goon's car and slammed it shut. "Weak ass nigga," Big Mel chuckled as he and the goons headed back inside.

Once Rell saw them carry Dave's body out it was on. "Lets make this happen," he ordered as he slid open the side door of the van as it cruised down the block five miles per hour. As soon as the van made it in front of the place, Rell and his crew opened fire. Immediately everybody hit the ground when they heard the shots ringing out, followed by the sound of shattering glass.

"Get down," Ali yelled as he helped Nancy to the ground safely so that she wouldn't hurt herself. Once the shots finished ringing out, people slowly started to make their way back to their feet, when out of nowhere a mini van came crashing through the front door running over anybody that was in its way. Once the van came to a complete stop, six masked men, holding some kind of machine gun jumped out the back of the van. Without hesitation, the gun men opened fire on whoever was closest to them.

Skip quickly snatched his .40 cal from the small of his back, and sent four hallow point bullets through one of the gunmen's chest. "Don't move," Ali ordered as he sprung from behind the table snatching his twin Beretta's from their holster. With a murderous look in his eyes Ali riddled, and rocked one of the gunmen full of bullets, leaving his chest smoking and full of holes. When Big Mel saw Ali jump into the gunfight, he quickly pulled out his Uzi and made his way to where Ali stood. His job was to protect him and that's what he planned on doing, even if it meant losing his own life. In the middle of the shootout one of the gunmen noticed Butch just sitting there in his wheelchair. Without a trace of emotion, the gunman pointed his weapon at Butch and pulled the trigger. Butch's body jerked and twisted like he was trying to brake dance, as he laid slumped over in his wheelchair.

Diesil, Wise, and the rest of the crew opened fire on the rest of the gunmen and van, moving closer with every shot. The remaining last two gunmen quickly threw some reckless shots over their shoulders, and tried to make their exit on foot. Without hesitation Skip, Diesil, and a few other soldiers quickly chased after the two gunmen.

Tears ran freely down Nancy's face when she realized what just happened. There were dead bodies everywhere; the pretty outfit she wore was now covered in blood. Even the D.J. had a bullet hole in his head. All the hard work Coco had done decorating had all been for nothing, and all that was left was carnage.

"You three get up," Ali said looking at Nancy, Coco, and Christie. "Yo Big Mel get these three to my crib safely," he ordered as he checked out the rest of the guests. Ali couldn't believe what just went down. Rell and Detective Nelson had really crossed the line this time. Minutes later Ali heard a sound he was too familiar with – sirens. One of Ali's soldiers quickly took each man's weapon and placed it into a duffle bag, then smoothly disappeared out the back door.

"What the hell happened up in here," Detective Nelson questioned with an evil smirk on his face. "Things didn't have to be like this; all you had to do was cooperate." Ali didn't respond, he just stared at the detective coldly. "Oh yeah, by the way I got your little note." "It won't be the last one," Ali growled through clenched teeth. "Was that a threat?" "No, a promise," Ali snarled. "All this can end today by just breaking me off forty percent, and I'll call off the wolves." "Kiss my ass. You'll never see another dime of my money, but you will be seeing more bloodshed…that's a promise," Ali said as he brushed past the detective. "Surrender Ali, your fighting a war you can't win," Detective Nelson yelled out. Ali didn't respond, he just hopped into his new Aston Martin convertible and headed home.

"Where's Big Mel," Ali asked as soon as he stepped foot into his house. "I don't know, he dropped us off and headed right back out the door," Nancy answered her face still full of tears. As soon as Ali looked at Nancy, Coco, and Christie all sitting down looking scared and hurt his heart melted. "Listen, I'm sorry about what happened back there. I promise I will never put anyone of you in harms way again," he told them as he quickly reloaded his twin

9mm's. "This fucking cop is trying to bring me down. The same crooked mutha fucka that locked up G-money. But I already spoke to Mr. Goldberg; he's trying to pull some strings, so hopefully G-money can be released at the end of the week." "I hope so," Coco rattled wishing the nightmare she was living would soon be over. "Everything is going to be alright. We're going to see what happen in court tomorrow."

* * * *

Meanwhile back in Detective Nelson's office he sat at his desk filling out paperwork, when Big Mel came busting into his office. By the look on the big man's face Detective Nelson could tell he was smoking mad. "What the fuck is wrong with you," Big Mel barked. "What are you talking about," Detective Nelson said faking ignorance. "You could of gave me the heads up about the baby shower today, I damn near got my head blown off", Big Mel laughed. "If I would've given you a heads up, then when it went down you wouldn't have been surprised."

Big Mel let those last words sink in before he spoke. "Yeah, I guess you're right, but next time try to give me a smoke signal or something." Detective Nelson chuckled as he handed Big Mel a brown paper bag full of cash. "What's this for?" "That's for the baby shower information, helping me lock up G-money, and leading me to Frankie. Keep up the good work and there'll be plenty more where that came from. Oh I almost forgot," Detective Nelson said pulling out another paper bag, but it was half the size of the first one. "Tell your partner, Wise, to keep up the good work also." "Will do," Big Mel said accepting the money. "Yo, next we're going to have to meet in a different location because I can't be seen coming in and out of this precinct, especially if I'm not in cuffs, you dig?" "I can dig it brother," Detective Nelson said disrespecting Big Mel right in his face. Only Big Mel wasn't smart enough to catch that last comment.

Big Mel quickly made his exit, and as soon as Big Mel got behind the wheel he felt like a piece of shit. He knew what he was doing was wrong, and very unnecessary because Ali paid him more than enough money. He was just being greedy. "Fuck that, I got my own plans," he said out loud.

The truth of the matter was, Big Mel wanted to be the man. He was tired of taking orders from Ali, and risking his life for him. So by setting Ali up, Big Mel could just take over the empire and run it however he felt like it.

"Yo, where the fuck was you at," Ali asked suspiciously. "I went back to the spot looking for you," Big Mel lied. "Yo, whoever did this is dead," he should've gotten an Oscar for the performance he was putting on. "It was Detective Nelson, and that faggot Rell," Ali huffed. "I say we just go to Rell's hood and body that nigga." "Sounds good, but we have to be a little smarter now. The odds are stacked against us. Rell has the money and the soldiers now, and Detective Nelson; so in order to get at him we're going to have to smoke him out," Ali stated harshly. "Oh, but don't get it twisted. We're going to definitely get at all of them mutha fuckas." "How are the girls holding up?" Big Mel changed the subject. "They cool; they're in the back laying down. You know chicks ain't used to being around shit like that, you dig?" "I can dig it." "Yo I'm a go lay down myself B. This day's over with so I can worry about tomorrow," Ali said as he disappeared in the master bedroom.

Chapter 32
ONLY GOD CAN JUDGE ME

Ali and the rest of the crew sat in the courtroom patiently waiting for them to call G-money's name. Seconds later, everyone's head turned when they heard Detective Nelson's hard bottom shoes clicking and clacking, as he made his entrance. "I can't stand this faggot," Ali said to himself shaking his head in disgust.

When G-money walked into the courtroom, he gave a head nod to all of his supporters as he stood next to Mr. Goldberg. Mr. Goldberg and the District Attorney went back and forth for about seven minutes only for the judge to remand G-money. G-money quickly had a word with Mr. Goldberg before he went back into the bullpen.

Ali and the rest of the crew stood outside, patiently awaiting Mr. Goldberg. "What's the word on G-money," one soldier yelled out when he saw Mr. Goldberg walk out the court house.

"Ali, can I have a word with you," Mr. Goldberg asked as he and Ali stepped to the side. "What's good, tell me something good," Ali said looking at Mr. Goldberg for a comment. "G-money told me to tell you somebody on the team is snitching." "Yeah I figured that. He didn't say who he thought it was," Ali asked rubbing his chin. "No, but he said it's somebody close who knows everything." "Aight, tell him I'm going to do a little investigation and get down to the bottom of this. Tell him not to worry, we're going to have him out of there soon," Ali said with a frown.

"He also told me to tell you to start doing shit on your own. He said it might be a little risky, but at least you know you won't snitch on yourself. But personally I think you should take a break for a minute. Maybe go on a little vacation until things cool off a little," Mr. Goldberg said sincerely. "I'll think about it," Ali said as he hugged Mr. Goldberg. "Meet me on 141st and 8th Ave at eleven p.m." He whispered in his lawyer's ear. "Will do," Mr. Goldberg retorted as he walked off swiftly.

"What that Jewish mutha fuck talking about," Big Mel asked nosily. "He ain't talking about shit; you know lawyer shit, he want his money," Ali said misleading his twenty-four hour bodyguard.

When Big Mel and Ali made it to the crib Big Mel noticed that Ali was acting and moving differently, not his motions but his actions. "Boos man everything aight?" "Yeah everything is cool, this fucking rat in the crew is driving me crazy," Ali stated plainly as he strapped on his Teflon vest over his white tee covering it up with his brand new Pelle leather jacket.

"Where we going," Big Mel asked. "I gotta go take care of something, but I have to do it alone," Ali told him. "You sure about that? It could be a little dangerous especially with all this beef shit going on; know what I mean," Big Mel stated. "I'll be aight, plus I'm not going far any way," Ali said as he headed out of the door.

"Fuck," Big Mel yelled out as he pulled out his cell phone and dialed a number. "Ali just left the crib alone." "Why did you let him out of your site," Detective Nelson snarled. "What you want me to do? Tell him he can't go out side," Big Mel asked sarcastically. "Don't be a wise guy. What car is he in?" "He took the grey Range Rover," Big Mel replied. "Okay, make sure you let me know every time he leaves that house and you're not with him," Detective Nelson said hanging up in Big Mel's ear.

Mr. Goldberg pulled up and saw Ali doubled parked on the corner of 141st Street. He quickly hopped out of his vehicle, and slid into the passenger seat of the Range Rover.

"Glad you could make it," Ali said as he pulled off. "So what seems to be the problem," Mr. Goldberg asked wanting to know why Ali had him out at this time of night. "I needed to speak to you in private. I had a few questions about G-money's case." "What kind of questions," Mr. Goldberg asked curiously.

"Aight, check it out…I got this soldier right he's willing to turn himself in for the cop murders, but if he turns himself in will G-money be released?" "Absolutely," Mr. Goldberg exclaimed loudly. "The murder charges would be dropped, but he's going to have to eat the gun charge." "Aight, that's all I want baby," Ali replied excitedly. "I'll have that soldier sent to your office first thing in the morning."

"Who would be crazy enough to turn them self in on a murder charge," Mr. Goldberg asked. "It's all part of the game. Taking care of your family if something happens to me or G-money a lot of men and their families will be fucked up you dig? We do a lot for our soldiers and their families, not to mention the community work we do, so a few people wouldn't even be a man if it wasn't for us. How can you call yourself a man, if you can't even put food on the table for your family?"

"I understand," Mr. Goldberg stated as Ali dropped him back off at his car. "I'll call you when your soldier finds his way to my office." "Aight do that," Ali replied as he watched Mr. Goldberg pull off.

Chapter 33
NO TURNING BACK

"Come on let's go," Freddie yelled as he beeped the horn on the Benz like a mad man. "Chill out old man," Spanky said as he slid into the passenger seat. "Today is the biggest fight conference of your life, and you in there bullshitting," Freddie huffed as he stepped on the gas. "I bet "The Terminator" won't be late," he taunted.

"Fuck the terminator, I'm going to terminate his ass when we step in that ring," Spanky said with a chill in his voice. Freddie's words had struck a cord within him only because what he said was true. "After this punk ass conference, it's hard work from here on," Freddie stated firmly. "I been training for about two months now already. We just signed the contract two weeks ago, so I'm focused right now B." "You better stay that way because "The Terminator" will be more than ready for action mentally and physically, come fight night," Freddie warned. "Likewise brother," Spanky countered as he stared blankly out the window. Spanky knew this next fight was his biggest one yet. He knew exactly what he had to do when fight night came around.

As soon as the Benz pulled up, dozens of reporters bum rushed the vehicle hoping to get a word with Spanky. “How do you plan on defeating James “The Terminator” Johnson,” a white reporter in her early thirties asked aiming her recorder towards Spanky’s mouth, looking for a comment. “Easy, he’s going to whip his ass just like he did the rest of his opponents,” Freddie answered as he and Spanky ignored the other reporters and cameramen as they made their way inside of the building.

“It’s a fucking circus out there B,” Spanky said getting a rush just from the anticipation of the fight. “Clash of the undefeated,” Freddie said reading the big poster that had a picture of both fighters on it out loud. “I can’t wait,” Spanky said out loud as he and Freddie took their seat on the stage and prepared themselves for the thousands of questions they knew they would be asked.

The mini crowd cheered loudly when James “The Terminator” Johnson stepped on the stage. The Terminator had his game face on as he grilled Spanky , before he sat down (gave him a hard stare). “First of all I want to thank God and The Terminator for giving me this opportunity,” Spanky cleared his throat as he stood at podium. “I just want to let all my fans know that I appreciate all their love and support, and come fight night they will get more than their money’s worth thank you,” Spanky smiled for the cameras, and waved to his fans before he took his seat.

When “The Terminator” stood, all eyes were on him as he made his way to the podium. “First of all I just want to ask the challenger one question,” he said turning to face Spanky. “Who have you fought so far? A bunch of bums and drug addicts,” The Terminator said answering his own question. “You’ve never been in the ring with a fighter like me, and come fight night I will expose you just like all the other fighters who came for my title. I think I will break more of a sweat doing twenty push ups than fighting this guy,” The Terminator chuckled then looked at Spanky one last time before he headed back to his seat. “I’m going to wake his ass up because he must be dreaming,” Spanky whispered in Freddie’s ear as the reporters got ready to ask their questions.

“Terminator, why do you hate all of your opponents,” a Chinese reporter asked aiming his tape recorder towards the champs mouth. “I don’t hate my opponents, I just don’t respect them…it’s a difference. You see with me if you want some respect, you going to have to earn it by going in that ring with me and make me respect you. It hasn’t happened yet, and I seriously doubt if it happens this time around,” The Terminator stated firmly.

“What’s your thoughts on what The Terminator had to say about you,” a black reporter asked looking at Spanky for a comment. “Well it’s simple, The Terminator doesn’t want to fight me but he has no choice. Me and him was suppose to fight two years ago, but it never happened because he was scared. He’s just talking right now, but come fight night I’m going to just sit back and watch his face beat up my hands,” Spanky said as he headed back towards the podium so he and The Terminator could pose face to face looking each other dead in the eyes. “You can run, but you can’t hide,” Spanky said looking dead in The Terminator’s eyes.

“Okay that’s enough, let’s get out of here

before a mini riot starts," Freddie said as he escorted Spanky out of the building back inside the Benz. "I'm going to whip his ass," Spanky exclaimed excitedly. "He really think he's the real Terminator." "You going to really have to hurt that guy because you know the judges love to show favor to the champ," Freddie reminded him. "I got this," Spanky said glancing at his watch. "I'm a go home real quick, shower and go pick Christie up from work." "Aight, cool. I'll see you in the gym first thing in the morning," Freddie said as he pulled up right in front of Spanky's crib.

* * * *

Maurice stood on the block watching the fiends come and go. Now that Dave was dead, he was the man. Maurice loved having power, he just hated that he had to lose his best friend in order to gain it. But he vowed to do his best on the job. As he stood on the block, he noticed Rell's Lexus coupe pull up. Without hesitation, Maurice walked over to the car and stuck his head in the passenger's window. "What's good my nigga," he asked. "You got that count ready for me," Rell asked placing his Lexus in park. "Yeah it's right here," Maurice said dropping a brown paper bag on the passenger seat of the car.

"So how's it looking out here," Rell asked thumbing through one of the stacks. "It's like Christmas out here," Maurice replied. "That's what I like to hear. You got those shooters on the roof like I asked?" "Yeah, two on each end of the block just like you asked," Maurice replied quickly. "Keep up the good work. If you need anything, make sure you call me, you hear," Rell said throwing the Lexus in drive as he slowly pulled off.

Life for Rell couldn't have been better for him. He did what he wanted, when he wanted, and how he wanted. Rell pulled up in his driveway blasting 50cents song, "I get money." He quickly noticed the front door to his house was slightly ajar. Rell quickly slid out of the driver seat snatching the P89 Ruger from his waistband as he slowly entered his house with caution.

Beverly came walking into the living room and almost shitted on herself as she looked down the barrel of Rell's Ruger. "Gees, put that gun away before you shoot me by accident," she huffed kissing Rell on both cheeks. "Sorry baby, but I saw the door halfway open and I thought something…never mind," he said placing his P89 back into his waistband. "I was baking a cake, but I fell asleep by accident, and when I woke up the house was kind of smokey, so I cracked the door trying to let in some fresh air," Beverly said innocently.

"It's cool," Rell said as he headed to the master bed room so that he could take a nap. Rell couldn't remember the last time he got a good night's rest and when Beverly entered the bedroom butt naked he knew he wouldn't be getting rest anytime soon. "You haven't been home in three days," she said seductively licking her lips. "You know what that means right?" "I'm guessing you about to tell me," Rell countered. "It means we got a lot of fucking to do," she said looking at Rell like he was a piece of meat.

Beverly aggressively unbuckled Rell's jeans, only to find his manhood standing up at attention. She quickly wrapped her lips around her man's dick pretending it was an icey. Beverly made loud slurping noises along with a few loud moans as her man's love tool glided in and out of her mouth at a nice rhythm. After fifteen minutes of sucking, Beverly smoothly rolled a condom on Rell's dick as she hopped up on it riding it like a race horse. Rell firmly cuffed both of Beverly's ass cheeks as she bounced up and down, screaming loudly in pleasure then pain. The bedsprings counted the humps until

Beverly collapsed on top of him, the two breathing heavy before Beverly broke the silence. "Daddy I want you to start staying home a little more," she whispered. "Why, what's going on," Rell asked suspiciously. "Nothing is going on, it's just I don't want nothing bad to happen to you," she said pouting like a baby. "Listen, you let me worry about the streets. You just worry about taking care of the house and shit like that." "The reason I'm bringing this up is because I'm afraid you going to get locked up again."

"I'm never going back there ever again," Rell said aggressively. "The whole time you were gone, it felt like a nightmare and as soon as you came home it's like the nightmare just stopped." "Everything is going to be fine baby," Rell stated as he answered his ringing cell phone.

"Yo, who dis?" "What's good? Its me, Debo, what you doing?" "Ain't shit, just chilling. What's good popping with you?" "About to hit up this strip club, you down," Debo asked. "If they got long hair, you know I don't care," Rell countered smoothly. "Aight, me and the goons will be over in about thirty minutes." "Aight 1," Rell said closing his cell phone shut as he headed for the shower.

Thirty minutes later Rell kissed Beverly on the lips as he headed out the door. Rell and his crew pulled up into the strip club's parking lot five cars deep. Each man stepped out looking like new money. Rell strolled up to the strip with seventeen soldiers behind him.

"What's good? We ain't going to have no trouble up in here tonight gentlemen," the big bouncer barked looking at Rell for an answer. "Come on B, we ain't looking for no trouble. We come up in here every week spending our hard earned money," Rell shot back as the big bouncer allowed Rell and his crew to enter the strip club.

As soon as Rell and his crew stepped foot into the strip club all eyes were on them. Strippers came from every direction; it was like they could smell money. In less than five minutes every member in the crew had a thick dancer on their lap or in their face. Everyone except Rell; he had his eye on this thick dancer wearing a red thong, along with some knee high red shinny boots with a three inch heel.

Rell wasted no time handling his business. He quickly made his way over to where she stood nursing a drink. "What's good, let me get you another drink," Rell said as he ordered a bottle on Hennessey. "So what's your name," he asked filling up her cup. "Christie," she answered. "So Christie, what you doing working in a spot like this?" "I'm trying to get paid like everybody else," she replied quickly. "Get with me and you'll never have to worry about money again," Rell said removing a thick stack of money from his pocket.

Christie chuckled before she responded. "Nah I'm good, besides I don't think my man would like that," she said turning to leave. Rell quickly grabbed

Christie's arm before she could leave. "Where you going ma?" "I'm about to hit up this pole; my brake is over." "How much for a lap dance," Rell asked looking at Christie's fat ass. "Twenty dollars," she answered. "Here's a hundred."

Christie placed the money in her small Gucci bag as she lead Rell to the lap dance section. As if right on Q, as soon as Rell sat down on the small couch the DJ threw on Luke's "Doo-doo Brown." When Christie heard the music blaring through the speakers she quickly began shaking her ass in Rell's face. After five minutes of watching Christie shake her ass in his face, Rell couldn't take it anymore so he grabbed Christie by the waist pulling her down on his lap.

Christie proceeded to give Rell a lap dance. She really didn't want to do it, but it was her job. After thirty minutes of grinding on Rell's dick, Christie decided she had given the man his money's worth. "Okay, I think that's enough," Christie said as she stood up. "Woo, woo where you going," Rell asked not wanting the woman to leave. "I think you had enough." "What you want more money? Is that it," Rell asked disrespectfully tossing money in Christie's face.

Out of reflex Christie grabbed her drink off of the floor and tossed it into Rell's face. Without thinking twice, Rell violently bust the Hennessey bottle over Christie's head sending shattered glass everywhere as Christie dropped to the floor. Seconds later a bouncer came swarming from every direction and escorted Rell and his crew out of the strip club.

"Do me a favor and don't put your hands on me," Rell barked as he and his crew made their exit. "Fucking dirty ass bitches in there," Debo yelled out as the crew headed back to the parking lot. Rell strolled through the parking lot reading a text message Beverly had sent him when something told him to look up. "Oh shit," he yelled out not believing his eyes. "This nigga must be crazy," Rell said tapping Debo on the shoulder.

Spanky strolled through the parking lot without a care in the world until he noticed about fifteen to eighteen thugs headed into his direction. Spanky didn't think anything of it until he identified Rell as one of the thugs. Something inside of Spanky told him to turn around, but his pride just wouldn't let him. "I hope this nigga don't try to act up since he got his boys with him."

Seconds later, Spanky knew something was about to pop off. "Yo what's poppin homey," Rell yelled out reaching for his strap. Spanky quickly came to a halt when he saw Rell holding a gun in his hand. Without thinking twice Spanky hit a 360 and took off running in the opposite direction. Spanky's attempt to escape was quickly ended when he felt a hot slug explode in the back of his thigh, sending him crashing down to the ground.

Once Debo and the crew saw Rell shoot the kid in the parking lot, they all quickly reached for their weapons. "Hold your fire yo," Rell said holding his crew back. "Yo Debo, go get me that baseball bat out the trunk," he ordered.

Rell slowly walked up on Spanky, who was on the ground trying to crawl leaving a blood trail on the concrete. "Let me give you what I owe you," Rell said as he knelt down and punched Spanky in his mouth. "Punk mutha fucka," he growled as he hogged spit in Spanky's face. "What's good boss? You want me to bat this nigga to death," Debo asked with fire dancing in his eyes. "Nah, you can't kill him, I got something even better than that," Rell grinned. "Yo lift his arm up," Rell ordered. Once Debo extended Spanky's arm, Rell swung the bat with all his might until Spanky's arm snapped like a number two pencil.

Spanky squealed in pain as he just laid on the ground helplessly. Pain shot through every inch of his body as he cried like a baby. "Yo grab his other arm B," Rell ordered tightening his grip on the bat. "No please don't," Spanky begged. His cowardly plea was silenced by the sound of his arm cracking. "Ahhhhhhhhhhhhhhh," Spanky screamed out in pain at the top of his lungs, wishing his attackers would just kill him and get it over with.

"Yo come on, that's enough," Rell said as he heard sirens. Rell and his crew quickly scrambled to get to their vehicles, leaving Spanky laid out in the parking lot squirming on the ground like a fish out of water.

A few bouncers helped Christie nurse her wounds when they heard a thunderous shot go off. Christie quickly shot to her feet when she remembered Spanky was supposed to be picking her up from work. "Get off me, I gotta go see if my husband is out there," she said pushing the bouncers off of her.

When Christie made it out to the front of the club, she saw a body sprawled out at the end of the parking lot. She jogged swiftly through the parking lot in her red thong, and red knee high heels. "Please Lord don't let that be my Spanky. Please Lord Jesus, don't let that be my baby," she prayed the whole way until she finally reached the body. "Oh my God," Christie broke down and screamed when she saw both of Spanky's arms bent in directions they didn't belong. "Helppppp," Christie screamed at the top of her lungs until a couple of bouncers came rushing from the club to see what the problem was. "Baby who did this to you," Christie asked afraid to touch Spanky. She could tell he was in a tremendous amount of pain. Spanky mumbled something back, but it was inaudible. Seconds later the bouncer lead the ambulance to where Spanky was laying in the parking lot.

Christie couldn't do anything but sit back and cry, as she watched the paramedics do their best to lift Spanky off the ground without putting him a painful position. "I love you baby, everything's going to be okay," Christie yelled out attempting to cheer her husband up the best she could. Spanky's lips were moving, but Christie couldn't make out what he was saying. She quickly moved in closer so she could hear what her husband was trying to say. "Call Ali," he whispered as the paramedics placed him in the back of the ambulance and shut the back doors.

"Let's get you inside so you can put some clothes on," one of the bouncers spoke softly as he placed his jacket over Christie shoulders. "Let me use your cell phone real quick," Christie demanded. She quickly dialed Ali's number.

On the fourth ring Ali answered. "Who dis?" "It's me Christie, I'm down at the club and some guys just attacked Spanky," she yelled hysterically in the phone. "Hold on baby, you going to have to slow down; now what's going on," Ali spoke firmly. "Some guy in the club assaulted me, then I heard a loud gunshot outside, when I rushed outside I saw Spanky laid out at the end of the parking lot." "Are you telling me my little brother is dead," Ali asked in a panic. "No, he's still alive, but he got shot in his leg and both of his arms are broken," Christie sobbed, then swallowed hard. "Fuck," Ali's voice boomed like thunder. "Aight call me back when you find out what hospital they taking him to," Ali said hanging up in Christie's ear.

"What's wrong boss man," Big Mel asked when he saw Ali's face buried in his hands. "Somebody just shot Spanky and broke both of his arms," Ali said through a sobs. "Get the fuck outta here; you serious;" Big Mel asked in total shock.

"Baby what's wrong," Nancy asked overhearing what happened. "Its Spanky, somebody shot him and broke both of his arms." "What," Nancy replied not believing her eyes. "Don't even worry, I'm going to handle this shit for you," Big Mel said. "Nah, I got this myself," Ali spat out of emotion not thinking about the consequences. "Round up all the soldiers, and tell 'em it's a meeting first thing in the morning," Ali ordered as he strapped on his Teflon vest, and headed out the door with Big Mel on his heels.

Once the doctors stitched up Christie's head, she was right by Spanky's side the whole way, sitting right next to his bed. Ali parked the Range Rover in the hospital's parking lot. Before he made his exit, he took one of his 9mm's from his holster and placed a silencer on the muzzle. "What you doing boss man," Big Mel asked somewhat confused. Ali didn't respond, instead he slid out of the driver seat of the Range Rover and headed straight for the police car that sat parked adjacent from the hospital.

"Good evening officers," Ali spoke politely leaning his head through the driver's window. "Could you tell me how to reach the main entrance?" "Sure, you go straight until you see..." The officer's words were quickly cut short as Ali aimed the nozzle at the cop's baldhead and squeezed the trigger. The bullet spit effortlessly out of the gun sounding like a bird chirp. Ali quickly raised his arm aiming the smoking silencer at the dead cop's partner painting the inside of the squad car with blood, leaving the two officers slumped over one another.

"Fucking pigs," he mumbled as he headed back towards the Range Rover. "Yo, go inside; I'm going to call you in an hour to see how my brother is doing. I can't stand to see him all fucked up," Ali said as his eyes welled up. "Look out for my call," he said as he hopped back into the driver's seat and peeled off.

Big Mel walked into the hospital feeling guilty inside. When he saw Detective Nelson he planned on giving him a piece of his mind. Big Mel was trying to come up, but he didn't know shit was going to get this out of hand. When he reached the waiting area he saw Freddie sitting in the corner crying like a baby. Skip and a few other goons sat next to Freddie trying to comfort the old man.

"It's on now! Them mutha fuckas went too far this time," Skip said getting misty eyed. "Ali called for a meeting tomorrow morning at the warehouse," Big Mel informed Skip and the rest of the soldiers who stood around.

The entire waiting room went silent as Detective Nelson spoke with a smirk on his face. "I'm glad you think this is funny, you white devil," Freddie yelled out from his seat. "That boy ain't never did nothing to nobody and you just snatched his dreams away," he said in a small near to tears voice. "Hey what are you mad at me for? I didn't do anything to that boy. He was just at the wrong place at the wrong time," he remarked snidely.

"You son of a bitch," Freddie screamed out in rage as he lunged towards the detective. Before Detective Nelson could react, Freddie already punched him in his face. Detective Nelson shook off the blow and proceeded to rough the old man up until Skip and the rest of the goons pulled the two men apart. "Old fart must be crazy," Detective Nelson hissed feeling good about assaulting the elderly man.

"Hey Detective, come quick it's an emergency," the young flashlight cop screamed out. Detective Nelson didn't ask any questions, he just followed the young flashlight cop who lead him to a police car outside.

When Detective Nelson looked inside the police car, his face looked as if he sunk his teeth into a lemon. "Mother fuckers," Detective Nelson exploded with rage.

* * * *

When Ali stepped into his house, he noticed that Nancy was fully dressed. "Where you going?" "I was about to go to the hospital and do my best to comfort Christie. I thought she might could use a shoulder to lean on," Nancy replied sincerely. "Aight, just be careful out there and call me if you need me for anything." "Okay baby I will," Nancy told him as she headed out the door. Nancy hopped into her Lexus truck that Ali had brought her as a baby shower gift. Her whole mood was depressed because this was the reason she never dated drug dealers. She hated the fact that any day you could lose your man to the graveyard, or the jail cell, maybe even to the groupies. Nancy really felt sorry for Spanky and Christie. She felt bad because she heard about the big up coming fight he had with The terminator. But she felt worst for Christie; she could only imagine how hard it had to be to watch her man just lay there in pain all day.

* * * *

Ali sat at the mini bar he had in his house and got twisted all night. "It's all my fault," he whispered over and over to himself as he turned up the Grey Goose bottle he held in his hand. Ali didn't know how to handle the pain that was inside of him. His little brother was laying up in a hospital bed because of some old street beef he had. The thought of it just made his stomach turn. Ali's thoughts were interrupted when he heard his throw away phone ringing. He glanced at the caller I.D and saw that it was Big Mel calling.

"Yeah what's up," he answered sourly. "Yo it's a circus down here, all the cops are going crazy," Big Mel said excitedly. "That's the third cop that's been murdered in the last two months." "And your point is," Ali asked with a sharp edge in his voice. "I think we might need to chill out for a minute." "Go tell that shit to Spanky," Ali growled hanging up in Big Mel's ear.

The next morning every soldier from every borough was in attendance. After minutes of waiting Ali, finally made his presence known. When Ali walked through the door, every soldier stood up and cheered. Ali strolled through the door with his Teflon vest visible, along with his twin 9mm's. "I take it we all know why we're here today," Ali paced in front of all his soldiers with his hands clasped behind his back. "We tried to do the right thing, but sometime doing the right thing ain't always doing the right thing." All the soldiers cheered again.

"They backed us into a corner and we all know pressure bust pipes," Ali spoke calmly as he continued to pace the floor. Before another word could leave his mouth G-money came strolling through the front door with Mr. Goldberg on his heels. All the soldiers went crazy at the sight of G-money. "They can't keep a good nigga down for long, you dig?" G-money smiled as he stood up front with Ali. "Okay, okay, I see ya'll thirsty to go put in this work so I'm going to wrap this up," Ali said silencing the crowd. "I want half of you soldiers to kill one cop every week until this faggot Detective Nelson know we mean business, and I want the rest of you to take care of Rell. The first person to put a bullet in that mutha fucka is going to get twenty thousand dollars," Ali said dismissing all the soldiers.

Once all the soldiers were gone Ali gave G-money a big hug. "Glad to have you home." "I'm glad to be home," G-money replied gratefully. "So what you need me to do," he asked ready to get back to work. "I need you to chill out and help me find this new connect because we running dry," Ali told him. "Now remember G-money, you have to be cool because you only out on bail," Mr. Goldberg jumped into the conversation. "Yeah I know; in eight months I gotta go do this time for the gun charge I copped out to," G-money said shaking his head in disgust.

"Damn, with that new law now they making mutha fuckas in New York do three and half years for a gun now," Ali added. "Yeah I know, but I can't cry over spilt milk, you dig." "Just keep your nose clean and you'll be fine," Mr. Goldberg assured him.

"Oh yeah, you ain't going to believe what I found out while I was locked up," G-money said snatching one of Ali's 9mm's from his holster. "What's up," Ali asked giving G-money his full attention. "Yo, one of my homey's I was locked up with said that he used to be Wise old cellmate when he was locked up." "And," Ali asked as his patience was running thin. "And he said Wise snitched on another inmate to get out of jail, so that means Wise is the fucking snitch." G-money fought to control his temper. "Who introduced you to that rat mutha fucka?"

Ali let those last words sink in before he quickly snatched his other 9mm from his holster, grabbed Big Mel by the throat and placed the burner to his head. "You brought that cock sucker into my family," Ali growled through clenched teeth. "Slow down Ali, I didn't know he was a fucking snitch," Big Mel lied in attempt to save his life. "You know I wouldn't do no shit like that, we go way back." "Fuck that, shoot that mutha fucka," G-money said from the side line. "Come on G-money, how long have I known you for," Big Mel pleaded. "I don't give a fuck," G-money replied coldly. "You brought in the snitch, so now you gotta go." "Ali you know I ain't no fucking snitch, as long as I been down on the team. Come on, don't do me like this." "Fuck that! Smoke this ugly mutha fucka now, so you won't have to do it later," G-money added. "You brought that nigga in, you take him out" Ali whispered never taking his gun off the big man.

Big Mel quickly pulled out his cell phone and dialed Wise's number. "Yo what's up," Wise answered. "Yo we need you to come back to the warehouse for second." "Why what's up, I just left there," Wise asked suspiciously. "I can't talk on the phone, just get back over here now," Big Mel yelled hanging up in Wise's ear.

"You better pray I don't find out you a fucking snitch," Ali warned. "If you can't trust me, then who you going to trust," Big Mel asked nervously.

G-money and Mr. Goldberg didn't say word, instead they just looked on from the sideline.

Twenty minutes later, Wise strolled into the warehouse with a confused look on his face. "What's good," he asked. "You snitching, that's what's up," Big Mel snarled looking at Wise with a murderous look in his eyes. "What you talking about," Wise asked looking from face to face. "I always knew you was fucking snitch," Big Mel said pulling a .357 magnum from the small of his back. "Bu…but you told me if I didn't…"

Big Mel quickly silenced Wise with three shots to the chest. "Why the fuck you ain't let him finish talking," G-money asked sensing something fishy was going on.

"I don't want to hear shit that snitch mother fucker has to say," Big Mel capped back helping himself to a drink. "I don't trust this mutha fucka," G-money said nonchalantly. "Get rid of this body," Ali ordered as he took a swig from his Grey Goose bottle.

Big Mel didn't say a word, he just did as he was told and dragged Wise's lifeless body out of the warehouse. Ali sat in deep thought as he watched Mr.

Goldberg explain a few things to G-money over in the corner.

"I need a fucking vacation," Ali said out loud as he heard his cell phone ringing.

"Who dis," he answered. "It's time," Nancy screamed into the receiver. "Time for what," Ali asked confused. "For the baby." "Oh shit, where you at?" "Coco is helping me into a cab right now," she answered in pain. "Aight, what hospital you going to?" "You know the one across the street from Burger King. I can't think of the name of it right now." "Aight, I'm on my way," Ali said ending the call.

"Yo, I gotta be out. Nancy about to have the baby." "That's what's up," G-money said giving Ali a hug. "You make sure you raise that kid right; treat it like your own. We need more brothers like you out there, these kids need us B." "I'm doing my best," Ali said as he headed out the door.

"I'm going to get out of here too," Mr. Goldberg said as he stood up to leave. "You make sure you stay out of trouble," "I'm going straight to the strip club tonight and show all my beautiful women some love, then I'm going straight to my girl Coco's crib," he boasted.

"Okay, just stay out of trouble." Mr. Goldberg patted G-money on the back and exited the warehouse.

Chapter 34
NEW LIFE

After five hours of pain, Nancy gave birth to a beautiful baby boy. "How you feel," Ali asked rubbing Nancy's head. "Much better now," she replied happy the hard part was over with. "I got so much I want to teach him," Ali said looking down at the blessing in front of him. "I'm going to teach him how to be a man." "Thank you," Nancy whispered. "For what?" "For everything," Nancy said looking Ali in his eyes. "I don't know where I would be or what I would be doing if I never met you. The crazy part about it is at the beginning I wasn't even going to take the job working for you at that apartment. But my girl, Coco, wouldn't take no for an answer," she chuckled. "That's how I know you are truly a blessing from God."

Those last words really touched Ali's heart. He never would've imagines in a million years that his presence alone would have saved someone's life. With that being said, Ali knew he had to raise that baby up the right way.

*　　*　　*　　*

"Yo where the fuck are we going," Diesil asked. "We going in circles." "Nah, I know these mutha fuckas be over here hanging out," Skip replied as he tripled the block. "Man ain't nobody even out here," Diesil said ready to go home. "Look what I told you," Skip yelled out as he double parked on the corner. "Look." He pointed at two cops entering a small coffee shop. "Aight, come on lets go kill these scum bags. I got some pussy at home waiting for me," Diesil said pulling his ski mask over his face.

Skip quickly threw on his black leather gloves and checked the magazine on his dessert eagle. "Aight lets be out," he ordered as he slid his ski mask over his face and exited the vehicle. "You should've seen the look on that boy's face when we kicked his door in," the officer bragged. "I said listen up boy you shouldn't sell crack if you don't want to go to jail." The entire coffee shop erupted with laughter. That laughter quickly came to an end when the owner heard the bell on top of the front door ring notifying him that someone was entering his store.

The shocked look on the owner's face caused the two cops to turn around on their bar stools. Both officers sat with their mouths hung wide open when they saw two men, wearing ski masks, blocking the entrance and holding firearms.

"Finish the story," Skip yelled out to the officer who was telling the story. "Have you lost your mind boy," the officer asked as he stood up. "If I was you I…"

The officer's sentence was cut short as his lungs filled with blood when three shots pierced through his chest and heart. Once the officer's lifeless body hit the floor, Skip and Diesil killed everybody in the small coffee shop. "Come on, let's get out of here," Diesil commented as he headed out the door only to find another cop car pulling up for some coffee. In a blink of an eye Diesil sent three shots through the cops' windshield as he and Skip ran to their car which was doubled parked on the corner.

"Officers down, officers down back up needed immediately," the officer yelled through his walkie talkie as he gained chase behind the stolen Acura.

"Be out, be out," Diesil yelled looking over his shoulder to see how far behind the cop car was. "Come on be out, this mutha fucka is right behind us." "I got this," Skip replied confidently as he hit a fish tailed right turn, causing Diesil's body to jerk left then right. "We ain't gon never get away like this," Diesil said as he quickly reloaded his fully automatic Israel Uzi. Diesil quickly hung half his body out the window and let his Uzi spit round after round spraying the windshield full of holes.

When the bullets came raining, the officer quickly lost control of the vehicle as he crashed into a parked car. Once Skip saw that the cop car crashed into a parked car, he quickly whipped a quick right bringing the car to a skidded stop. "What the fuck you doing," Diesil asked looking at Skip like he was crazy. "We going to have to brake on foot, that's our only chance; you know that cop called for back up," Skip replied. With that being said the two fled into the woods on foot, never looking back.

Detective Nelson pulled up behind the stolen Acura left in the middle of the street with both the doors wide open. All he could do was chuckle, his boss had been digging him a new asshole about finding out who had been dropping cops like it was nothing. Detective Nelson knew it was only one thing left for him to do. He pulled out his cell phone and dialed Big Mel's number.

When Big Mel recognized the number, he quickly took the call in the next room. "Yeah," he answered in a hushed voice. "I should blow your fucking head off," Detective Nelson barked into the receiver. "I got two more dead cops on my hands and one with a huge gash on his head from a car crash." "I'm doing the best I can. What more do you want me to do?" "Anything that's about to go down I need to know about it," Detective Nelson growled.

"Look I'm going to have to be cool for a while, Ali and G-money are on to me. They made me kill Wise the other day because they found out he was one of the snitches, so I gotta be cool; my ass is on the line." "Well my ass is on the line too and I guarantee you want me as a friend instead of an enemy," Detective Nelson threatened. "What do you want me to do?" "The next time Ali leaves the house alone contact me. I'm going to have a unit parked three blocks away from his house first thing in the morning. Make sure I get that call from you within forty-eight hours," Detective Nelson demanded as he hung up in Big Mel's ear. Big Mel hung up the phone with a sour taste in his mouth. He knew he was stuck between a rock and a hard place. "I should've never started fucking with this cop in the first place," Big Mel said shaking his head. He knew he had to do something and he had forty-eight hours.

* * * *

Rell sat in his new mid-night black Lambo entertaining a stripper in the parking lot at Sue's Rendezvous. "I got my drink, and my two step," blared through the car speakers as the stripper head bobbed up and down, and in and out of Rell's lap until Rell filled her mouth with his juices. Debo and the rest of the crew sat inside the strip club doing their own thing, while Rell slid off to the parking lot with one of the strippers. "Damn that was delicious," Erica said wiping her mouth and chin. "We been seeing each other now for six months, I think we should start spending a little more time together." Before Rell could respond he noticed a doo-doo brown station wagon circle his Lambo twice. "Yo if this station wagon circle around us one more time I'm a kill everybody in that mutha fucka," Rell said placing his P89 Ruger on his lap. "Are you sure that's him in that Lamborghini," Skip asked circling the parking lot one more time. Diesil slowly cruised up in the parking lot on his R1 Yamaha motorcycle; he made sure he wore his helmet to disguise his identity. "Yo, look in the glove compartment and grab what's in there," Rell ordered as he carefully watched the station wagon. Erica quickly opened up the glove compartment and saw a .380 with a marble handle sitting there along with a box of .380 bullets and a box of P89 bullets. Erica quickly grabbed the .380 and cocked it back. "These clowns must think I'm stupid," Rell said as he pulled out in front of the station wagon blocking them off. He quickly pointed his Ruger at the passenger, who was holding some kind of assault riffle and pumped four shots through the windshield. “Bak, Bak, Bak, Bak.” Skip quickly took cover as the bullets came blasting through the windshield. Rell quickly swerved up out of the parking lot like a bat out of hell. “These niggas are some characters,” he boasted until he saw the motorcycle speeding up on him from behind. Without thinking twice, Rell ran the red light and jumped on the highway going ninety down the ramp. Diesil breezed through the light, doing about eighty-five causing other drivers to beep their horns at the reckless driver. He flew down the ramp on his back wheel to pick up more speed. The R1 engine sounded like a speed boat as Diesil picked up speed. Once in firing range, Diesil pulled out his .45 instead of the Uzi because of how fast he was going; any wrong movement would have caused him to lose control of the bike.

Once in an empty lane, Rell quickly stomped on his brakes. Once the motorcycle past by, Rell put the pedal to the medal. “Fuck,” Diesil screamed out because now Rell was chasing him. “Fuck it, I’ll catch his ass next time,” he said to himself as he quickly got off at the next exit.

Chapter 35
THE RECOVERY

Ever since Spanky's accident, Christie quit working at the strip club. Her whole way of thinking had changed; nothing was worth having Spanky leave her. Everything in the future would be for Spanky. Christie jumped with fright when Freddie entered the room. "Hey Freddie, I didn't even hear you come in," Christie said. "I didn't mean to startle you," Freddie said politely as he kissed Christie on the cheek.

"How's it going champ," Freddie asked looking at Spanky. "I'm cool," he replied with a smile. "That's what I like to hear," Freddie said feeling sorry for the young man that he basically raised in the gym. "The doctor said my arms should be back to normal in eight to ten weeks, giving me six months to get ready for the fight," Spanky said excitedly.

Freddie looked at the floor before he spoke. "Umm…I was thinking you should cancel the fight and give your body a whole year to recover." "A whole year," Spanky echoed. "If I don't fight The Terminator now, I ain't going to never get another title shot and you know it."

"You just going to have to work your way back up to the top." "You talking like it's just that simple," Spanky said as a tear escaped his eye. "I worked all my life for this fight, now you want me to cancel it because of a few broken bones?"

"This is not a game. You could get killed out there in that ring if you ain't careful," Freddie warned. "Well I'd rather die in the ring instead of a hospital bed any day," Spanky said with a disgusted look on his face. "I don't care if I get killed in the ring or if I lose, you know why? Because later on in life people can say, "Damn I remember when Spanky fought for the title," not, "Damn he would've fought for the title if he didn't get jumped in the parking lot." I've worked my whole life for this opportunity, I can't just sit back and let it slip away like that."

"I'm guessing you okay with this since you ain't saying nothing," Freddie said looking at Christie for a comment. "Whatever Spanky decides to do I'm going to back him up a hundred percent," Christie retorted calmly.

"Spanky listen to me, you are like the son I never had and I don't want to see you get hurt, so please think this over," Freddie pleaded.

"There's nothing to think about," Spanky replied coldly. "I'm not missing up on this opportunity no matter what! A opportunity like this only comes around once in a lifetime and I'm not missing my opportunity," he said looking at Christie and Freddie.

"You right, there's a chance I could get hurt but there's also a chance I won't. Now what I need to know is will you be there to train me when I step foot back in that gym?"

"I don't know, I'll have to think about this. I need a drink," Freddie said as he stormed out of the hospital room.

"Well fuck you then," Spanky yelled as loud as he could. "I'll train by my fucking self," he said mad at the world because he was laid up in a hospital bed. "It's going to be okay boo," Christie said as she placed the straw in Spanky's mouth so he could drink some water.

Seconds later Ali entered the room with a look of concern on his face. "How you feeling little bro," he asked fiddling his thumbs. "Much better now," Spanky said smiling from ear to ear. "What took you so long to come see me?" "You know it hurts me to see you all fucked up like this, especially when it's my beef that got you laying up in this fucking hospital in the first place."

"Nah, it's not your fault. This could've happened to anybody," he told his older brother. "No, everybody knows that this is all my fault, but don't worry I got my best soldiers out hunting that cock sucker right now."

"Thank you, I appreciate it," Spanky said feeling sorry for his older brother. "I feel horrible inside," Ali said emptily. "Don't worry about it everything happens for a reason," Spanky spoke calmly.

"When you get up out of here?" "Tomorrow, I can't wait." "When does your cast get removed?" "In eight to ten weeks," Spanky said proudly.

"Aight, I'm out of here. Keep your head up," Ali said as he headed for the door.

"Why you leaving so soon," Spanky asked.

"Because I can't stand to see you all fucked up like this," Ali said as he kissed Christie on the cheek and made his exit.

Chapter 36
WHAT YOU WANNA DO?

"I shot his whole back window out. I know I had to hit whoever was in the back seat," Diesil boasted. "So you want me and the goons to stay on this Rell nigga?" "I really don't even care no more," Ali spoke calmly. Everyone looked on in amazement. "Yo, you felling alright," G-money asked.

"Yeah I'm just tired of all this killing," Ali said emptily. "If we keep this thing going on the killing is never going to stop," he said trying to drop some knowledge.

"I started doing this to get up enough money so I could open up some businesses to uplift our people. If we keep this war going, all I'm going to be doing is killing my own people, and basically what I'm trying to say is I don't want that blood on my hands no more, so from now on G-money is in charge. Anybody have any questions ya'll go see G-money," Ali said dryly.

"I understand what you going through," G-money whispered in Ali's ear as he gave his best friend a hug. "I want all of ya'll to know that I love all of ya'll, and I'm officially out of the game. If ever anybody want to change their life and get out the game ya'll know where to find me," Ali said depressingly as he made his exit.

Once Ali was out the door G-money took over. "Ali is just feeling down about his little brother. We going to continue on with the regular plan; Rell and Detective Nelson have to go no questions asked," G-money confirmed. "Lets make Ali proud and get rid of these two scum bags."

With that being said Skip, Diesil and the rest of the soldiers went back out on their man hunt.

* * * *

"What the fuck you mean, he out the game," Detective Nelson barked into the phone. "He just up and quit out the blue," Big Mel spoke softly. "What do I pay you for," Detective Nelson asked making Big Mel feel like a child.

"Listen, you told me to keep you updated on what's going on and that's exactly what I'm doing. If you don't like how I do it, then I suggest you find somebody better for the job," Big Mel raved. "I think I just might do that," Detective Nelson said hanging up in Big Mel's ear.

"Who was you on the phone with," Ali asked suspiciously. "Oh…that was my mom's," Big Mel lied quickly. "Tell her I said hello next time you speak to her." "I will," Big Mel said relieved Ali didn't fish for more questions.

"Yo Ali can I ask you something?" "Yeah, what's on your mind?" "Why did you just up and quit like that," Big Mel asked. "It comes a time in your life when you just have to grow up; you know what I'm saying? Butch is dead, Spanky's in the hospital all fucked up, G-money about to do three and a half years in a couple of months, and a whole bunch of other soldiers is locked up and in jail all because of me! I'm the leader, so I'm responsible. Oh I almost forgot about lil' Andre. He was only sixteen and he got his head blown off for pumping crack for me," Ali said disgustedly.

"I never looked at it like that," Big Mel said letting Ali's words marinate for a minute. "You see what I'm saying Mel? I could've been got out the game, but then that would've been selfish of me. The reason I stayed in it so long was so I could build up something for my people and try to give back. I've accomplished that, now I'm done."

"I ain't mad at you for that," Big Mel said as he poured him and Ali a drink. "To a new beginning," Big Mel said raising his glass. "To a new beginning," Ali echoed as the two clinked their glasses.

*   *   *   *

"So what's the baby's name," Coco asked as she held the cute little baby in her arms. "Ali," Nancy answered. "Word," Coco asked in disbelief. "Yeah I'm serious." "Ali didn't have a problem with that," Coco asked as she began to feed the baby. "Not at all; he's the best man in the world," Nancy boasted as she continued to get dressed. “He does things that other men are not willing to do or are scared to do,” she said as she slid her feet into her three inch heels. Nancy was the happiest chick in the world. Not only did she have a good man and a beautiful baby boy, but most of all she could wear her old clothes again. When it was all said and done, Nancy looked like a million bucks when she finished getting dress.

“Where you going,” Ali asked as he entered the master bedroom. “Me and Coco about to go shopping and pick up a few things. What’s wrong, you need me to do something,” Nancy asked noticing the worried look on Ali’s face. “Nah, I just need to talk to you real quick before you go,” he spoke softly.

“Coco can you excuse us for a second.” “No problem; I’ll be downstairs in the living room when ya’ll done,” Coco said as she excused herself. “Baby what’s wrong? It look like something has been bothering you for this past week,” Nancy said rubbing Ali’s lower back.

“I quit the game,” Ali said. “It’s all over.” “That’s great, but why do you look so sad?” “I just been thinking about all the people who got hurt because of me,” he said looking at the floor.

“It’s okay baby you can’t change the past. Look at me,” she said lifting up Ali’s head. “It’s okay, you did what you had to do, now it’s all over,” Nancy whispered placing a soft kiss on Ali’s lips.

“It’s like my whole life has been fucked up. I been doing this for as long as I can remember; I’m just happy it’s finally over.” He paused and then said, “I’m just happy it’s over.”

“Poor baby,” Nancy said giving Ali a big hug. “So what are you going to do now?” “Well now I’m going to start focusing all of my attention on these businesses, and my wife." "Wife," Nancy echoed loudly. "I know you joking right," she asked seriously. "Yeah, I said wife," he said lifting his eyes from the floor.

Nancy looked at Ali closely. "You mean to tell me you been married all this time," she asked coldly. "Of course not," Ali replied as he stood up only to drop down to one knee. "I'm not married yet," he remarked as he fished around his pocket until he found what he was looking for.

"Nancy will you marry me," he asked opening up the ring box revealing a five karat rock. "Of course I will," Nancy sobbed happily as tears rolled freely down her cheeks.

Ali placed the ring on her finger, and kissed his new fiancée with passion. "I knew you was the one from the day I first laid eyes on you," he whispered in her ear as they hugged each other for about five minutes.

Nancy wanted to hold on to the feeling she was feeling forever. "From this day forward I'm starting off fresh. Everything I do is going to be done right," Ali vowed. "Whatever you choose to do, I just want you to know that I'm behind you one hundred percent," Nancy said sincerely. "I know boo," Ali replied with a smile.

"Go enjoy your self with Coco. When you get back we'll go out to eat." "Okay babes," Nancy said planting a wet juicy kiss on Ali's lips. She then rushed to the living room to show off her new ring.

"Girl you ain't going to believe this." Nancy excitedly ran to the living room. "Damn you scared the shit outta me," Coco jumped slightly startled. "Look," Nancy said as she flashed the fat rock in Coco's face. "Tell me that's not what I think it is,"

Coco asked smiling from ear to ear.

Nancy didn't reply, she just nodded her head slowly with a big kool-aid smile on her face.

"You lucky bitch," Coco spat playfully. "You don't know how much I love that man," Nancy sobbed as she began to cry again. "I am so happy for you," Coco said emotionally. "If anybody deserves it, its you."

"Thanks for always being there for me." Nancy sobbed as she gave Coco and little Ali a hug. "Stop all that crying, today is suppose to be the happiest day of your life! Now lets go shop until we drop, and get this baby some more clothes." Coco grinned.

* * * *

"Go and your money little duffle bag boy," Skip hummed along with Lil' Wayne as he and G-money sat staked out in a stolen Honda. "Yo that's her right there," Skip said pointing. "Who, that white bitch right there," G-money asked making sure they were on the same page.

"Yeah, the snow bunny," Skip chuckled. "I guess a sistah ain't good enough for that clown," G-money snickered as he threw the Honda into drive and pulled out of the parking spot.

Beverly stood on the sidewalk patiently waiting for the street light to change so that she could cross the street and go get into her S.U.V.

When the light finally changed Beverly crossed the street without a care in the world,, the whole time fishing around in her purse looking for her keys. Seconds later, all that could be heard was the sharp squealing sound of a car burning rubber.

Beverly quickly looked up, only to see a green Honda speeding in her direction. Before she got a chance to do anything, her body bounced viciously off of the Honda.

"Yo, speed up son," Skip chanted from the passenger seat. "I got this," G-money said with a smirk on his face as he sped up. "Here we go," he said his adrenaline pumped in anticipation. "Ohhh shit," G-money yelled as Beverly's head came crashing into his windshield.

Beverly's body flew over the hood of the Honda, and hit the ground making a loud thud sound like she just fell out of a window. "That's what I'm talking about B," Skip said. G-money quickly parked the Honda on a deserted block and bailed on foot.

* * * *

"What's good for tomorrow," Skip asked as G-money pulled up in front of his house. "Some stripper is throwing a party tomorrow night at some club downtown. I'm going to probably swing through there, you wanna role?" "Yeah I'm down. Come scoop me up tomorrow." "Matter of fact I'm going to this stripper's crib I bagged the other day; she always got friends over there, you wanna roll," G-money asked.

"Nah B, I gotta go home. I haven't been home in a week following that fucking white bitch around all week," Skip said as he slid out the passenger seat heading towards his front door.

As soon as Skip stepped foot inside his house, April was right there waiting for him. She rolled her eyes before she spoke. "So where the fuck you been all week," she asked in a snotty tone snaking her neck.

"Working," Skip answered quickly as he headed to the kitchen. "For a whole week?" "Yeah," he answered drinking some orange juice straight from the carton. "You're such a liar. Do I look stupid to you," April asked in a challenging tone.

"Yo I ain't been in the house for five minutes yet and you already on my back. Damn, can I at least take a shower first," Skip huffed.

"No fuck that, you can take a shower later, right now I want to know where the fuck you been all week," April hissed placing her hand on her hip.

"I already told you, I been working; out getting this money," Skip said pulling out a big wad of cash wrapped in two rubber bands for extra emphasis.

Don't be a smart ass," she sucked her teeth. "I don't know if you forgot, but you do have a family and we need you too you know?"

"Yeah I know, but these bills still have to get paid no matter what you say."

"Don't you dare try to throw your money in my face. I'm in school so I can better myself, but if that's not good enough I'll go get a job." "Listen I don't want to fight or argue with you, all I'm saying is what I do out in the streets is for my family. You and my son, in that backroom, is my main focus."

"Is it another woman?" "Yo, you bugging," Skip said dryly as he brushed past his wife. "Don't you walk away from me while I'm talking to you." She grabbed his wrist. "Where you going?" "To take a shower."

"Why you rushing to take a shower, huh?" "Because I'm tired and want to take a shower and get some rest." "Skip are you cheating on me?" "I'm not even going to answer that," he said disgusted. "I'm going to take a shower." "Not until I smell your dick first," April demanded as she reached for her husband's belt buckle.

"What fuck is wrong with you," Skip's voice boomed like thunder. "Look at yourself, you bugging," he said in a tone of disgust. "Well what you expect me to think? You have never not been home for a week straight before."

Listen April, you are my wife, not some bitch I'm fucking – remember that," Skip said leaving her in the kitchen to think on it.

Chapter 37
WHAT GOES AROUND COMES AROUND

"Yo shorty, go to the store and get me a slice," Diesil ordered giving one of the young soldiers a ten dollar bill. "And a Snapple," he yelled out.

Diesil sat on top of the bench watching the other soldiers roll dice. It was just another day in the hood until he saw Rell strolling through the hood talking on his cell phone. "This nigga must be crazy," Diesil thought as he looked on in amazement.

"A yo, look at this clown walking through like he tough," Diesil said to his soldiers pointing at Rell. "Yo ya'll niggas go twist his fucking cap back and get that reward money."

The seven goons quickly loaded their weapons and headed in Rell's direction. Rell strolled through the hood without a care in the world talking freely on his cell phone.

"Yeah it's about seven bitch ass niggas

headed in my direction." "Aight, just lead them in the building," Debo said ending the conversation. Debo stood in the lobby of the building with five killers by his side. It's about seven mutha fucka headed this way," he said as he and his shooters got their weapons ready.

Rell quickly stepped inside the building and snatched his P89 from his waist. "Click Clack," as Debo buzzed him in the building. "Aight, here they come," Rell said as he and his crew waited patiently for their prey to enter the building. "Yo, I'm going to blow this nigga's head off," one of Diesil's soldiers boasted as the seven of them entered the building.

"Oh shit," a soldier yelled as he watched one of his partner's head get popped off right in front of his eyes. He tried to fire back, but Rell's crew swarmed in like a pack of wolves leaving no prisoners. Once all seven off Diesil's goons were left for dead in the lobby. Rell and his crew made their exit.

Diesil sat on the bench and watched Rell and his crew walk out of the building without a scratch on them. "Fuck," he yelled out as the two exchanged glares.

* * * *

"I hope this Spanish cat ain't working with no garbage," G-money said as he and Skip slid into his new Porsche. "We running dry as a mutha fucka." "Yeah I know," Skip agreed.

"It seems like nobody got good work no more. Everything I've been seeing lately been all stepped on shit." "Well I heard this Spanish cat is supposed to have some butter (good coke)," G-money said stopping at a red light.

Skip sat looking out the window, when he felt his cell phone vibrating on his hip. "Yo what's poppin five," he answered. "Yo this nigga, Rell, just came through the hood and smoked like seven of my niggas," Diesil said hotly. "Aight, I'm a get back to you," Skip said hanging up not wanting to speak too much about that situation over the phone.

"Diesil just called; he said Rell just came through the hood and took out like seven of his soldiers." "How they let him come in the hood and do that," G-money asked keeping his eyes on the road. "I don't know. I told him I would holla at him later." "Yeah we'll handle that shit later; first we gotta get our hands on some work," G-money said sharply.

G-money quickly pulled over to the curb and beeped the horn. Seconds later a filthy crack head slid into the backseat. "Hey, I thought you wasn't coming for a second," Dirty Larry said flashing his rotten tooth smile.

"I told you I was coming Dirty Larry," G-money said as he and Skip busted out laughing. "Ya'll some funny mutha fuckas," Dirty Larry chuckled feeling embarrassed.

"Don't get all sensitive on me, Larry you know I'm just fucking with you," G-money half-apologized, as he pulled up into the warehouse's parking lot. Both men checked and cocked their weapons before they exited the vehicle.

"Pedro what's poppin?" G-money greeted the Spanish man. "Tired," he replied dryly. "Lets get this over with so I can go home," Pedro said handing G-money a duffle bag.

"You got the money," he asked greedily. "Yeah one second," G-money said as he unzipped the duffle bag and removed one of the bags of cocaine. He flicked open his pocket knife and plunged it into the plastic.

Right on point Dirty Larry tested the product. He snorted a half a gram of cocaine off the tip of the knife. His nose turned into a mini vacuum as the cocaine quickly disappeared up his nose.

Dirty Larry stood there with a stupid look on his face for about a minute, before he spoke in a light stutter. "Ye…yeah its straight; its not all that but its definitely sellable," he mumbled as his mouth started to foam on the corners.

"Nice doing business with you," G-money said as he handed Pedro the duffle bag full of money. "The pleasure was all mine," Pedro said as he and his bodyguard made their exit.

*　　*　　*　　*

"I'm going to kill everyone of them mutha fuckas, especially Gerald," Rell sobbed as he looked at Beverly's shinny casket. Hundreds of people stood in the funeral polar to pay their respects to Beverly. "It's all your fault, you cold hearted bastard," Beverly's mother yelled as she spat in Rell's face.

Without thinking twice, Erica slapped the shit out of Beverly's mother. Before things could escalate, Debo grabbed Erica and restrained her.

Erica might have been Rell's side chick, but she wasn't going to sit back and let no white lady spit in Rell's face; to her that was just so disrespectful.

"Bitch don't you ever do no shit like that again," Erica barked trying her best to get free from Debo's hold.

Seconds later the sound of gunfire sent everybody dropping down to the floor. Shots flew through the front door taking down innocent people who just came to attend a funeral.

Diesil cruised by on his motorcycle with a shooter on the back. The shooter hung on tight with one hand, as he squeezed the trigger on his Uzi with the other hand.

Once the shots finished ringing out, Rell and the rest of his crew quickly ran outside and let off about fifty shots in the direction of the motorcycle.

"These niggas have to go," Rell barked as he pulled out his cell phone and dialed Detective Nelson's number. "Yeah what's up," he answered on the forth ring. "Yo, G-money and his crew have to go," Rell yelled.

"Calm down. What's wrong?" "They just shot up my baby's funeral," Rell sobbed. "Who was it, G-money?" "Nah, it was Diesil. He's the only one out the crew with a motorcycle," Rell spoke sharply.

"Okay I'm going to take care of him and Ali, but I'm going to leave G-money to you." "I'm not playing with these fools no more; it's on." "Okay stay in touch," Detective Nelson said as he ended the conversation.

Chapter 38
ON THE LOW

Ali laid on the bed watching the news. He looked on in disgust as he listened to the reporter give the world the run down about the "Jena 6" situation. "Fucking racist mutha fuckas," Ali said shaking his head as he noticed Nancy enter the room. "Hey baby, what's up?" "Hey boo, what you doing," she asked kissing him on the lips.

"Watching this "Jena 6" shit," he replied. "White folks about to get back on they bullshit again," Nancy said sourly. "I'm going to take a quick shower…oh, and don't forget to wear all black tomorrow for those poor babies," she said shaking her head at the T.V. as she headed to the master bedroom's bathroom.

Ali quickly cut the T.V. off and popped in a Jay-z C.D. Ali was quickly snatched out of his zone when he heard Nancy clear her throat. When he looked up he saw Nancy posing in the middle of the bathroom's doorway.

Nancy stood in the doorway wearing a yellow thong, a sexy yellow bra, and a pair of bright yellow pumps. Her body glowed from all the baby oil she covered herself with. "Hey daddy, you busy," she asked seductively.

Ali looked on in amazement as he examined Nancy's body from head to toe. Nancy slowly made her way from the doorway over to the bed; her shapely figure swayed as she walked.

Nancy was walking too slow for Ali. He quickly hopped off the bed and met her halfway.

Nancy threw her arms around Ali's neck and kissed him passionately. She had been waiting for this moment to come ever since she met Ali. Ali cupped both of Nancy's chunky ass cheeks in both hands as he began licking and sucking on Nancy's neck.

Nancy moaned as she felt Ali's tongue glide up and down her neck. Ali roughly scooped Nancy in the air as they continued to kiss. Nancy smoothly locked her legs around Ali's waist as he pinned her back up against the wall.

"Fuck me daddy," she whispered in his ear as she nibbled on it. "Fuck me daddy," she begged as she felt her pussy juices about to leak down her inner thighs. "Wait, first I gotta see how that pussy taste," Ali stated plainly as he laid Nancy down on the bed and removed her soaking wet thong.

When Ali saw Nancy's pretty pink pussy lips looking at him, he quickly dove in head first.

His expert tongue found her most sensitive spot along her inner thighs causing Nancy's body to squirm like a snake as he licked and sucked all over her clit. After Ali finished handling his business, he quickly got in between Nancy's legs and slid right in.

Nancy moaned loudly when she felt the pipe.

Ali started off with long slow strokes as he plunged in and out of Nancy's walls. After about ten minutes of that, Nancy pushed Ali off of her. "What's wrong baby," Ali asked confused.

Nancy didn't speak, she just held his dick in her hand and played with the pre-cum with her thumb before she placed the whole thing in her warm mouth.

Nancy sucked and polished the shit out of Ali's dick. She rubbed it all over her face as she ran her tongue across his balls and up his shaft, then back in her mouth where she continued to give him head a hundred miles per hour.

Nancy kept sucking until Ali filled her mouth with his fluids. She did her best not to let any escape her mouth as she swallowed every last drop.

To Ali's amazement Nancy didn't stop there, she continued to please her fiancé orally until he was ready for round two. Ali watched as Nancy crawled on the bed getting on all fours.

Nancy laid with her face down and her ass poking in the air waiting for the dick. Ali just sat back for a second and looked at Nancy's fat ass sticking up in the air. He quickly hopped on the bed with her. Ali spread both of her ass cheeks apart as he entered her from behind.

"Ohh shit," Nancy purred as she buried her face in a pillow as Ali went to work. Ali pounded Nancy's pussy roughly as he watched her fat ass bounce off his torso with each stroke. He pulled her hair as he continued to pipe her down.

"Oh yes, this pussy is all yours," she screamed out from a mixture of pain and pleasure. Ali watched Nancy's ass jiggle all over the place until he couldn't take it no more and exploded.

Chapter 39
WHEN YOU TRY HARD YOU DIE HARD

"What's good, this that new package," Diesil asked excitedly. "Yeah, I got this from that Spanish cat from uptown only until I find a better connect," G-money informed him. "It's about time, shit," Diesil said happy the block was about to be poppin again.

"Oh yeah, what's that I'm hearing, Rell came to the hood the other day," G-money pressed as he took a long hard drag on his blunt. "This nigga strolled through the hood like he owned the whole shit," Diesil exclaimed loudly. "He wet up a few of my goons God bless they soul, but me and my man right here strolled through his girl's funeral and swiss cheesed the whole place, smell me," Diesil boasted giving G-money a pound. "That's what I'm talking about. You gotta go hard, it's crunch time," G-money said passing the blunt to Diesil. "Go hard or go home, you already know how I do," Diesil said coolly as he passed G-money back the blunt.

"Yo I'm out. I'm about to go set shop back up, you dig. I'm a scream at you later," Diesil said tossing the duffle bag strap over his shoulder as he headed for the door with his main goon, Marcus, in tow. "Come on B, hurry up I gotta go see one of my shorties after this," Diesil said as he tossed the duffle bag in the trunk, then quickly slid into the driver's seat of his old school Chevy that was tricked out. "Why you copped this country ass whip," Marcus asked. "Because I fucks wit the south. That's where all the money is at," Diesil replied as he turned his key making the car come to life. "Plies" song "100 years" blasted through the speakers as Diesil pulled out into traffic.

Diesil drove dropping knowledge to Marcus when he spotted flashing lights in his rearview mirror. "Fuck," Diesil cursed loudly. "Yo, put this in the glove compartment," he ordered handing Marcus his .45. Marcus quickly tossed the handgun into the glove compartment along with his .357 magnum.
"Yo just be cool," Diesil said nervously as he pulled over to the side of the road.

Two red faced officers slowly approached the Chevy cautiously with their pistols already drawn. "Driver slowly step out of the vehicle." "What seems to be the problem officer," Diesil yelled out of the driver's window as he placed his hands on the steering wheel. "Driver slowly step out of the vehicle," the officer asked again.

"Yo, I'm about to pop off," Marcus whispered looking at the glove compartment. "Nah chill," Diesil ordered as he slowly slid out of the driver's seat with his hands up in surrender. "Slowly hand me your driver's license," the officer asked sternly. "Damn, be easy," Diesil said shooting the officer a look that screamed trouble as he slowly reached for his wallet in his back pocket. Once Diesil got his hand in his back pocket. The other officer screamed out, "HE'S GOT A GUN!"

Both officers immediately opened fire on Diesil riddling his body with bullets. The bullets slightly lifted Diesil off of his feet sending him crashing to the ground smoking.

When Marcus heard the officers' guns start poppin, he quickly popped open the glove compartment and snatched Diesil's .45 and let it blast. "BOOM, BOOM, BOOM, BOOM." The officers quickly took cover as the young goon let his cannon bang out. Marcus quickly pulled out his cell phone and called Skip.

Skip sat in the warehouse with G-money counting money and listening to Young Jeezy. "Yo you think Ali gonna stay retired," Skip asked taking a sip of his yak.

"I don't know? Ali been in the game for a long ass time," G-money said downing the shot of liquid fire in one gulp. "Whatever he decides to do, I'm going to support him." "I guess when I get older I'll understand," Skip said wrapping a rubber band over a stack of money. G-money just chuckled. "What's so funny," Skip asked. "You just a straight goon, a full blooded goon. The reason I'm laughing is because I'm the same way," G-money said helping himself to another drink. "I might have to take a little vacation soon." "Why, what's up," G-money asked. "April think I'm cheating on her, so I was thinking about taking her on a little vacation." "Yeah make sure you take care your home before anything."

"Yeah, I'm probably going to take that trip at the end of the week," Skip said as he answered his ringing phone.

"Yo, what's poppin," he answered. "Yo, the fucking cops just smoked Diesil. Yo son, its crazy! These crooked ass cops got it out for us," Marcus yelled into the receiver peeking through the shattered windshield. "Slow down. Where you at right now," Skip asked.

Before Marcus could reply, both of the officers opened fire on the vehicle causing him to drop his cell phone. "Fuck that, I ain't going out like no chump," Marcus said to himself as he grabbed his .357 from the glove compartment.

By this time four more police cars had pulled up to the scene. Marcus recited a quick prayer before he made his move. Marcus quickly sprung out of the vehicle with a gun in each hand. Marcus shot one of the officers in the shoulder before the cops silenced him forever.

Skip and G-money listened in on speaker phone as they heard at least seven different guns going off at the same time before the call ended.

"Fuck," G-money cursed loudly as he buried his head in the palm of his hands. "Not my nigga, Diesil," he cried out. Skip was also at a loss for words. He just sat there looking blankly at the floor. "Yo, we was just with him," G-money sobbed still in shock. "Fuck that shit, I'm riding out," Skip growled as he snatched his dessert eagle from his waistband and checked the magazine, making sure it was full.

"It's on," G-money said through clenched teeth as he and Skip finished counting the last bit of money before they left.

Chapter 40
HEART OF A LION

Everybody in the gym stopped what they were doing when they saw Spanky walk through the front door with his wife by his side. Freddie stepped out of the restroom and was at a lost of words when he saw Spanky standing in the entrance with his gym bag hung over his shoulder.

"Old man I'm back," Spanky said with a smile. "I see," Freddie replied with a stone look on his face. "I'm going to win this fight; no matter what it takes I'm going to do it. Will you help me," Spanky asked sternly.

Freddie didn't respond, instead he just stared at Spanky blankly. After one minute of the two staring each other down a warm smile appeared on Freddie's face as he gave Spanky a big hug. "I'm glad you're back. We got a lot of work to do and not much time, so lets get to work," he said leading Spanky over to the training table so he could get his hands wrapped up.

"Later on tonight I got a few more tapes of The Terminator that we have to go over," Freddie spoke in a matter of fact tone. "No doubt," Spanky replied. "Thanks for taking me back." "Don't mention it kid. I had a lot of time to think about what you had said to me," Freddie said. "And you were right; you only get a chance like this once in a lifetime, so you better win," Freddie joked as he hugged Spanky. "I ain't come this far to lose," Spanky answered stiffly. "That's what I like to hear," Freddie said as he and Spanky headed over to the weight room section.

"Okay for the next two weeks you're going to have to lift weights, so you can get your strength back in your arms," Freddie told him.

Spanky started off with the fifteen pound dumb bells. He threw slow punches with a dumb bell in each hand, as Christie sat on the sideline watching to support her man. "Start off light baby, you been gone for a while," Freddie said taking the fifteen pound dumb bells from Spanky's hands and replacing them with ten pound dumb bells instead. "You gotta crawl before you walk."

Spanky worked his ass off for four hours straight. Christie sat on the side with a smile on her face. She was so proud of her husband. She watched his body drip of sweat as he worked the jump rope. Christie knew Spanky wanted to win the title more than anything in the world, and she was going to do everything in her power to comfort and support him. "Go ahead baby," she cheered from the sideline.

Spanky didn't respond, he just winked at his wife and continued what he was doing.

Chapter 41
NOT A GOOD FEELING

G-money slid out of the backseat of the black Yukon and was met by eight of his goons waiting by the curb for him. The goons quickly escorted G-money inside the funeral parlor. G-money strolled up in the funeral parlor wearing some dark shades, and an all black Dickie suit. His Dickie pants hug low from the weight of the pistol he concealed on his waist. "I want at least ten mutha fuckas outside to make sure nobody don't try to shoot this mutha fucka up," G-money ordered as he made his way towards Diesil's mother.

As soon as Diesil's mother saw G-money headed in her direction, she quickly met him halfway and melted in his arms. "What happened to my baby," Ms Jones sobbed as she buried her face in G-money's chest. "I don't know," G-money answered shamefully. "Those crackers been killing kids left and right, and they had the nerve to tell me that they were just doing their jobs, that's why it took seventy shots to kill two men." "Yeah you know the NYPD is the biggest gang in New York," G-money said removing his sunglasses. "G-money please promise me that you'll kill the person responsible for taking my son away from me," Ms Jones sobbed crying like a baby. "Promise me." "I promise," G-money whispered in Ms Jones' ear. The soft funeral music playing in the background only made the mood feel even worse.

A few family members stood and said a few good things about Diesil in front of everyone in attendance. Seconds later Ali and Big Mel strolled into the funeral parlor and took a seat in the back.

G-money sat next to Ms Jones when he heard a scuffle break out at the front door. Everybody stood up in unison and headed towards the entrance, where they were met by Detective Nelson with fifteen officers behind him. G-money's goons blocked the entrance refusing to let the police enter. "What the fuck ya'll want," G-money asked with about seventy goons behind him. "We're just here looking for Ali," Detective Nelson said calmly. "What's the problem," Ali asked making his way to the front of the crowd. "We need you to come downtown and participate in a line up," Detective Nelson grinned. "We got a witness who said she witnessed the murder of those two police officers in a small coffee shop a few weeks ago." "So what the fuck does that have to do with me," Ali asked in a nasty tone. "You fit the description," Detective Nelson responded pulling out a shinny pair of handcuffs.

Get four cars to follow me down to the station to make sure that's where they taking me," Ali whispered in G-money's ear. G-money nodded in agreement. Detective Nelson quickly handcuffed Ali and escorted him to a squad car.

"Fuck the police," A few goons yelled out as they watched the Detective lower Ali's head into the backseat of the squad car. Just like Ali had instructed, four cars full of goons followed the squad car, all the way down to the station. "I'm going to kill that mutha fucka," G-money said out loud shaking his head in disgust. "Yo, let me holla at you real quick," Skip said pulling G-money off to the side. "What's up?" "A few of the goons snatched up those two racist cops that smoked Diesil and Marcus," Skip said excitedly. "Say word." "Yeah they got 'em tied up in the basement in some abandoned building out in Queens," Skip said anxiously. "Come on, we out," G-money said as he, Skip, and about five goons hopped in two awaited vehicles and headed to Queens.

* * * *

"Why are you looking at me like that," Detective Nelson chuckled looking at Ali through the rearview mirror. "You're not my friend no more?" "We were never friends. Fuck you," Ali replied coldly. "You see a bitch, you use a bitch." "You the one looking like the bitch right now," Detective Nelson countered. "Ali, I hate to be the one to break the bad news to you, but…I'm going to kill you, and I'm going to do it real soon," he said raising an eyebrow. "Don't worry, I'll be prepared when the time comes," Ali said as the two exchanged challenging glares. "If you say so," Detective Nelson replied smiling at Ali weakly.

* * * *

"Yeah what's up," G-money answered his ringing cell phone. "Hey baby you busy," Coco asked innocently. "Kind of; why what's up?" "Oh, just wanted to talk to you about something." "Aight, I'm going to talk to you when I get home. I should be there in about an hour." "Okay boo, I'll see you then." Coco said ending the conversation.

G-money headed into the abandoned building with Skip and the rest of the goons on his heels. When G-money entered the basement, he could tell that the goons, who had bought the two cops in, had beat the shit out of them from the dried up blood and bruises they sported on their faces. "These the mutha fuckas who killed Diesil," a young goon growled as he slapped the shit out of one of the cops. G-money slowly walked up to one of the officers, slowly pulling his .45 from his waistband. He placed the barrel on the cop's forehead and pulled the trigger without a trace of emotion. The impact from the shot caused the cop's body to fall backwards, out of the chair he once sat in. "Please don't kill me…I got four children," the other officer begged. His cowardly plea was answered with a punch in his face. "I have to go home and take care of something; ya'll can have fun with this mutha fucka," G-money yelled over his shoulder as he made his exit. When G-money reached his S.U.V. he could hear the other cop screaming like a bitch. He just shook his head and headed home.

* * * *

Ali stood in the line up with six other men.

"Okay, turn to your left," a voice ordered over the loudspeaker. After three hours of bullshit, Ali was finally released. Detective Nelson knew Ali wasn't the cop killer, he only brought him downtown to fuck with his mind. Detective Nelson knew he was going to kill, Ali he just didn't know how yet.

*　　*　　*　　*

G-money stepped into his crib and saw Coco laying on the couch wearing a small tee shirt that looked like a mini skirt on her. "Hey babes what's up," he asked kissing Coco on the lips. "You cooked anything?" "Nah, I thought you might want to order something," Coco said as she stood up. "I'm glad you're here because I need to talk to you." "What's on ya mind," G-money asked as he took off his shirt revealing his thirteen tattoos that covered his body.

"Do you love me," Coco asked. "Yeah, I love you," G-money answered quickly. "Why you think I asked you to move in here with me?" "Well if you love me, then why are you out fucking other women," Coco asked snaking her neck. G-money sucked his teeth. "What you talking about," he asked faking ignorance. "You know exactly what I'm talking about," Coco folded her arms. "I was in the beauty polar and all I heard was G-money this and G-money that, from all those groupie, gold digging bitches," Coco said trying her hardest to control her temper. "What am I, not good enough for you?" "Of course you're good enough for me." "So why do you fuck other women then?" "I don't know," G-money answered feeling sorry for Coco. "I'm sorry baby, I'm just used to having a lot of women. I'm going to be straight up with you, I can't change overnight but I will slow down until I can control it." "Slow it down," Coco echoed rolling her eyes. "You must be crazy if you think I'm just going to sit here while you fucking all these other bitches," she spat as stomped down the hallway heading towards the bedroom. "Bring ya fine ass over here," G-money huffed as he followed behind her. "Listen babes, you my wifey aight? Them other bitches ain't got shit on you, if they did you wouldn't be living in my house," G-money said as he placed a soft kiss on Coco's neck. "I don't know why you kissing me for, you ain't getting none of this pussy," Coco hissed looking G-money up and down.

Three minutes later, G-money watched Coco's fat ass bounce and grind as she rode his dick backwards nice and slow. Coco moaned, sucking in air through clenched teeth, as she took the dick like a big girl. "I love you baby," she moaned loving every stroke.

After twenty five minutes of intense lovemaking, Coco came three times and went straight to sleep. G-money just laid in bed listening to Coco's slow and regular breathing as she slept.

Chapter 42
TRUTH BE TOLD

"Detective Nelson really got it out for you I see," Big Mel stated plainly. "Fuck Detective Nelson," Ali huffed. "He can kiss my ass." "You got out the game right on time," Big Mel said pouring him and Ali both a drink. "I'm in the game for life," Ali corrected him. "I'm just not participating in certain activities no more. I'm participating in building instead of destroying." "I ain't mad at you for that." Big Mel said shaking around the ice in his glass. "So how do you plan on building?" "I've been building from day one. I took all those mutha fuckas just sitting around in the hood and gave them all jobs; it might not have been a 9 to 5 but it still was a job. I done gave out so many turkeys on Thanksgiving that I lost count. Now I got these businesses poppin, giving my people more jobs and opportunities. I've done a lot for my people and the hood. People praise me everywhere I go, not because of the bad I've done, but for the good I've done," Ali said sipping on his yak. "I done shook more people's hands then a preacher," he chuckled as he noticed Nancy fingering for him to come into the bedroom.

"What's up baby?" "Nothing, I'm about to go shopping with Coco." "So what you need me for," Ali asked confused. "I wanted to get a quickie before Coco got here," she said seductively pulling down Ali's sweatpants.

Before Ali could respond, he felt Nancy's soft wet lips wrap around his dick. Nancy loved when Ali fucked her mouth; something about that made her pussy get wet. Nancy slowly removed her pants, revealing her firm juicy caramel ass. Ali quickly bent Nancy over the dresser, pulled her red laced panties down to her ankles and went inside her from behind. Ali delivered fast quick strokes and quickly exploded as he heard Big Mel in the living room talking to Coco.

"Thanks baby, I love you. I'll be back in a couple of hours," Nancy said as she kissed Ali on the lips then headed into the living room. Ali turned on the T.V. as he glanced over and saw the baby sleeping peacefully in his crib.

"Hey girl you ready to go," Nancy asked as she kissed Coco on the cheek. "I'm waiting on you," Coco replied as the two headed out the door. The two divas hopped into Ali's Lexus and headed to their favorite stores.

"I think I'm going to tie the knot real soon," Ali said reentering the living room. "You sure she's the right one for you?" "Yeah, I just feel good when I'm around her; you know what I mean?" "Yeah, I can dig it. I was in love once in myself," Big Mel chuckled thinking back on when he was in love. "Hopefully I'll stay alive or out of prison long enough to get married," Ali said in deep thought. "Why you say that?" "You know how you just get one of those fillings that something bad is just going to happen," Ali said looking at Big Mel. "I just been feeling like something bad is about to happen." "We just going to have to stay on point and make sure nothing bad happens." Ali chuckled, "Whatever happens is meant to be, it's all in God's plan." "Fuck that, I'm taking my life in my own hands," Big Mel huffed. "If I wait for God, I'll be waiting forever," he said sourly. The two men's conversation came to an end when Ali heard the baby crying.

* * * *

Nancy stood in the small dressing room trying on some new jeans, when she overheard some loud ghetto chicks enter the store. She looked at how the jeans hugged her ass and hips and decided to purchase them. When Nancy stepped out of the dressing room she noticed a strange look on Coco's face.

"What's wrong Coco?" "These loud ass bitches coming up in here giving black women a bad name," Coco said looking over at the hood rats. "Excuse me, you got a problem with your eyes," one of the ghetto girls asked with an attitude. "Yup, I sure do," Coco shot back looking the hood rat up and down.

Nancy was about to tell Coco to chill until she noticed one of hood rats was Dave's girlfriend, Rita. Rita stared at Nancy for about ten seconds until the face registered in her brain. "Yeah bitch, what's poppin now," Rita growled as she headed in Nancy and Coco's direction with her two home girls behind her. "It's your fault Dave is dead right now," she screamed as she ran full speed towards Nancy tackling her on a table that had some shirts neatly folded on top.

Coco quickly jumped into the fight, landing four punches to the back of Rita's head before one of Rita's girlfriends pulled Coco down to the floor by her hair. As soon as the fight broke out, the young clerk immediately picked up the phone and dialed 911.

Rita did her best to pull out as much of Nancy's hair as she could, the whole time clawing away at Nancy's face. Meanwhile Rita's two girlfriends assaulted Coco over in the corner. But Coco wasn't going out like a chump, she just dropped her head and swung wildly delivering blows as she took some.

When Nancy and Rita finally made it back to their feet, it was on. Both women grabbed each other's hair with one hand and threw vicious punches to one another's face with their free hand, knocking over racks of clothes in the process as they got their scrap on.

Seconds later, three police officers stormed into the store and pulled the women apart. Nancy fought her hardest to get loose from the officer's hold. "Bitch, every time I see you I'm a bust ya ass," Rita yelled out as one of the officer's handcuffed her. "You ain't saying nothing, hoe," Nancy capped back as the officers escorted her and Coco out of the store, placing them into the backseat of the squad car.

* * * *

Rell sat on his couch in the living room watching Killa Season, thinking on how he could find G-money. Rell had been going to all of the hot spots in the city, hoping to run into G-money, but he had no such luck. Rell started to think that G-money was hiding from him. Rell's thoughts were interrupted when Erica came strolling into the living room wearing nothing but her panties.

"Hey baby, you want something to eat," she asked innocently. "Yeah can you make me a sandwich please?" "Sure, turkey and cheese?" "Yeah, and make sure you toast the bread," Rell said as he slapped Erica on the ass and watched it jiggle as she headed towards the kitchen barefooted. "Don't start something you can't finish," Erica said flirtatiously as she disappeared into the kitchen to make Rell's sandwich.

Now that Beverly was gone, Erica was doing her best to fill her shoes and replace her. Deep down inside she really loved Rell and was willing to do whatever she had to do to prove it. Rell, on the other hand, had feelings for Erica but it wasn't anything serious. Of course he still loved his white women, but Erica was just the flavor of the month. Now that Beverly was gone, Rell vowed to never get into a strong relationship again to avoid the same thing from happening all over again.

"Here you go baby," Erica said reappearing from the kitchen carrying a plate in one hand and a cup in the other. "Thanks babes," Rell said gratefully as he took a bite out of his sandwich. Rell's lunch was interrupted by his ringing cell phone.

"Yeah what's up," his voice grumbled through the phone. "You ready for some good news," Debo asked excitedly. "Lay it on me," Rell said sipping on the fresh lemonade that Erica had made for him. "Yo, we just snatched one of G-money's workers from off the corner." "So where he at now," Rell asked. "I got the bitch ass nigga in the trunk right now." "Aight, I'll meet you at the spot. I'm on my way now." Rell said ending the conversation.

"Baby you leaving," Erica asked putting on her best sad puppy face. "Yeah, I gotta go take care of business real quick," he said grabbing his P89 from off the coffee table. "Will you be home for dinner later? I was going to cook some steak." "I'm not sure. I'll call you and let you know, okay," Rell said as he kissed Erica on the forehead, then headed out the door.

* * * *

"In jail," Ali said confused. "Yeah, some bum ass bitches ran up on me and Coco while we was out shopping. I think it was Dave's girlfriend and her people," Nancy said over the filthy phone that was stationed in the bullpen. "Aight, I'm going to send Mr. Goldberg down there with some bail money to get you out." "Don't forget about Coco," Nancy said not wanting to leave her best friend behind. "I got you baby. You should be out in about two hours," Ali said ending the conversation. Once he ended the call he quickly dialed Mr. Goldberg's number.

* * * *

“Where is this bitch ass nigga,” Rell asked impatiently. “He’s right over here,” Debo said leading him to the young soldier. The young soldier sat in a chair nursing a black eye when he saw Rell enter the room. “I want to know where I can find Gerald,” Rell huffed getting straight to the point. “I don’t know nobody named Gerald,” the young soldier said through a pair of bloody lips. “G-money, does that ring a bell?” “Yeah, I know G-money,” the soldier answered looking confused. “So where is he,” Rell asked calmly. “I don’t know man, I just want to go home,” the young soldier whined.

“Fuck this shit,” Rell huffed as he snatched his P89 from his waist and let a shot off in the floor. “Where the fuck can I find G-money? I’m not going to ask you again,” Rell said sitting the hot barrel on the young soldier’s forehead. “I don’t know where he’s at. I’m just a worker,” The young soldier pleaded. “But I do know when you’ll be able to find him.” “Where?” “He’s going to be at this big party downtown tomorrow night,” the young worker answered. “Who’s party is it,” Rell asked. “I’m not sure, I think some stripper maybe. I’m not too sure.”

Once Rell got the information he needed, he quickly squeezed the trigger on his Ruger. “Debo get all the soldiers ready for this party tomorrow night,” Rell ordered as he made his exit.

Chapter 43
HUSTLE HARD

"Why you so quiet for," Skip asked slowing down for the red light up ahead. "I got a lot of pressure on me now that Ali stepped down, you dig," G-money said sipping on some yak. "I have to start doing a better job. I got a lot of people depending on me" "What you talking about? I thought everything was straight," Skip asked. "Nah, this month our numbers been down by fifteen percent, plus when Diesil and Marcus got popped the cops took all the work from out the trunk – the whole re-up," G-money said looking stressed out. "Then I called Pedro trying to buy more product, but he said some other cat had already cleaned him out." "Damn, so we dead," Skip asked depressingly. "Nah, I got some work from some cat out in the Bronx, but the new soldier, Knowledge, I got in the hood said all the fiends been complaining about how weak it is; so basically we have to find a new connect soon." "I'm going to see if I can find a connect too," Skip said as he pulled up in front of a bodega. "Nah, I got this, plus you can't afford no more trouble. Don't you have to go do some time for those two guns Detective Nelson found on you that night he stopped us," G-money asked. "Yeah, I took a deal for five years," Skip shrugged his shoulders nonchalantly. "When you suppose to go in to do the five?" "Next week, but you know I'm a get on my Ginger bread man shit, you dig?. Those mutha fuckas going to have to catch me to get that time out of me. Make them crackers do they job for once," Skip said as he and G-money exited the vehicle and entered the bodega.

"Yo, Oscar what's good baby?" "You know it's all good," Oscar replied giving G-money a pound. "What its looking like," G-money asked helping himself to a bag of hot cheese popcorn. "It's looking good," Oscar said handing G-money a brown paper bag full of money. "But I need to talk to you." "What's on ya mind?" "I think I'm going to need some protection around here," Oscar said looking a little too nervous. "Why, what's poppin?" "Well last week this guy named Rell came up in here with about twenty thugs with him, demanding that I pay him instead of you because he run the streets now." "And what you told him," G-money asked. "I told him I was going to pay him because I had twelve to fifteen guns in my face," Oscar said as beads of sweat appeared on his forehead. "I got you Oscar, I'll send some guys up here first thing in the morning to watch over the place," G-money said calmly as he and Skip made their exit.

"I'm going to kill that nigga, Rell, when I catch his punk ass," G-money said as soon as they made it back inside the vehicle. "He must be hiding out somewhere because I've been going to all the hot spots and I ain't seen him once." "Don't worry, he'll pop up sooner or later," Skip said as he pulled off into traffic.

Chapter 44
KNOW YOUR OPPONENT

"You see his footwork is fantastic," Freddie said rewinding the tape so that Spanky could see what he was talking about. "He doesn't make many mistakes, so you going to have to be sharp in there." "I'm bringing my "A" game," Spanky said as he continued to watch the tape of his opponent. Spanky hated to admit it, but The Terminator was very talented and exciting to watch at the same time. Deep down inside Spanky knew he was going to have to come with it. "Now when you're in there with this guy remember he loves to counter punch so try not to throw single punches. Try to throw combinations and make sure you attack his body. We want to drag this mutha fucka in deep waters so we can drown his ass," Freddie said sternly. "I'm willing to die out there if I have to."

That last comment caught Freddie off guard. He knew Spanky wanted to win, but damn dying was something else. The reason that last comment bothered Freddie so much was because he knew Spanky meant exactly what he said. "You can take this guy Spank, you just have to stay focused and have control." "Don't worry Freddie, I won't let you down," Spanky said as he winked at his mentor / trainer. "I'm going to put these miles in. When I get back, I'm going to work on my foot work and ring awareness," Spanky said as he threw his I-pod head phones in his ear and headed out door.

Once Spanky was out the door, Christie walked over to Freddie and sat down. "Can I help you," he asked politely. "Yeah, I need to know honestly how Spanky's doing," she asked sincerely. "Honestly," he echoed. "Well Spanky is coming along fine, it's only one problem; his reflexes are off a little and I can tell when he swings too hard it still hurts him." "Will any of these things affect him in the fight," Christie asked nervously. "I'm not going to lie to you, this is a very dangerous sport and I know, just like Spanky, that anything can happen once you step in that ring," Freddie said looking down at the floor. "Do you think he can win?" "Well anything is possible when you step in that ring," Freddie replied quickly."I didn't ask you that, I asked you do you think he can win," Christie repeated the question. "Yes I do, but it's going to be hard," Freddie admitted honestly. "But yes I think he can and will win the fight."

* * * *

"How much is that," G-money asked taking the money from his newly promoted soldier. "Twenty-five hundred," Knowledge answered shamefully. "This must be a mistake, how many times you counted this shit?" "Twice," Knowledge answered. "The fiends don't like this shit. They been buying twice as much and getting less high, so now most of the fiends are starting to get they shit from some cat Rell, who got a spot a couple of blocks down the way." "Aight, I'm going to send a few soldiers down here. I want you to take them over to the block and shut that shit down," G-money said as he and Skip broke out.

Knowledge had been down with the crew for a couple of years now, but he was nothing but a pick up man. Now the Diesil was gone, Knowledge knew he had to step up to the plate and take on some more responsibilities. "Pull over right here." "Why what's up," Skip asked. "Just pull over, I have to go take care of some thing real quick," G-money huffed.

Skip pulled over right in front of the house that G-money had instructed. G-money quickly slid out of the passenger's seat and made his way towards the front door of the house slowly ringing the doorbell.

Seconds later Ms Jones cracked the door and peeked her head through the crack. When she realized who it was she quickly opened the door all the way. "Hey G-money, how you doing baby? You want to come inside," she asked stepping to the side so that G-money could enter. "No, that won't be necessary Ms. Jones. I'm just here to let you know that I took care of my promise," G-money spoke softly looking in Ms. Jones' soft brown eyes. "God bless your soul baby," she said stroking G-money's cheek. "Now my poor baby can finally rest in peace. Thank you Jesus." "Okay Ms Jones, I have to get going now. You take care of yourself, you hear," he said kissing Ms. Jones on both cheeks as he made his way back down the path to his awaited vehicle. "Thank you Jesus," Ms. Jones said out loud as she looked up to the sky.

* * * *

Maurice stood on the corner yelling at one of his workers when he noticed Rell's Lamborghini pull up to the curb. "Listen, stop letting these fiends sit around. Get 'em in and get 'em right the fuck back out," Maurice said dismissing the young man before Rell approached. "What's good? You out here schooling these youngins," Rell asked giving Maurice a pound. "Yeah, you know how it is out here," Maurice chuckled as he gave Rell and Debo a pound. "You been doing a good job; keep up the good work," Rell said over his shoulder as he and Debo disappeared inside the building. Rell stepped foot inside the stash crib and immediately smelled crack in the air, bringing a smile to his face as he entered the apartment.

Maurice stood on the block glancing up and down the street, when he noticed an old school car slowly creeping down the block. "What the fuck," he said to himself. The car and the speed they were driving just didn't seem right to him. Maurice quickly signaled to one of his shooters on the roof. The shooter nodded his head in understanding and gripped his Mac 11, never taking his eyes off of the vehicle.

"G-money said he wants this whole block cleared out," Knowledge informed the four soldiers in the car with him. "I want ya'll to bust them niggas' heads and get the fuck back," he growled.

With that being said, the four soldiers hopped out of the vehicle carrying wooden bats. Before they could even reach the curb, the gunman on the roof let his Mac 11 sing, "Pat, pat, pat, pat, pat." In less then ten seconds, all four soldiers laid sprawled out on the concrete. The gunman on the roof didn't stop there; after he gunned down the four soldiers, he quickly aimed his weapon at the old school car.

Knowledge sat behind the wheel looking on in amazement, wondering where the shots came from when suddenly his windshield exploded in a spray of glass. Knowledge quickly ducked his head and stomped on the gas, as bullets assaulted his vehicle.

When Rell heard the shots go off he quickly turned and looked at Debo. The look Rell gave him said it all. Debo quickly snatched his twin .45's out and headed downstairs to see what the problem was.

Rell continued stuffing stacks of money into his duffle bag like nothing had ever happened. Once he was done he met Debo in the lobby. "What happened?"

"Four of G-money's people hopped out a car with baseball bats," Debo chuckled.

"Baseball bats," Rell said his face turning into a frown. "What this nigga think this is the eighties?" Debo chuckled before he continued, "Don't worry the gunman on the roof took care of those clowns." "That's what he gets paid to do," Rell commented as he and Debo made their exit through the back door.

*   *   *   *

"What you doing out there fighting in the street like some hood rat bitch," Ali asked as he and Nancy sat at a quiet table in the back of Ali's new restaurant. "That big bitch ran up on me, so I had to fight her. I wasn't just going to sit there and let her whip my ass," Nancy shot back sipping on some champagne. "You had to do what you had to do, right?" "Yup, and I think I might whip her ass again if I see her," Nancy said strongly. "Save that for later baby, right now I need your help," "You need my help," Nancy asked in shock. "Yeah, your help." "Cool, what do you need me to do," she asked happy to finally be needed. "Well basically I'm going to need you to be my accountant and I'm going to need you to manage all the money and bills for each one of my businesses." "Oh my God are you serious," Nancy asked in total shock. "Yeah, I need someone who I know I can trust to handle this for me," Ali said seriously. "Yes, I would do that for you," Nancy said excitedly. "Okay cool; me and Mr. Goldberg will go over everything with you tomorrow," Ali said shoveling some yellow rice into his mouth.

Meanwhile Big Mel sat in his Yukon on a deserted block with Detective Nelson in the front seat. "So what's been going on," Detective Nelson asked suspiciously. "Nothing much; I told you Ali is out the game now. He hasn't been doing anything illegal lately." "Well then we have no other choice but to set him up," Detective Nelson said stiffly. "One way or another Ali has to go down and you're going to help me." "Why don't you just leave him alone? He's already out of the game; I don't understand why continue bothering him when you can go after G-money who's still deep in the game." "Don't worry G-money is next on my list, but first Ali must take a dive for breaking our deal." "You doing all this over a stupid deal," Big Mel huffed. "It might be stupid to you, but to me your word is everything," Detective Nelson spoke calmly as he dug down in a small bag. "Here take this," he said handing Big Mel a big zip lock bag containing a 9mm inside. "What's this for?" "You got three weeks to bring me this gun back dirty, so I can frame Ali." "Are you crazy," Big Mel asked in disbelief. "Do I look crazy?" "Yes you must be crazy," Big Mel said raising his voice. "You trying to get me killed." "If you scared get a dog and gun, simple as that. You came to me with a plan to take Ali out and that's just what we're going to do," Detective Nelson said flatly as he slid out of the vehicle.

Big Mel wanted to be the man, but Detective Nelson was trying to get him killed. Big Mel promised himself that he would complete this last mission, but afterwards if that wasn't good enough he was just going to have to kill Detective Nelson or die trying.

Chapter 45
THE TERMINATOR

"Come on, you only got ten more to go," Mr. Wilson coached from the sideline. The Terminator hung off the edge of the ring doing his sit ups. "Fifteen hundred," he huffed. "What you huffing for," Mr. Wilson asked.

The Terminator sucked his teeth. "Because I don't understand why I have to train so hard for," he said wiping the sweat off his face with a towel. "I'm going to beat the shit out of this Spanky kid. I was already going to spank him, now he got two broken arms I'm really going to kill him." "I seriously doubt that, if Spanky's arms weren't in good shape he would still be fighting. Plus he passed his physical, meaning the doctor cleared him to fight," Mr. Wilson spoke calmly. "Plus anybody who's willing to step in the ring when they're not a hundred percent is always dangerous because that means he has nothing to lose." "You talking like I'm not going to go out there and give it my all," The Terminator protested. "I'm not saying that, all I'm saying is never underestimate a man's heart, and will," Mr. Wilson countered. "I'm just trying to keep you on top of your game." "Oh you know when the lights is on I'm going to shine, The Terminator boasted throwing a quick combination in the air. "I'm telling you now it's not going to be easy," Mr. Wilson commented. "I don't want nothing easy," The Terminator replied with a smile. "Ain't nothing like a good fight." "Be careful what you ask for because you just might receive it," Mr. Wilson mumbled under his breath.

Chapter 46
PRESSURE

"What's wrong boo," Coco asked sensing that something was bothering her man. "Everything," G-money replied. "Is there anything I can do to help," she asked massaging the top of G-money's shoulders. "No not really; I'm going to get it together in a minute," he said downing his shot of Henny. "You want me to make you something to eat," Coco asked as she popped in her slow jams C.D. "Nah, I'm cool." "Ahww baby cheer up," Coco said as she slid in G-money's lap. "Everything's going to be okay," she whispered as she slowly began kissing him. One thing led to another and Coco found herself on the receiving end of some back shots.

G-money aggressively pulled Coco's hair, as he delivered powerful strokes to her love tunnel. He then slid his fingers in her mouth, as he continued to pipe her down. Coco sucked and licked G-money's fingers as she took the back shots like a soldier. When it was all said and done she laid her head on G-money's chest and fell asleep naked.

Chapter 47
CLEAN UP TIME

"Everybody listen up," Detective Nelson spoke loudly so that everyone could hear him. "Today we're taking down six houses looking for weapons, drugs or whatever. My boss told me it's time to clean this mess up and make some arrests, so when it hits the news it can look like we're doing something about the situation" He paced back and forth. "Now let's go take our streets back over," Detective Nelson announced as he and all the other officers suited up.

* * * *

"Can't you see I'm on the phone," Knowledge hushed one of his workers as he continued on with his conversation. The money flow in the hood had really slowed down and that put a lot of people in an unpleasant mood, especially

Knowledge. He had been brought in to replace Diesil and keep the number up, but ever since Knowledge took over his numbers had been way down; not because of him personally, but because of the quality of drugs G-money had been getting lately. Knowledge sat on the bench yelling at his baby mother on the phone, when he noticed cop cars coming from every direction circling the projects. Knowledge tried to smoothly get up and walk off, but seconds later two officers tackled him. One officer placed a knee on his neck as the other one cuffed him. "Fucking pussys, ya'll always gotta bring a hundred mutha fuckas with ya'll in order to do something," Knowledge huffed as he watched all of his workers get slammed down to the ground and put in cuffs. Detective Nelson quickly walked to where Knowledge laid on the ground and squatted down. "You're Diesil's replacement right," he asked placing a Winston between his lips. "I don't know no Diesil," Knowledge replied faking ignorance. "Listen kid I'll make you a deal; you tell me where the stash crib is, and I'll let you go free," Detective Nelson said with a smile. "I don't know what you talking about," Knowledge answered. "You sure," Detective Nelson asked. "Positive." "Okay gentlemen take this dick head to jail with the rest of the dick heads," Detective Nelson ordered.

* * * *

April had been up all day cleaning up the house, listening to her Alicia Keys C.D. She walked past her son's room and saw Michael peacefully resting with his mouth open. She just chuckled and thanked God for such a blessing, as she headed to the kitchen so that she could wash the dishes. April stood over the sink with her hands plunged in warm dish water, when she heard a loud boom at the front door. Her heart leaped into her throat when she saw about twenty officers with shields and guns run into her house. "On the floor now," one officer yelled as he roughly tossed April to the floor, placing his knee on her neck as he hand cuffed her. Once that was done, the officer quickly searched the rest of the kitchen. "The kitchen's clear," he yelled out to another officer. With that being said the rest of the officers began to search the rest of the house. April fought and struggled her hardest to get to her feet, when she heard little Michael crying from the backroom. "Get off of me. I have to go see what's wrong with my son," April huffed struggling to get to her feet but it was no use. April laid face down in the kitchen as she heard the police officers tearing her house apart. "What are they looking for," she asked curiously. "Contraband," the officer answered stiffly. "Well can you at least bring my son in here with me," April begged. "No," the officer answered sharply. All April could do was cry and listen to the police tear her house up for no reason because Skip never kept anything in the house. "I want to see a warrant," April demanded as she laid face down on her kitchen floor. "Ya'll crooked ass mutha fuckas better have a warrant," she threatened.

Seconds later, Detective Nelson strolled into the kitchen holding a piece of paper in his hand. "Your boyfriend, Skippy, didn't show up for court the other day. He owes the state five years and they want it," Detective Nelson said calmly as he dropped the warrant on top of April's head. "Tell your boyfriend if he doesn't turn himself in, we'll be back every week until he gets the message," Detective Nelson said as he slowly uncuffed April. "Have a nice day."

Chapter 48
PARTY TIME

G-money's black Lamborghini flowed smoothly with the rest of the traffic. It seemed like everybody and their momma was going to this party. "Damn B, it's gonna be mad bitches up in this joint tonight," G-money said looking at the bumper to bumper traffic as he slowly sipped his cup of vodka. "Yeah, it's definitely going to be poppin up in there tonight," Skip agreed as he felt his cell phone vibrating against his hip.

"Hey baby what's up," he answered. "They just kicked in our door and trashed the place," April sobbed. "Who kicked in our door," Skip barked sitting straight up. "The police," she answered drying her eyes with a piece of tissue. "They had a warrant for your arrest." "Okay are you and Michael alright?" "Yeah we're fine, but they destroyed our house; anything that could be broke they broke it." "It's okay baby, I'll get you new furniture. I'm just happy that you and the lil' one is okay," Skip said trying to lighten up the mood. "I don't want new furniture, I want to stop living like this," April said angrily as she continued to rant. "This shit has got to stop, I'm fucking sick of this shit," she sobbed loudly. "Listen, just calm down aight. Everything's going to be alright." "How's it going to be alright," she demanded to know. "Because I got everything…" "I don't want to hear that shit no more! You been saying that same shit for the last five years now," she snarled cutting him off. "Now on top of all this shit, you on the run. Let me guess? You going to take care of that too, right." "Yeah, whatever; I'm a talk to you later cause the way you talking you gonna make me break ya face when I see you. And keep ya ass off the fucking phone," Skip growled as he hung up in April's ear.

"What's good? Everything aight," G-money asked curiously. "Yeah, everything's cool. April just called talking about they just kicked in my door looking for me. She said they had a warrant," Skip said as he tossed his phone out of the window. "I know them crackers got my house phone tapped."

"Definitely," G-money agreed. "Let me guess? April spazzed out, right." "You know she did. I think she's going to leave me soon," Skip spoke softly. "She's tired of living like this." "You know at anytime you can bail out and go take care of your family, you dig?" "Nah, I can't just jump off the boat now; especially while it's sinking," Skip stated plainly. "I'm just letting you know that whenever you want to make things right with your family, you got my approval," G-money said as he pulled into the club's parking lot. "Good looking; I'll keep that in mind," Skip said distractedly as he looked at all the beautiful women scattered around the parking lot.

"Hard to stay focused with all this ass all in ya face, huh?" G-money chuckled as he searched for a parking spot.

All the groupies, and gold diggers strained their eyes as they tried their hardest to see through the limo tints on the Lamborghini. Once G-money found a parking spot, the rising suicide doors caught the attention of two chicks, who were half naked. "Yooo," G-money yelled out to the divas. The two women quickly swayed over to the Lambo. "What's good? Where the party at," The tallest one spoke seductively looking at G-money for an answer. "Right here," G-money yelled over the blasting music that blared through his speakers. "I know ya'll wasn't going inside without getting right first," he said grabbing the bottle of Grey Goose from under the driver's seat.

As G-money and Skip sat parking lot pimping, G-money noticed the rest of his goons pull up into the club's parking lot. "So what's good, ya'll got names," G-money asked smoothly. "I'm Ashley and this is Wanda," the taller one spoke as she pointed to her friend who was now sitting on Skip's lap as he sat on the hood of the vehicle. "So Ashley what you doing after the club," G-money asked undressing Ashley with his eyes. "Nothing, I was going to go home. I don't really know my way around the city too well yet," she said in a soft voice.

G-money could tell that neither one of the girls were from New York by their strong accents. "So where ya'll from?" "We just moved out here from Florida," Ashley answered proudly, showing all of her teeth. "Florida," G-money echoed looking Ashley up and down.

Ashley wore a skimpy dress that looked like it

had to have been painted on because the bottom of her dress barely covered her caramel ass cheeks. As her knee high leather go-go boots completed her outfit. “What’s wrong,” Ashley asked looking at her clothes when she noticed how G-money was hungrily eye balling her. “Oh my bad, I was just checking you out,” he admitted honestly. “Well do you like what you see,” she asked brushing a piece of hair out of her face. “I think like is an understatement,” he capped finishing off his drink. “Well that’s a good sign because I like what I see as well,” she said placing her freshly done weave in a ponytail. “Aight cool, so let me get your number now before we go inside that loud ass club.” As G-money took down Ashley’s number he noticed about fifteen of his goons headed in his direction. Ashley quickly stored her number in G-money’s I-Phone before the rest of the posse arrived. “Make sure you give me a call lil’ daddy,” she said in a southern drawl as her and Wanda made their way to the club’s entrance.

“Damn, where the bitches going,” Knowledge asked with fourteen thugs behind him. “You scared them off as usual,” Skip said playfully giving Knowledge a nudge. “Shiiiiit, I look so good I had to slap my momma the other day,” Knowledge said as the whole crew fell out in laughter. “Fuck this shit, let’s get up in here and be stars,” G-money said as he and his crew made their way towards the entrance.

“How many you got with you tonight G-money,?” the bouncer asked giving G-money a pound. “Ummm…sixteen,” G-money answered slipping the bouncer three hundred dollar bills discreetly. “Aight, only one problem…no weapons allowed,” the bouncer announced. “Come on homey, you can’t let us slide just for tonight,” G-money pleaded. "Sorry I can't. We had a bad shootout in here last month; another incident like that and we get shut down for good," the bouncer spoke like a gentleman. "Aight, we'll be right back," G-money said as he and his crew headed back to the parking lot, so that they could drop off their firearms.

"Something ain't feeling right," Skip said removing his dessert eagle from his waist and tossing it on the passenger seat. "What's wrong," G-money asked placing his .45 on top of the front tire on the driver side. "You know how you just get a feeling that something ain't right?" "Listen Skip, if this ain't right its going to get much righter," G-money slurred as the alcohol began to take it's affect. "Yeah, I guess you right," Skip agreed as he, G-money and the rest of their crew headed back towards the entrance of the club.

* * * *

"Hey boss man, it's some guy out here who say's he needs to talk to you and it's an emergency," Big Mel said peaking his head through the door. "Who is this guy," Ali asked standing in front of his pool table playing by himself. "Some cat named Bob," Big Mel chuckled. "A real filthy looking brother." "Send him in," Ali ordered as he poured himself a glass of Belve with some orange juice. When Ali looked up from sipping his drink he saw a dusty looking man enter his office. "How can I help you," Ali asked as he continued with his game. "How you doing Mr. Ali," Bob spoke nervously. "Umm…I heard you were the man to see about a job." "What kind of job are looking for," Ali asked. "It doesn't matter. If you supply me with any kind of job, I will be very grateful," Bob said nervously as he glanced at Ali's two 9mm's resting in his shoulder holsters. "Why should I hire you?" "Ummm…because I'm a hard worker and I'm willing to work at the bottom until I reach the top," Bob replied honestly.

Ali looked up from the pool table and studied Bob's face as he took another sip from his drink. "How would you like to be a waiter in my restaurant?" "I would love that; that would be great," Bob said smiling from ear to ear. "You know where my restaurant is, right?" "Yeah, I know where it's at." "Aight, show up there bright and early on Monday. I'm going to call the manager and let her know that you're coming," Ali said giving Bob a pound. "Thank you so much Mr. Ali. I really appreciate this and I promise I won't let you down." "Aight cool, I'm happy I could help you; but I got one question, how did you know you could find me here," Ali asked curiously. "A few people from the hood told me I might could catch you here, and that you were the man to see about a job." "Aight Bob, you be cool and if you know anybody else who needs a job make sure you send them this way," Ali said as he walked Bob to the door.

"Damn that's like the eighth person you gave a job to today," Big Mel huffed. "What's wrong with that? You talking like you giving them money straight out of your pocket," Ali said checking his twenty-four hour bodyguard. "Now let's use your phone because my battery died." "Here," Big Mel handed Ali his cell phone as he headed to the bathroom.

Ali started to dial Nancy's number, but before he could finish a restricted call came through, catching Ali off guard. "Who the fuck is this calling with a blocked number?" "Hello," Ali answered. No answer came back. "Who is this," Ali asked again. Still no answer, then suddenly the line went dead. "Did you get through," Big Mel asked suspiciously as he returned from the bathroom. "Yeah I got through," Ali said flatly as his mind started to wonder.

* * * *

The whole club went crazy when Swizz Beatz, "She ain't got not no money in the bank," came bumping through the speakers. Every female in the club began to shake their asses. Knowledge quickly eased up behind a freak whose red thong rose above her jeans as she shook her ass to the beat.

Knowledge did his best to control himself, as he watched the fat ass in front of him grind up and down on his dick. G-money sat on the couch in the V.I.P. section with Ashley curled up in his lap, sipping on some strong vodka. "Damn you got my dick harder than putting together a thousand piece jigsaw puzzle," G-money flirted as he kissed Ashley's neck. "You're very freaky I see," Ashley whispered seductively in G-money's ear. "I'm not freaky; you just bring the freak out in me," G-money replied as he pulled out one of Ashley nice sized titties and slowly placed it in his mouth. Ashley let out a light moan as she rubbed G-money's neatly corn rowed hair. "Damn ya titties taste good," G-money said as he noticed Ashley's nipples get hard. "Lets save this for later," Ashley said sticking her breasts back in her dress. "Sorry I couldn't help myself," G-money stated plainly as he refilled his glass with vodka. “Fill me up too,” Ashley chimed as she heard her favorite Reggae song come blaring through the speakers. Immediately her body began to sway with the beat as she found herself giving G-money a magic city type of lap dance. G-money just sat back and let his hands explore the rest of the Diva’s sexy body.

* * * *

Rell pulled up in the club’s parking lot, seven cars deep each man ready for action. “The plan is simple; we going to go in there, find G-money and kill him,” Rell spat, his voice dripping with venom. Each man behind Rell had the same murderous look on their face, as Rell led his crew towards the entrance of the club.

“Big man, what’s up,” Rell said giving the bouncer a pound. “I’m chilling,” he replied quickly. “How much is it going to cost for me and my crew to get up in here without waiting on this long ass line, and without getting searched,” Rell asked pulling out a huge stack of money from his pocket. “Sorry brother, but I can’t allow nobody inside without getting searched,” the bouncer stated firmly. “Why,” Rell asked curiously. “We had a bad shootout in here last month; another incident like that and we get shutdown for good.” “Aight, I can respect that,” Rell said as he and his crew headed back to the parking lot.

“Aight, I want four of you to hang out here in the parking lot. As soon as ya’ll see G-money come out, I want ya’ll to light his ass up. Me and the rest of the soldiers about to run up in this club and bring his ass out." Rell flicked his cigarette as he and the rest of his soldiers headed towards the entrance.

* * * *

Nancy laid spread out on the king sized water bed butt naked, listening to the soft sound of Alicia Keys humming softly through her speakers. She laid down quietly, watching the muted T.V. as the ringing of the house phone startled her causing her to jump a little. Nancy slowly slid out of her comfortable bed and walked towards the dresser where she had left the cordless phone.

"Hello," she answered. Silence came back. "Helloooooo," she said again. When she didn't get an answer the second time she quickly hung up. "I wonder who the fuck that was," she asked herself as she headed back towards the bed. Her fat ass jiggled with each step she took.

Nancy quickly grabbed the .22 caliber handgun that Ali had given her for emergencies. For the past week, someone had been ringing the house phone without saying anything.

When Ali entered the bedroom he looked at his fiancé's beautiful naked body, until he noticed the small handgun laying inches away from her. "What's the gun for," Ali asked sitting at the foot of the bed. "Somebody keeps on calling here and hanging up," Nancy whined. "I want this number changed." "Okay baby, change it whenever you want." "Baby I'm starting to get scared," Nancy whispered as she moved to the foot of the bed so she could sit next to her man. “Scared about what,” Ali asked taking Nancy’s hand. “I’m scared that something bad is going to happen to you.” “Something bad, like what?” “I don’t know. I just don’t have a good feeling about our safety. I’m getting the feeling that somebody knows something that we don’t.” “I’ve been getting the same feeling lately,” Ali said in deep thought. “I’m not sure, but I think Big Mel is up to something fishy.” “I have been noticing him acting a little weird lately,” Nancy agreed. “Weird like what,” Ali asked curiously. “Like the other day right, I was coming out of the kitchen and I heard Big Mel talking in a real low voice to somebody on his cell phone. I’ve never heard him whispering on the phone before.” “Don’t even worry about that clown. I got something for that ungrateful mutha fucka,” Ali hissed. “Me and you are going on a long vacation next week and while were gone I’m going to have Big Mel murdered.” “Why next week? Why can’t we leave tomorrow,” Nancy asked knowing a lot could happen in a week. “Because Spanky’s big fight is next Saturday. We can leave that night as soon as the fight is over.” “Oh yeah, I forgot about that,” Nancy said mad that it had slipped her mind. “So where are we going?” “I was thinking maybe the Bahamas,” Ali answered with a smile. “You ever been there before?” “Never, I never even been out of New York before,” Nancy said shamefully. “There’s a first time for everything, even marriage,” Ali said throwing in the curve ball at the end of his sentence. “Marriage,” Nancy echoed. “Yeah, I was thinking we should get married next week in the Bahamas and spend about six months there on our honeymoon,” Ali suggested.

“You’re the best,” Nancy said as she happily pushed Ali down on the bed and quickly removed his love stick, not hesitating to put it in her mouth.

Ali just laid back, with his eyes closed as he felt his soon to be wife polish and lick all over his dick. It seemed like no matter how far Ali moved away, he still couldn't escape the ghetto. He quickly broke out of his trance when he saw Nancy plant her feet on the bed, as she began to slowly bounce and grind on Ali's dick.

"Damn baby," he moaned as he watched his dick disappear in and out of Nancy's wet pussy. "This pussy is all yours daddy," Nancy screamed out as she began bouncing harder, and harder on Ali's dick, screaming loudly. Minutes later, Nancy came hard as she felt her thick juices slid down Ali's shaft. Ali let out a loud groan, as he exploded inside his fiancé. The two laid on the bed, exhausted from their sexual escapade.

* * * *

G-money sat in the V.I.P. section, nursing a drink with Ashley still on his lap when he saw Rell and his crew snaking through the crowded club.

G-money quickly jumped up almost tossing Ashley on the floor. "Sorry sweetheart, but I have to go handle something real quick," he said as he and the four goons who sat in the V.I.P. section watching over him followed his lead. G-money squeezed past all the sweaty bodies that stood in front of him as he tried his best to catch up to Rell.

Skip stood over in the cut, sweet talking to some shorty he knew from around the way, when he saw G-money and the goons pushing their way through the crowd. "Yo, stay right here; I'll be right back," Skip told his lady friend as he followed G-money and the rest of the goons, to see what was up. "That bitch ass nigga probably hiding somewhere," Debo yelled over the loud music. "I wouldn't put it past that coward," Rell replied as he continued to scan over the crowd. When Rell turned to his left, a fist smashed into his face like a blunt object, causing him to stumble backwards. G-money went in for the kill, but was caught off guard when Debo snuffed him with a powerful right hook, dropping G-money off of impact.

Once the goons saw G-money hit the floor, it was on. The two crews collided with one another; each man throwing vicious blows. When the fight broke out the rest of the crowd quickly parted not wanting to get hit by a wild punch. When G-money made it back to his feet, he quickly rushed Rell swinging wildly. Out of reflex, Rell swiftly ducked down and scooped G-money's legs from up under him dumping him on his head. "Bitch ass nigga," Rell growled.

G-money quickly sprung from the floor, catching Rell with a clean sharp upper cut to the chin, followed by a left hook to the body. When Rell doubled over clutching his stomach, G-money grabbed the back of Rell's head and viciously kneed him in his face. G-money watched Rell's head bounce off the hard club floor as he continued to stomp him out until he felt a strong pair of arms wrap around his neck from behind. G-money struggled with all his might to get loose from the man's hold but it was no use.

When Knowledge realized what was going on he quickly made his way over to where the action was going down at. He violently busted a Heineken bottle over Debo's head. But the bottle didn't faze the big man, Debo continued to try to squeeze the life out of G-money.

When Skip saw G-money gasping for air he quickly ran over and tried to loosen up Debo's grip along with Knowledge, but it was no use the big man's hold was too strong.

Just as G-money was about to run out of air four big bouncers came to his rescue and released Debo's arms from around G-money's neck. G-money dropped down to his knees as he tried to suck in ass much air as he could, rubbing his throat.

The bouncers literally tossed each man out the club one by one. When G-money finally got tossed out of the club, his vision was still a little blurry from Debo's choke hold. As G-money visions started to clear up he noticed four men walking swiftly in his direction looking like they were holding a weapon behind their backs.

G-money quickly reached for hip, then remembered he was unarmed. "Fuck!" He spat as he quickly dashed in the direction of all the other club goers who scrabbled for their lives. Without a trace of emotion the four gun men opened fire into the crowd not caring who they hit.

G-money was to grab the guy who was running next to him, and use him as a shield, but he was a bit too slow. He felt a bullet rip through the back of his thigh, as he watched the people around him drop like flies. G-money stumbled but some how remained on his feet, as he tried to limp his way to safety.

When Skip made his way out of the club he

heard a loud series of gun shots go off. Once Skip heard the gun shots he already knew what time it was. He quickly ran towards the Lamborghini and snatched G-money's .45 from off of the front tire. With time working against him, Skip let off six rounds in rapid fire. "Boom, Boom, Boom, Boom, Boom, Boom." One shot entered one of the gunmen's collarbone, while another shot ripped through another gunman's leg.

G-money limped as fast as he could, as one of his goons tried to help him, but one of the gunmen quickly caught up to the wounded soldier and opened fire on G-money again. G-money's goon quickly shoved him to the ground and took the hot slugs for his boss. But before the soldier pushed G-money out of the way he took another shot to his shoulder as he went crashing to the ground.

As the gunman quickly tried to reload his weapon, he never saw the minivan coming full speed, directly at him. When the gunman finally looked up, he was like a deer stuck in headlights.

Knowledge put the pedal to the medal, as he watched the gunman violently bounce off of the windshield. When the minivan came to a screeching stop, G-money thought it was the enemy. He closed his eyes and said a quick prayer as he prepared himself for the next life.

"Ahww shit, not my fucking nigga," Knowledge said to himself as he saw G-money laid out on the concrete covered in blood. Knowledge quickly slid out of the van and ran to G-money's aid. As Knowledge knelt down to see if G-money was still breathing, he heard a woman screaming hysterically as her heels clicked on the concrete. "Who did this," Ashley screamed out as she placed her hand over her mouth in shock. "Help me get him in the van," Knowledge yelled nervously as he lifted half of G-money's body off of the ground and dragged the rest of his body over toward the van. Ashley didn't help, instead she just stood there in shock not knowing what to do. "Oh shit, you scared the shit out of me," Knowledge jumped as Skip grabbed G-money's lower body and helped Knowledge get G-money in the van.

Before G-money was all the way in the van, bullets pumped through the back windshield showering G-money's body with glass. Knowledge quickly slid from the back into the driver's seat.

Skip grabbed Ashley, who stood frozen and aggressively tossed her into the back of the van with G-money. Skip quickly hopped on top of Ashley, as Knowledge put the pedal to the medal.

"I'm going to kill this mutha fucka," G-money's voice grumbled as he coughed and spat out a little blood. "Try not to talk, we taking you to the hospital now," Skip whispered as he rubbed G-money's forehead. "Ahwww this shit; its burning and I think my shoulder is broke," G-money squealed out in pain. "I'm going to get you there as fast as I can," Knowledge yelled over his shoulder as he weaved from lane to lane doing about seventy miles per hour.

"Somebody call Ali," G-money groaned. "Let him know what happened." "Don't worry, I'm going to call him as soon as we get you to a hospital," Skip replied as he tightly gripped G-money's hand. "Mutha fucka caught me slipping," G-money hissed shamefully. "Don't sweat it; shit like this happens to the best of them," Skip replied trying to cheer his friend up.

Knowledge pulled up in front of the hospital,

beeping the horn like a madman. "Come on, help me get him out of the van," Skip yelled out as he and Knowledge lifted G-money out of the van and rushed him into the hospital.

Four doctors quickly rushed to G-money's aid. "What happened," a tall white doctor asked sternly. "He got shot in the thigh and shoulder," Skip replied nervously. "Okay, we'll take it from here," the doctor said as he and the other doctor slowly placed G-money on the stretcher and rolled him back towards the emergency room.

* * * *

Ali laid in his bed knocked out with Nancy laying right next to him, when the ringing of the house phone caused the two to wake up.

"Hello," Ali yawned into the phone. "Yo, G-money just got shot twice," Skip yelled into the receiver. "Hold on; what happened," Ali asked sitting up in his bed. "We bumped into Rell and his crew at this club and shit popped off." "So how did G-money get shot?" "When we left the club; the shit was a fucking set up," Skip hissed. "It was my fault I should've never took my eyes off G-money. I lost site of him when one of the fucking bouncers threw me out the club." "Don't even sweat it Skip. What hospital is he in," Ali asked. "St. Luke's," Skip answered quickly. "Aight, I'll be there in a minute," Ali said ending the call.

"Baby what's wrong," Nancy asked with a nervous look on her face. "G-money just got shot twice. He's in the hospital right now," Ali said as he quickly got dressed. "Oh my God! Is he…," Nancy asked with her hand covering her mouth. "No, he's still alive," Ali confirmed. "Thank God," Nancy said relieved. "Call up Coco and let her know what happened," Ali yelled over his shoulder as he stormed out the house.

Nancy quickly picked up the cordless phone and dialed Coco's number. "Hello," she answered sleepily. "Wake up, G-money just got shot twice," Nancy yelled into the receiver. "What," Coco echoed quickly sitting up in her bed. "G-money just got shot twice. Hurry up and get dressed, I'll be at your crib in five minutes," Nancy said ending the conversation.

Coco quickly hopped out of bed and threw on the outfit she had on the night before. As soon as Coco finished getting dressed, she heard somebody ringing her door bell. Coco hurried to the door and was relieved when she saw Nancy on the other side of it.

"Come on girl," Nancy yelled out as she hopped back in the driver seat. She quickly glanced in the backseat to make sure little Ali was still sleeping peacefully before she pulled off.

* * * *

"That nigga ,G-money, is a fucking pussy," Rell huffed as he felt a puffy bruise forming under his eye. "That nigga lucky he snuck me." "It's all good boss. When I came out the club I seen that faggot, G-money, laid out on the concrete crying like a little bitch," Debo said excitingly as he stopped for the red light. "Say word," Rell said seriously. "Word to everything," Debo replied with a grin on his face. "Hopefully that mutha fucka dies in the hospital tonight." "If he don't die, when I catch his ass he's going to wish he was dead," Rell hissed as he stared blankly out of the window. "Don't worry, we going to get his ass," Debo said out loud as he cruised smoothly along with the traffic.

Chapter 49
ALL WORK AND NO PLAY

"Kill or be killed," Spanky repeated as he worked his jump rope. "That's right; when you step in that ring it's kill or be killed," Freddie said out loud watching every move Spanky made.

Freddie really stayed on Spanky's back, not to be a pain in the ass but because he knew how important this fight was to the young man. Freddie did his best to prepare Spanky for what lied ahead, but he didn't know if Spanky knew how difficult it was going to be to defeat his opponent. It was only one thing that bothered Freddie about the up coming fight and that was Spanky's reflexes. Ever since his accident, Spanky's reflexes had been slightly off. Freddie knew this was going to be a problem, but no matter what Freddie told Spanky he was still going to fight so Freddie decided not to mention it.

Once Spanky finished jumping rope, he then headed in front of the full length mirror where he began shadow boxing. Christie just sat on the sideline with a nervous look on her face. At first she wasn't nervous, but with the fight being only three days away she couldn't help but have a few butterflies in her stomach. Her worse fear was Spanky being seriously hurt in the ring. "Three days and it's going down," Spanky yelled out looking over at Christie. "I know, you doing good," Christie said blowing Spanky a kiss. Spanky playfully caught the kiss and placed it on his lips. "Thanks boo, I needed that." "Anything for you baby," Christie whispered as she continued to watch her husband workout.

Spanky's mind was already made up, he wasn't going to leave that ring without The Terminator's belt around his waist. He made sure he overworked himself everyday just to make sure his body was ready. Spanky knew it wasn't going to be easy, but he was willing to go through hell if he had to. When Spanky and Christie made it home, Christie gave Spanky a long oiled massage. "Baby after I win the title, I think we should take a little vacation. What you think," Spanky asked with his eyes closed. "That would be great. Where would you like to go?" "I was going to let you pick the place this time. It'll be my gift to you, for putting up with me for all these years," Spanky said sincerely. "Ahw baby, that was sweet but you know you don't have to reward me for loving you." "What you talking about? You're my Queen; you're supposed to be getting rewarded everyday," Spanky said in a matter of fact tone. "I know baby, but now I think it's your turn to be rewarded for all of your hard work. You been working hard since we got married." "Okay, how about after the fight we just go somewhere so we can escape all this real life shit for a little while," Spanky said as he hopped up and headed for the shower. "How does that sound to you?" "That sounds perfect," Christie replied with a smile as she watched her husband disappear in the bathroom.

Chapter 50
THE DAY BEFORE

Nancy walked the streets of Harlem pushing little Ali in his stroller, as she did a little last minute shopping before her big trip with Ali. Nancy was so excited because not only was she going to the Bahamas, but she was also getting married to the man she loved.

Nancy strolled down the block minding her business when she heard a familiar voice calling her name. When Nancy turned around, she was shocked to see her mother, Jasmin, headed in her direction with her boyfriend, Rick, on her heels.

"Hey mommy what's up," Nancy said very friendly. "Don't you hey mommy me," Jasmin snarled looking Nancy and little Ali up and down. "You should be ashamed of yourself." "A shamed of myself for what," Nancy asked not knowing what her mother was talking about. "Now you going to sit here and play stupid, like you don't know what I'm talking about," Jasmin huffed as she swiftly slapped Nancy across her face.

Nancy took a few steps backwards only because the slap caught her off guard. Once she regained her balance, she quickly punched her mother dead in her moth, causing her to drop to one knee. Nancy quickly went to grab the handle on the stroller so that she could leave, but when she looked up she saw Rick approaching with fire dancing in his eyes. As he moved forward, Nancy retreated a step.

"You disrespectful little bitch," he growled. "How dare you hit your mother," Rick spat as he threw a vicious right hook that landed right on the side of Nancy's head. The impact of the punch caused Nancy to hit the ground. Once she was on the ground, Jasmin and Rick started viciously kicking her in the ribs and back area.

"How dare you have Dave murdered," Jasmin yelled as she continued to kick her daughter. "Now that poor bastard baby of yours will never have a father because of your stupid ass," she yelled.

The real reason Jasmin and Rick were angry that Dave had been murdered was because he would give them money every week since he started hustling. Now that Dave was dead, Jasmin and Rick had no extra money to support their nasty drug habit which made the two furious.

"That's enough," Jasmin yelled pushing Rick off of her daughter. "Don't you ever fuck with my money again bitch," Jasmin said through a pair of clenched teeth as she gave Nancy one last kick.

When Nancy looked up, tears started running freely down her cheeks as she saw little Ali staring at her innocently. "Mommy is sorry baby. Let me get you up out of these streets and back in your crib where you belong," Nancy whispered as she quickly headed back to her vehicle. She sat little Ali in his car seat, tossed the stroller in the trunk, and hopped into the driver seat heading straight home.

* * * *

"Boss man you going somewhere," Big Mel asked suspiciously as he noticed Ali packing away a few things. "Yeah, after the fight tomorrow me and Nancy going on a little vacation, you dig." "That's cool. Were ya'll going," Big Mel asked. "I'm not sure yet," Ali lied sensing that Big Mel was up to something. "While I'm gone, I'm going to need you to watch over the crib for me," he said setting Big Mel up for the kill.

"I hope Spanky does well tomorrow," Big Mel said changing the subject. "I already know Spanky's going to thrash that clown tomorrow," Ali said in an even tone.

Ali was about to say something else, but he held onto his words as he noticed Nancy storm into the house with a defeated look on her face. "What's wrong boo," Ali asked following Nancy into the master bedroom.

Once inside the room, Nancy removed her shirt so Ali could see the bruises by her ribs and down her back. "What the fuck happened to you," Ali asked his face turning into a coat of anger. "My mother and her boyfriend attacked me in the middle of the street, in front of the baby," Nancy sobbed. "Talking about I got Dave murdered." "Here write down your mother's address," Ali said calmly as he handed Nancy a piece of paper and a pen.

Without thinking twice, Nancy quickly scribbled down her mother's address. Once he had the address Ali quickly picked up his throw away phone and dialed a number.

* * * *

Skip parked a block away from the hideout crib, that only he and April knew about. Skip still couldn't believe what had happened to G-money. Skip bopped down the street with a lot on his mind; not only did his best friend just get shot, but his marriage was also going down the drain.

Skip quietly stuck his key through the keyhole and entered the two bedroom shack. "Hey baby what's up," he asked as he tried to kiss April on the lips. "We need to talk," April said quickly turning her head so that Skip couldn't kiss her. "I'm tired of this shit, Skip." "I know baby, I promise I'm going to fix it and make things right," Skip pleaded. "How are you going to make things right and you're on the run," April asked angrily, placing her hand on her hip waiting for an answer. "Baby, have some faith in your husband please; shit is going to be alright." "No, shit is not going to be alright. I want you to leave," April said sternly. "Baby please don't do this," Skip begged. "I love you baby and right now I need you more than ever; please don't do this." "You did it to yourself Skip," April said as she opened up the door so that Skip could make his exit. "Damn, it's like that," Skip asked innocently. "You're just going to throw everything out the window just like that," he asked with a hurt and defeated look on his face. "I don't want Michael growing up around this shit, when you're getting yourself together. My door will always be open. I love you baby, but you really need to change your lifestyle…if not for me, then for your son."

Skip was about to respond, but his ringing cell phone caused a distraction. "You see what I'm talking about? Every five minutes your phone is ringing. Skip get yourself together and when you're ready to be a family, you know where to find me," April said as tears ran freely down her cheeks as she closed the door on her husband.

"Fuck," Skip yelled out due to frustration. Nothing in his life seemed to be going right. "Yeah what's up," he spoke into the receiver. "I need you to handle something for me," Ali said in a mellow tone. "Write this address down." "Hold on gimme a second," Skip said fishing around in his pocket for a pen. "Aight, go ahead."

Once Skip had the address written down, he quickly ended the call and hopped back into his ride and headed to the address Ali had just given him.

* * * *

Nancy angrily packed her things; she still couldn't believe what her mother had done to her.

"Don't even worry about it; you know your man is going to handle this for you," Ali spoke softly as he wrapped his arms around her waist. "I know boo, I just can't wait to go on this vacation. I just want to get away from all this bullshit."

Before Ali could respond, he heard a light

knock at his bedroom door. He opened the door to find Big Mel on the other side dressed in all black. "What's up?" "I'm about to run and get some KFC, ya'll want anything while I'm out," Big Mel asked. "Nah we cool; good looking though," Ali said as he gave Big Mel a pound.

Once Ali closed the door, Big Mel quickly threw on his black gloves and grabbed the 9mm that Detective Nelson had given him and headed out the door.

* * * *

Skip entered the raggedy apartment building and quickly took the stairs to the apartment he was looking for. Once in front of the door, Skip smoothly slid on his hoody and pulled out his dessert eagle. On the count of three, Skip shot the lock off of the door, then viciously kicked the door in. He ran into the house like a madman only to find Rick and Jasmin having sex on the living room floor.

"What the fuck is going on," Rick asked throwing his hands up in surrender. "Damn, I know the rent is late, but damn you gotta kick the mutha fucking door in? I told you I was going to pay you mutha fuckas next week," Rick slurred as a bullet to his head shut him the fuck up once and for all.

Skip quickly stood over Rick's body and pumped five more bullets into his lifeless body. Jasmin was getting ready to scream, until Skip pointed his cannon directly at her. "Go ahead and scream, I dare you," Skip challenged. "Close ya fucking eyes and count to a hundred."

Once Skip saw Jasmin close her eyes and start counting, he quickly made his exit. Skip quickly glanced down the block making sure that the gun shots didn't draw any attention as he made his exit.

* * * *

Big Mel doubled parked his vehicle and slowly stepped out with the 9mm hanging down by his side. With his free hand, he smoothly slid his ski mask over his face as he entered the small bodega.

Once the clerk saw the masked man enter the store, she quickly reached for the shotgun that rested under the counter, but three shots to her chest removed the thought from her mind. After he shot the clerk, Big Mel quickly hopped over the counter and cleaned out the cash register.

As Big Mel stuffed the bills into his pocket, he noticed a customer enter the store. Without a trace of emotion, Big Mel raised the 9mm and sent three shots into the customer's upper body. Once his work was done, Big Mel quickly exited the bodega and slid back into his vehicle.

Big Mel knew that he was fucked up, but unfortunately he was in too deep and couldn't turn back now. He loved Ali like a brother, but if it was his ass or Ali's it would definitely have to be Ali's ass. Big Mel quickly picked up his cell phone, and dialed Detective Nelson's number. "Yeah what's up," Detective Nelson growled into the phone. "Wake the fuck up. I need to see you; I got what you been waiting for," Big Mel huffed. "It's about time. Meet me at that small coffee shop two blocks away from my house," Detective Nelson said hanging up in Big Mel's ear.

Big Mel was furious when Detective Nelson hung up on him. He wanted to snap the Detective's neck with his bare hands, but he knew he couldn't because Detective Nelson was down with the NYPD. When Big Mel pulled up, he spotted Detective Nelson's unmarked car double parked on the corner. He slowly rolled up right beside him and rolled down his window. "I hope you happy now," Big Mel hissed as he tossed the 9mm on the passenger seat of the Detective's car. "What's this," Detective Nelson asked with a wicked smirk on his face. "Two murdered in a small bodega downtown," Big Mel replied dryly. "Good work. I'll call you ten minutes before we raid Ali's house tomorrow," Detective Nelson said coldly as he pulled off leaving Big Mel with a lot to think about.

Chapter 51
FIGHT NIGHT

Ali and Nancy packed the remainder of their things, while Mary j. Blige hummed softly through the speakers putting the couple in an even better mood. Things couldn't have been better for the two. "Did you hear what happened at the hospital," Nancy asked as she packed away all of her sexy underwear. "Nah, what happen?" "Coco told me she went to go pick G-money up from the hospital, and some model looking chick was there all up in G-money's face." "Word, that's O.D.," Ali asked with a smile on his face. "That's not funny. Coco really loves him." "And he loves her too, but that's just how he is," Ali said honestly. "So what else happened?" "Nothing, Coco and the girl got into a little argument but the other girl left before things got out of hand." "That's good, Coco don't need no more drama in her life anyway," Ali chuckled lightly. "You stupid," Nancy exhaled.

The conversation was momentarily paused

when Ali heard the house phone ringing. "Hello," he answered. "You already know what time it is," Spanky yelled excitedly into the phone. Ali laughed before he spoke. "I see you already hyped up for the fight." "You already know it's on tonight. Either go hard or go home!" "You got any predictions," Ali asked. "Yeah, I think I'm going to knock this chump out in the fifth round," Spanky boasted. "Yo, I gotta go, but make sure I see you in that front row tonight, aight." "You know I'm going to be there supporting my little brother." "Aight bet, I'll see you later; one," Spanky said ending the call.

"Damn this going to be a good ass fight tonight," Ali said out loud. "Spanky better win," Nancy said as she changed little Ali's stinking diaper.

Big Mel sat on the couch in the living room watching Sport Center when he felt his cell phone vibrating. "Hello," he answered in an even tone. "You got ten minutes to get out that house," Detective Nelson said calmly as the phone went dead.

Big Mel quickly shot to his feet and grabbed his car keys and his Uzi. He reached the door and something inside of him made him stop. "I can't go out like this," he said to himself as he stood in the doorway and tried to think of a plan.

Big Mel knocked lightly on Ali and Nancy's bedroom door. "What's good my nigga," Ali asked giving the big man a pound. "I was about to run to the store and get some snacks, ya'll want anything," he asked. "Nah, we cool," Ali answered with little emotion. "Do ya'll mind if I take the baby out to get some air with me," Big Mel innocently. "Sure, I don't see no harm in that," Nancy said as she gently placed little Ali in Big Mel's strong arms. "How long you going to be gone for?" "Like ten minutes," Big Mel yelled over his shoulder as he quickly headed out the door. When Big Mel looked at his watch, he saw that he had three minutes left. He quickly sat little Ali in his car seat, slid into the driver's seat and pulled out of the driveway.

As Big Mel cruised down the street, he noticed about ten to fifteen vans speed past him. Inside, Big Mel wanted to die, but the least he could do was get the baby out of harm's way. That made him feel a little better inside with himself, as he glanced at little Ali in the back sitting in his car seat drooling.

Nancy sat curled up in Ali's lap as the two watched a classic episode of Jerry Springer. When out of the blue, all the lights and electricity went out. "What the fuck," Ali said as he and Nancy glanced at each other. Seconds later, Ali heard three loud "Booms" coming from downstairs. He quickly tossed Nancy off his lap and made his way toward the hallway where he looked over the balcony and saw ten to fifteen cops bust through his front door. Three of them held up a big bullet proof shield, that had police written on the front, while the rest of them clutched sub-machine guns.

Without thinking twice, Ali quickly snatched his twin 9mm's from their holsters and got the party started. Bullets flew from every direction, filling Ali's lovely home with bullet holes. When Ali noticed about twenty more officers storm through the front door, he continued to fire, back peddling inside his bedroom.

Once in the room, Ali quickly headed straight to his closet where he grabbed two Teflon vests, he threw one on and tossed the other to Nancy along with a 9mm. "If anybody come in this mutha fucka you better light they ass up" Ali barked as he grabbed his A.K. 47 with the hundred round clip out of his closet. "Come on mutha fucka this what ya'll wanted," Ali yelled as he stormed back out towards the balcony.

As soon as Ali made it back towards the balcony, he saw four officers trying to creep their way up the stairs. Ali immediately aimed his A.K. at the four cops and watched round after round pump out of the it effortlessly. The slugs caused the four officers to fly right back down the stairs, which they just came up.

Once that was done, Ali quickly took cover behind a wall as bullets came raining in from every direction. On the count of three, Ali sprung from behind the wall blasting. The officers quickly took cover the best they could.

Nancy laid on the floor, trying not to get hit with a stray bullet. As soon as Nancy tried to get to her feet, about twenty shots flew through the door missing her by inches. "Oh shit," she whispered as she heard more and more shots being fired.

In a quick motion, Nancy threw her hair into a ponytail, grabbed the 9mm that Ali had tossed to her, and quickly took cover behind a wall. Nancy's heart pumped about a thousand miles per second from anticipation on what was about to go down. She quickly came from around, and fired her 9mm at a cop who was creeping up on Ali from behind. Seconds later, a shot hit Nancy in the middle of her stomach sending her instantly to the floor where she held her stomach, trying to get her wind back.

When Ali saw that Nancy hit the floor, he went crazy. "Mutha fuckas," he yelled as he quickly made his way over to his fiancé. On his way to his girl's rescue, a bullet penetrated Ali's thigh. He quickly brushed it off because his adrenaline was pumping too fast to feel the pain.

"Baby, you okay," Ali asked nervously. "Yeah, I'm cool. The bullet didn't go through, it just knocked the wind out of me," Nancy squealed in pain. As Ali stood kneeled down by Nancy's side, he noticed tear gas bullets come flying in from every direction. Ali quickly grabbed a pillow from off of the bed and snatched off the case. "Here, cover ya mouth and nose with this."

As Ali stood helping Nancy nurse her wound, he saw three pairs of feet block the light coming from beneath the door. Ali sprung to his feet, firing recklessly through the door. His A.K. rounds found fatal homes in the flesh of two of the three officers.

Ali stood next to Nancy with his smoking A.K. aimed directly at the door, but the tear gas burned his eyes making it hard for him to focus. Seconds later, the gas took it's toll on Ali causing him to fall flat on his face.

When officers finally made it inside the bedroom, they found Ali laid out cold on top of Nancy. The officers quickly handcuffed the two and dragged them outside.

Once outside, Detective Nelson stood over Ali's body shaking his head in disgust. "Stupid mother fucker; look what I found," he taunted as he held up the 9mm that Big Mel had given him the night before. "Not to mention you just killed eight cops." He grinned wickedly.

Ali was still drowsy from the tear gas, so he didn't know what was going on; but he did recognize the white man who stood over him. Ali might not have known what was going on at the moment but, he knew it wasn't good.

*   *   *   *

"You been waiting for this moment your whole life," Freddie whispered in Spanky's ear as he got his hands wrapped up. Spanky didn't respond, instead he just soaked it all in. His mind was stuck on The Terminator. "When you step in that ring, you gotta be ready to take some to give some. I want you to take the fight to this mutha fucka," Freddie yelled trying to get Spanky fired up.

Spanky just shook his head, signaling that he understood. Once his gloves were on Spanky was ready to go. "Did Ali get here yet," he asked. "I'm not sure. He's probably running a little late," Freddie said.

Christie stood in the locker room with a nervous look on her face. Her vibrating cell phone brought her back to reality. She saw Coco's name flashing across the screen and quickly answered. "Hello?" "Where you at," Coco asked in desperate tone. "I'm in the locker room with Spanky, getting ready for his fight. Why, what's up?" "You ain't going to believe this, but Ali and Nancy are in jail for killing eight cops," Coco said weakly. "Are you serious," Christie asked in shock. "Where did you hear that at?" "It's all over the news, plus Big Mel just dropped little Ali off with me. He was at the store when the police raided the house," Coco said in a light tone. "Girl let me call you right back; it's time for the fight," Christie said hanging up the phone.

"What's up," Spanky asked sensing that

something was wrong. Christie thought about telling Spanky, but decided to wait until after the fight. "Oh nothing; that was just Coco; she just wanted to wish you good luck," she lied. "That's what's up! I'll see you in the front row boo," Spanky said as he and Freddie headed down towards the ring.

Spanky stepped in the ring and knew it wasn't no turning back. "It's either going to be you or him," Freddie yelled out.

The crowd went crazy as soon as The Terminator made his way towards the ring. "That ain't nothing but a mind thing," Freddie whispered in Spanky's ear. "A lot of mutha fuckas going to leave here broke when this fight is over." "Tonight is my night," Spanky replied as he bounced up and down trying to get himself loose.

When The Terminator stepped into the ring, he had his game face on as he stared at Spanky coldly. Spanky just continued to bounce up and down as he returned the stare.

The referee called both fighters to the middle of the ring so that he could go over the rules one last time. "Okay I want a nice clean fight. I already went over the rules with both of ya'll in the locker room, so keep it clean and break when I say brake," the referee announced as the two fighters headed back to their separate corners.

"You know what you gotta do," Freddie said as he placed Spanky's mouth piece in his mouth. "Remember, be the counter puncher; you let him come in and you just counter punch his ass all night," Mr. Wilson reminded The Terminator. "This lil' nigga can't fuck with me," The Terminator boasted as the bell rung signaling the beginning of round one.

The two fighters met in the middle of the ring.

Spanky quickly threw a double jab only to watch The Terminator dance out of his reach. The Terminator faked a right cross and threw an awkward left hook that landed perfectly on Spanky's chin. Spanky shook off the punch and continued to come forward. Once Spanky saw an opening, he fired a quick jab. The Terminator smoothly took a step back and countered with a sweeping left hook, causing everybody in the crowd to rise to their feet anticipating a first round knock out. The cheering made The Terminator get a little big headed. He quickly fired another sweeping hook, but this time Spanky ducked the hook and came up with a vicious upper cut, causing The Terminator to back pedal into the corner.

Once Spanky saw The Terminator stumble back into the corner, he quickly boxed him in by throwing punches from every direction. The Terminator blocked as many punches as he could before his foot work got him out of the corner and back into the middle of the ring. Spanky didn't stop there; he threw a lightening fast jab, followed by a hook. Both punches landed perfectly. To Spanky's surprise The Terminator kept his feet and fired back. The Terminator got off two good punches before the bell sounded.

"Bitch ass nigga," Spanky yelled in The Terminator's face as the two brushed past each other heading to their separate corners. "That's what I'm talking about. You gotta make this a dog fight," Freddie yelled as he squeezed a wet sponge over Spanky's head. "I think I hurt him with that upper cut," Spanky said taking in some water. "Of course you did! You have to throw more combinations because he's looking to counter punch." "I got you," Spanky replied as he glanced at Christie and gave her a wink. He stared at the empty seat next to her and wondered where his big brother was.

"What the fuck is going on out here," Mr. Wilson growled all up in The Terminator's face. "Don't just run up in there swinging! Use your head, God damn it," Mr. Wilson yelled as the bell rung letting both fighters know it was time for round two.

The Terminator immediately fired two jabs, causing Spanky's head to violently jerk back. "I'm about to teach you how to box chump," The Terminator grumbled as he threw another quick jab followed by a hook to the lower body. Spanky took both punches well, as he threw a wild upper cut. The Terminator smoothly side stepped the wild punch and countered with a sharp hook to Spanky's temple. The last punch dazed Spanky, fucking up his equilibrium. The Terminator threw a series of combinations, until Spanky hit the canvas.

Spanky laid on his back, still a little dizzy, as he tried to sit up. He knew what was going on, but at the same time he didn't. Everything quickly came to Spanky when he saw the referee counting loudly in his face. Somehow Spanky made it back to his feet at the count of eight.

"You alright," the referee asked looking in Spanky's eyes. "Yeah, I'm good," Spanky replied trying to shake of his dizziness. As soon as Spanky made it back to the middle of the ring, the bell quickly sounded ending round two.

"Wake the fuck up Spanky," Freddie yelled in Spanky's face trying to wake him up. "Nah, I'm good. Mutha fucka just caught at me with a luck y shot," Spanky said taking in some water as he felt a puffy bruise forming under his eye.

"That's what I'm talking about. Give me

another round just like that," Mr. Wilson said rubbing some grease on The Terminators face.

Spanky quickly began working his jab at the beginning of round three. "Stop running like a little bitch," Spanky taunted as both men threw wild vicious combinations; each man taking a punch to throw one. Both fighters went in to throw a punch at the same time and by accident the two clashed heads.

The Terminator instantly felt warm blood trickling down his right eye, as he proceeded to ease back into the corner. Once Spanky had The Terminator trapped in the corner, he quickly pounded him out until he heard the bell ring.

"You see that cut on his eye? I want you to bust that shit open," Freddie ordered as he poured water in Spanky's mouth. "Don't worry about that cut, just keep doing what you do," Mr. Wilson said as the cut man did his best to patch up The Terminator's eye.

At the beginning of the fourth round, Spanky went straight after The Terminator's eye. Spanky could tell that the cut was really bothering him. Spanky quickly threw a jab followed by a hard hook, which caused The Terminator's mouth piece to fly out of his mouth. The Terminator quickly threw a head fake followed by a right cross. Spanky stood with his hands up because he knew that The Terminator was about to throw another sweeping hook. He planned on countering the hook with a sharp upper cut, but The Terminator's punch was fired awkwardly, catching Spanky dead on his chin causing him to drop to the canvas for the second time.

Once The Terminator saw Spanky hit the floor, he immediately threw his hands up in the air signaling that he had already won the fight. The referee reached the count of ten, before Spanky could make it back to his feet.

Freddie quickly hopped in the ring and helped Spanky get back on his feet. "You did good son. You did real good, I'm proud of you," he whispered in Spanky's ear.

The Terminator made his way over to Spanky's corner and gave him a big hug. "You fought your ass off. Keep your head up baby." Spanky didn't respond, instead he, Freddie and his cut man quickly exited the ring and headed back to the locker room.

"Fuck," Spanky cursed loudly as soon as he stepped foot in the locker room. "I had that mutha fucka. I knew he was going to throw that hook, I just couldn't get out the way fast enough," he said tossing a towel over his head.

"Baby, are you okay," Christie asked as she stormed in the locker room. "I almost had him, baby," Spanky said with tears running down his cheek. "I almost had him." "It's okay baby. You're going to get another shot at the title." "Yeah, I know boo," Spanky said. "Thanks for everything. I really appreciate it," he spoke softly as he kissed Freddie on the cheek and tossed his duffle bag strap over his shoulder. "You want me to ride with you in the limo," Freddie asked noticing the look of defeat on Spanky's face."Nah, I'm cool," Spanky said in a weak and shaky voice as he and Christie made their exit. Once inside of the limo, Spanky just sat quietly as tears rolled freely down his face.

Not knowing what to do, Christie just grabbed Spanky's hand and held on tight as the limo driver pulled off into traffic. "Baby I have to tell you something," Christie said in a frail voice. "Yeah what's up," he said uninterested. "I didn't want to tell you before the fight because I didn't want to distract you, but Coco called me earlier and told me that Ali and Nancy are in jail." "In jail for what?" "Coco said that they killed eight cops." "Eight fucking cops," Spanky said not believing his ears. "Fuck…today must not have been our day," he chuckled as he stared blankly out the window with tears still rolling down his face.

For the entire ride home the two sat in tense silence as the limo driver pulled up to their house. As soon as Christie stepped foot in the house, she threw on a relaxing R&B mixtape. "Come here baby," she said grabbing Spanky by the wrist. "You sit right here. I'm going to run you some bath water, then give you a nice massage," Christie said as she disappeared inside the bathroom. "Okay, I got your bath water running. Would you like for me to give you a massage now or after you get out the tub," Christie asked innocently. "When I get out the tub," Spanky replied as he stood up and kissed Christie passionately . "I'll be right back, I gotta go take a shit real quick," Spanky yelled over his shoulder as he disappeared inside the bathroom.

Once Spanky was in the bathroom, Christie slowly peeled out of her dress and kicked off her heels. She walked freely around the house in nothing but her white thong as she headed to the kitchen to grab a bottle of champagne. On her way back to the bedroom, she nosily placed her ear against the bathroom door. When she didn't hear anything, she began to panic.

"Baby, you okay in there," she asked as she knocked lightly on the door. No answer came back. Christie quickly reached for the doorknob only to find out that it was locked. "Baby, stop playing around and open up the door," she yelled in a worried tone. Seconds later, Christie heard a single gunshot go off. Instantly her heart leaped up into her throat.

Christie quickly took three steps backwards and came forward with a hard kick which busted the door wide open. She slowly melted down to her knees with her mouth hung wide open. Spanky sat on top of the toilet seat with half of his brains painted on the wall behind him while the rest of his brains rested on his shoulders.

"Noooooooooooooooooooooooo," Christie screamed at the top of her lungs as she rested her head on Spanky's lap. "Why did you do this," she asked herself over and over again as she just cried like a baby. "WHY?"

TO BE CONTINUED...

A Novel By: $ILK WHITE

"The End"

Now Available:
Paperback

TEARS
OF A
HUSTLER
A NOVEL BY
SILK WHITE

TEARS
OF A
HUSTLER
2
A NOVEL BY
SILK WHITE

GOOD 2 GO PUBLISHING PRESENTS
TEARS
OF A
HUSTLER
3
A NOVEL BY
SILK WHITE

THE
TEFLON
QUEEN
A NOVEL BY
SILK WHITE

TRA VERDEJO MONIQUE BAILEY SILK WHITE
BLACK BARBIE
HOLLIDAY MAFIA STORY

NO WAY OUT THE MOVIE
STARRING SILK WHITE